CHARLIE'S DOCTOR

SHADOW ELITE
BOOK 1

JOCELYNN DRAKE

Cover art by Cate Ashwood

Photograph by Wander Aguiar

Edited and proofed by Flat Earth Editing.

DID YOU KNOW SHADOW ELITE IS A SPIN-OFF?

The Shadow Elite is a spin-off series from the assassin series Exit Strategy.

Binge both series and get your fill of assassins, mercenaries, and the adorable men they love!

Exit Strategy
Deadly Lover: Special Edition
Vengeful Lover
Final Lover
Forbidden Lover
Accidental Lover

Shadow Elite
Stephen's Translator (novella)
Charlie's Doctor
Kairo's Billionaire
Edison's Professor
Westin's Prince

1

CHARLIE SANDS

July 2030

BUENOS AIRES WAS NOT TURNING OUT TO BE AS MUCH FUN AS he'd initially expected.

He'd thought tracing the roots of previously unknown paintings for an artist who'd supposedly died more than fifty years ago would be an exciting romp through the Argentine art world. Mix in danger, intrigue, sex, and some time on the beach, and Charlie would've called it a success.

But he and his team had been in Buenos Aires for nearly a week with nothing to show for it except for indigestion from lunch, and West had a sunburn on the back of his neck.

No danger.

No intrigue.

And no sex.

He was planning to at least fix that egregious oversight tonight, though. There were plenty of hot playthings strolling the gallery show, giving off those "come fuck me" vibes. It would be rude of him not to oblige.

"How do you do it?" The low rumble of Edison's voice

rolled through Charlie's ear, and he turned to regard his undercover companion for the night. His demolitions expert looked good in his bespoke suit. Of course, it wasn't like something off the rack was going to fit his broad shoulders, thick chest, and massive arms. The man was a walking tank. And yet the tailor had wrapped him in a soft camel-brown suit with a white shirt that perfectly complimented his dark, rich skin tone.

"Do what?" Charlie inquired, giving the left cuff of his midnight-blue shirt a small tug. His own suit for the evening was a mix of blues and blacks that set well against his tanned complexion and salt-and-pepper hair.

"In the land of sex and machismo, you still stand out as an old-school god of sex," Edison replied.

There was a low snickering in his ear, and Kairo immediately added over their private communication system, "A stallion in heat."

"Or just an old tomcat in heat," Westin interjected for good measure.

Charlie didn't react beyond a twitch of his mouth as he continued to stare at the post-modern painting in front of him that was an explosion of reds and grays. He wasn't quite sure what it was supposed to be, but he hadn't actually noticed most of the art in the showing. His attention was now on the members of his team who weren't in the gallery.

Currently, Kairo was in the safe house they'd rented, digging into famed and supposedly dead painter Thiago Vergara as well as the gallery owners who were known to have sold his work. Kairo Jones was the best reconnaissance guy he'd ever worked with. There was nothing he couldn't hack, no bit of information he couldn't uncover. But even he was running into a wall when it came to what happened to Thiago Vergara after he disappeared in 1977.

Westin St. James had elected to find a dark and shadowy perch outside the gallery from which to watch people coming and going. The former Marine sniper didn't do crowds or situations where he might be forced to have a face-to-face conversation with someone.

Ed was plenty backup for this reconnaissance mission, especially since Charlie didn't expect to run into a single ounce of trouble.

Not that Buenos Aires didn't offer up ample trouble. The lovely South American city had her fair share of crime, corruption, violence, and greed. They didn't even have to turn over that many rocks to locate it. They just had trouble pinpointing the dark side that matched their problem: What really happened to Thiago Vergara?

When his brother's new boyfriend, Ehren Galanis, discovered that he'd inherited four "lost" Thiago Vergara paintings, Charlie's mind had immediately spun out an exciting tale of drugs, corruption, and smuggling between crime families in Argentina and Turkey. Maybe they'd even find Thiago Vergara locked up in some crime boss's basement, forced to churn out masterpiece after masterpiece to fund his operations.

And that Erhen's honest uncle had somehow gotten his hands on the paintings to protect them from the dirty thieves.

At the very least, he thought he'd find something interesting. A clue. A dead body. Another painting.

So far, it was nothing.

Thiago Vergara disappeared in 1977 along with more than thirty thousand others in the late seventies and early eighties as part of *Los Desaparecidos*—a giant purge conducted by the right-wing military government that had seized control of the country.

Where the fuck had the paintings come from?

They'd had three separate experts confirm that all six paintings in Ehren's possession were made by Thiago Vergara. What's more, the four "lost" paintings had been done in the last twenty-five years—well after the man's supposed death.

Charlie loved a good mystery. But he hated ones that refused to cough up even the smallest clues.

"No offense, Charlie, but I'm thinking we should have called in Soren," Ed started anew. While Charlie was grateful they'd dropped the conversation about his "come fuck me" vibes, he wasn't too keen on this new direction.

But it was hard to argue with the truth.

"Soren knows how to schmooze the artsy types. They love talking to him," Kairo chimed in.

Of course, that had been Soren's job while they'd all worked for the CIA. Soren had been the agent in the field, and the man knew how to be charming. He could get anyone to talk to him with minimal trouble, and the amount of knowledge he had in his head with regard to art and historical artifacts was terrifying.

"It seems you're forgetting that he's on vacation with his new, hot, and scary boyfriend. Would you want to leave that bed to come play with us?" Charlie answered while staring at Edison.

"I don't know why you call Alexei scary. I thought he was sweet," Kairo teased.

Charlie decided to let that one go. Sure, Alexei appeared to be sweet and too pretty for his own good, but he needed to only look in the kid's eyes to know he was a ruthless killer. It also didn't hurt to know that his pedigree was impeccable. Two uncles who were accomplished assassins. No, Alexei was scary, and he was going to be more than a handful for Soren.

"But yeah, you're probably right," Kairo continued with a laugh. "Why find trouble with us when he's got a hot boyfriend?"

"Besides, Charlie can handle this," Edison added with a wide grin.

"Can we move this along? I'm bored," West moaned, and that was enough to get Charlie's mind into the game again. They didn't want Westin to get bored. He'd start searching for things to shoot at with the idea that no one would notice him peppering said things with bullets. West was a crack shot and could easily do it, but it was also asking for trouble.

"I've spotted my target," Charlie murmured. He turned and picked up a flute of champagne from a passing server in black pants and shirt. The young man carrying the tray paused long enough to let his dark eyes sweep along Charlie from his head to his feet and back. He offered a smile that included a bite of his bottom lip prior to moving on. Certainly not the most blatant invitation he'd received since entering the gallery, but it was the most enticing.

As the server continued to cut a lazy path through the crowd, Charlie moved in the opposite direction. The Blue Wind was the third gallery he'd ventured into in as many days, and like the other two, it was filled with pieces of art that he didn't quite get. Some of it was pretty and some of it was interesting, but none of it was like the works of Thiago Vergara.

The Argentine artist had been in his early twenties when he'd broken out as a shining star. Both the works that Erhan Galanis possessed as well as what he'd been able to find online had a vibrant realism that managed to strike straight to the core of the viewer. If Thiago Vergara was dead, it was a damn shame. The world needed more of his work.

But the reason they were at The Blue Wind wasn't because the gallery showed works similar to Vergara. No, it was because the gallery owner had sold several pieces decades ago before Vergara's disappearance. Right now, the closest they could get to the owner was his daughter.

Isabella Romero was a tall, elegant woman in her early fifties with exotic dark almond-shaped eyes and a large, lush mouth. Her black hair was liberally threaded with gray and was artfully twisted up on her head, revealing the long slope of her neck. There was a frostiness to her demeanor as if she were the queen of her domain and everyone else were merely supplicants hoping for a moment of her precious time.

Charlie was very tempted to see how much of her time he could steal away, and not just for the job.

"*Señora* Romero?" Charlie murmured politely as he came to stand beside her. "Congratulations on your *coup* of obtaining the sale of the Bautista Blanco collection."

The woman arched a perfectly sculpted eyebrow at him, her sharp eyes assessing him as she granted him the barest nod. "Thank you. It was only natural that the Blanco family elected to go with The Blue Wind to handle the sale of his most critically acclaimed period."

Charlie took a leisurely sip of his champagne as he looked over the painting in front of him while listening to Kairo rattle off some important background details. Bautista Blanco was a highly successful painter and sculptor who hated to sell his work. That meant when he died three years ago, every gallery in Buenos Aires and quite a few overseas fought for the right to show and sell some of his most valuable pieces. It was Isabella Romero who beat out the competition in the end.

"His *Endless Road* series was a personal favorite of mine. How Blanco captured the isolation and hopelessness of man nearing the end of his life was quite stunning," Charlie said, repeating almost word for word another reviewer's criticism.

Isabella's expression thawed a little, and the arms she'd been holding across her stomach loosened as she turned toward him a fraction. "Interesting. Most people find the austerity of the work too off-putting. They prefer the warmer, more hope-filled pieces of his youth."

Charlie affected a nonchalant shrug. "If I want warmth and hope, I will turn to Thiago Vergara."

The laugh that escaped Isabella was deep and throaty with a burn that warmed his chest, reminding him of good scotch. "Don't we all. No one could do hope like Thiago."

"Yes, but he managed it without the whimsy and feeling of

childishness. It was drenched in realism and starkness. That no matter how bleak the moment, you felt justified clinging to that hope."

As he spoke, the gallery manager shifted fully toward him, her arms falling to her side while her expression blossomed into a bright smile. "Exactly. Thiago Vergara never shied away from the reality that glared back at him."

"I knew you'd understand," Charlie warmly murmured. As a new server passed close by, he snagged a fresh glass of champagne and held it out to Isabella. "I understand your father was quite a fan of Mr. Vergara. I'll admit that I was curious if he passed his appreciation of Vergara's work on to you."

She accepted the glass, a speculative look entering her eye. "My father taught me to appreciate true genius. He was lucky enough to have been friends with Thiago when they were both young."

"His was a genius that was cut short far too soon. The world was gifted with too few of his paintings." Charlie took a sip of his champagne and grinned at Isabella. "Though, I have heard whispers that some lost paintings have been discovered in recent years. I would love your professional opinion on those rumors."

She sighed, but there was still a tolerant air about her. "Those rumors surface every few years about most dead geniuses. Doesn't the world have enough Picassos?"

"So, it's utter bullshit."

Isabella shrugged one shoulder. "For the most part. There were a handful uncovered in the late eighties after the fall of the military government. They'd been stolen from Vergara's studio. His girlfriend confirmed they were the last pieces he'd been working on or completed. At that time, all his work was accounted for. No more so-called lost pieces to be uncovered. But those that were found in the eighties tend to give people irrational hope that there might be more out there."

With a smirk, Charlie lightly clinked the edge of his flute against Isabella's. "The world could always use a little hope in the form of Thiago Vergara's light."

"Thiago Vergara was a fucking hack and a blight on our society," a harsh, angry voice interjected into their conversation.

Charlie twisted about to narrow his eyes on a short man with nearly black hair and a beard that lined his angular jaw. The stranger's gaze skimmed over Edison, who was standing a few feet away by Charlie's elbow and seemed to dismiss him. Charlie received the same brief appraisal before moving on to Isabella. The woman's entire demeanor froze over, and while she didn't turn her back on him and snub him directly, Charlie had a feeling that she very much wanted to.

"You don't consider Vergara to be a national treasure? Most of the world does," Charlie drawled.

"The world is filled with sheep and idiots," the man sniped with a curl of his upper lip. "Vergara was a known drunk and hedonist. His wild leftist ideals were a monstrosity and an embarrassment."

"So, you think the government was justified in making him disappear," Charlie replied tightly. It was becoming harder to watch his tone when he very much wanted to slug the bastard right in his nose.

The asshole snorted. "Those tales are an exaggeration at best, and utter bullshit at worst. As if any government would have an interest in Vergara. The man likely ran away to escape the husband of whichever woman he was sleeping with at the time. It's more rational to believe that he was killed by an angry husband and his corpse buried in the woods."

"That is certainly one theory," Charlie murmured. He tipped his glass up, downing the last of his champagne.

The asshole sniffed at him and then turned his attention fully to Isabella. "I believe we have some business to discuss. I'd like to sign the paperwork tonight and have it done. I'll be waiting in your office." Without waiting for a response from her, the guy turned and strode away with a pair of large men who screamed "bodyguard" flanking him.

"I'm sorry to cut our conversation short," Isabella paused and exhaled, "and to end it on such a sour note."

Charlie held out his hand and Isabella instantly placed hers into it. With a warm smile, he graciously bowed over it. "Not the parting I would have preferred. May I ask who that was?"

"Benicio Perez, and I would suggest avoiding him, if at all possible," she replied, slowly sliding her hand free from Charlie's.

"Only if it increases my chances of seeing you again. Possibly over dinner. We could continue our more enjoyable discussion."

The frost melted from her demeanor, replaced by a welcoming smile. "I think that could be arranged. You know where to find me." She gave a wave to the gallery around them as she turned and strode in the direction of Benicio Perez.

"Yeah, I don't think Soren could have done better. That was fucking smooth," Edison purred beside Charlie like a giant cat.

"I could have done without the interruption from the truth-denying little shit," Charlie grumbled. He placed his empty glass on a passing tray. He gave the server a glance this time to make sure he was one of the workers they'd identified when they arrived. Old habits were hard to break, and posing as temporary hired staff was always the easiest way into an event while remaining part of the scenery.

He and Edison continued through the gallery, pretending to view the art as they slowly made their way toward the exit.

"What did you think of Romero?" West inquired.

"Other than the fact that she's hot and ready to climb into Charlie's bed?" Edison joked.

"I think she believes what she told me—there are no lost paintings and Vergara has been dead for fifty years," Charlie murmured, trying not to clench his teeth. "Apparently this was another dead end."

"Maybe not," Kairo countered.

"What do you mean?" Edison asked.

"That little shit Benicio Perez is the son of Lorenzo Perez, a prominent right-wing political leader. Not only is Lorenzo a member of the Chamber of Deputies with aspirations of the presidency, but he is also the chairman of one of the largest banks in Argentina. One of the most profitable, too, despite the country's near-constant financial troubles." Kairo fell silent for a moment, and Charlie glanced over to find Edison giving him a somewhat speculative look. "Huh. Seems like that bank was extremely profitable during the military's dicta-torship in the seventies and eighties."

"The Perez family would likely prefer it if the country happened to forget about *Los Desaparecidos*, especially iconic figures such as Thiago Vergara," Edison stated.

"True, but it's not much to go on. There's no specific link between Vergara and Perez," West argued.

"Unfortunately, we're running out of potential leads. The gallery owners and art world have been a bust. Our next step is to dig into the military leaders who had a hand in the *coup* and those who disappeared," Kairo said through a clatter of keystrokes in the background. "And most of those old bastards are dead now."

"Let's add a tail to Little Shit and dig into his daddy's past. See who he knows and if his path ever crossed Vergara's," Charlie decided. All this might turn up nothing, but he was starting to get the sneaking suspicion that they would need to walk away from this mystery. This was the kind of thing a person could spend a lifetime digging into with zero results. There were people out in the world hurting right now who could use their help. "We'll give this one more week."

"Got it, Boss," Kairo agreed. The other two men grunted. No one was happy when a job didn't go the way they expected, but it was something they'd all learned to accept over the years.

Charlie stepped outside the gallery and held the door for his companion, flashing him a grin as they stepped into the cool night air. It was hard to remember sometimes that July in Argentina was the height of winter. The temperature had dipped into the low forties, and the wind was biting through his jacket. Most of his missions, both with the CIA and after they'd parted ways, had been in Europe and parts of Asia—all locations north of the equator. In his mind, it should be sweltering hot, not a bitter wind nipping at his balls.

"Head to the house? Or grab a drink? The night is still young," Edison prodded.

Charlie opened his mouth to answer when Little Shit swept past them at a brisk pace, hurrying down the stairs to a black sedan that screeched to a halt in front of the gallery to a bevy of honking horns. As Benicio threw himself into the back seat, Charlie lifted his eyes to look around the busy street. His gaze caught on a lean figure standing across the street.

It couldn't be.

A truck lurched and rumbled by in a flash of bright headlights. When the truck was gone, so was the figure. Charlie couldn't shake the image burned into his brain. His heart raced and he suddenly couldn't breathe.

Will…

Was that really Will?

2

WILL MONROE

WILL JUMPED INTO THE TAXI, SHOVED A WAD OF PESOS AT THE driver, and demanded he follow the black sedan sliding into traffic. Thankfully, the driver didn't argue. He just stepped on the gas and raced forward.

Slumping low in the back seat, Will exhaled loudly and scrubbed both shaking hands over his face. Yes, he was nervous about confronting Benicio Perez, but that was nothing compared to seeing Charlie Sands in the flesh.

What the fuck was he doing in Buenos Aires?

He almost laughed out loud at himself and that stupid thought. Charlie could and would travel wherever he wanted to go. It was simply unfortunate that they had to show up at the same place at the same time.

Will dropped his hands to his lap and glared out the window at the blur of lights as they streaked by. It was barely after nine in the evening in the middle of the week, but Buenos Aires was still a mess of traffic and people rushing from one place to another. He'd lived in a lot of places in his lifetime, but this city was one that struck him as restless, as if the people refused to stop for more than a few minutes. He'd been told that it changed during the summer months, when people turned sluggish during the height of the afternoon thanks to the oppressive heat, but as soon as the sun set, the city came alive.

Charlie fucking Sands.

His mind traitorously circled. It had taken him years to stop thinking about him, and now in the span of a minute, his brain was clawing at those old memories.

Will would be the first to admit that his life was full of mistakes and missteps, just like everyone else, but if he made a list, Charlie Sands would go to the top as the biggest damn mistake of his life.

How long had it been since he'd last set eyes on Charlie? Six years? At least. Maybe even longer. He wasn't even sure anymore. The years had blurred together following that night in Paris.

It was his own fault. Why should he have expected more from the man, even if they had been dating for a year? They weren't exactly living together at the time, even though Charlie had spent nearly every night in his bed, allowing them to wake together to slow kisses and coffee.

That stupid year had been the longest, most exhausting, best of his life. He'd been finishing up the last year of his residency in Paris. It was pure luck that he'd met Charlie in the first place. He'd been little more than a shuffling zombie as he left the hospital and had literally run right into the sexy man.

Their relationship might have started as purely sex, but it evolved into something sweet and beautiful. Charlie had been there to listen to his bad nights and to hold him when he was so exhausted, he couldn't hold himself upright. They'd giggled and Charlie had even introduced him to his coworkers and friends.

They'd had something.

It wasn't his imagination. It wasn't a fantasy.

Charlie had loved him.

But not enough.

And when the time came for Will to return home to the States, Charlie had said good-bye so easily. As if their year together had been nothing more than a few laughs and a good fuck. There had been no offers to try to stay in contact or pleading for him to remain in France. Nope. Charlie was already heading off on a new job to Austria or Poland. Will didn't know. He'd gone deaf and numb at that point. He wasn't entirely sure what Charlie did. Some kind of team leader for a specialized IT department, though he'd even started to have doubts about that toward the end of their relationship.

Fuck it. Fuck it all.

Why was he thinking about Charlie? That man was just another ex, and he didn't deserve one more second of his brainpower. They meant nothing to each other now.

A bitter laugh escaped Will before he could catch it. It was pretty clear that he'd meant nothing to Charlie even when they were dating.

It didn't matter.

Charlie didn't matter.

He had more important things that needed his full attention. Buenos Aires was a large city. The odds of them crossing paths once again while Charlie was here were astronomical. It wasn't going to happen.

Will forcibly shoved thoughts of Charlie to the back of his mind and glanced around, taking in where he was. The Blue Wind art gallery had been located in Palermo Viejo, which wasn't surprising considering the *barrio* contained some of the hottest and trendiest restaurants and shops in Buenos Aires. It looked as if the black sedan was headed south toward San Telmo. That meant Benicio was going to his steak-house restaurant rather than his ostentatious home in Recoleta. Will couldn't decide if this was a good development or a bad one. A public place might make Benicio more willing to talk or at least keep the conversation civil.

But he was skeptical of even that. If he'd learned anything in the past few months, it was that Benicio Perez was all ego and hot temper—two things that made him utterly impossible to deal with.

As the black sedan parked in front of the *parrilla*, Will grabbed the seats in front of him and pulled himself upright. He directed the driver to continue past the restaurant and pull over to the next block. After thanking the driver and handing him another wad of pesos, Will stepped onto the sidewalk.

He gathered his peacoat a bit tighter around him as the wind slipped through the city and tugged at his clothes with an added bite. His hair fell in front of his eyes, and he shoved it back. Overdue for a haircut yet again, but life had been too busy for basic personal chores beyond food and sleep.

With his hands tucked into his pockets, he strolled down the block toward the *parrilla* that was ablaze with warm lights. As he pulled the door open, boisterous laughter and the rich scent of cooked meat assailed him. While the Perez family tried to position themselves among the elite within Argentine society, Benicio hadn't attempted to create an exclusive posh dining experience. No, the place was warm and lively, welcoming both the monied and the middle-class families.

From what he'd heard, the food was damn good at Parrilla 1880. It was just unfortunate that he'd never intended to eat there.

At the hostess station, a tiny woman in a tight black dress and a flirtatious smile greeted him. "Do you have a reservation with us tonight?"

"I am here for my meeting with *Señor* Perez. My name is Dr. William Monroe. He is expecting me."

The young woman seemed at a loss for words for a moment, her bright-red lips parting only to close without a sound escaping her.

Will flashed his most ingratiating grin. "I'll wait at the bar.

I know he arrived only minutes ago. I'm sure he needs to check a few things prior to meeting with me."

Before she could argue with him, he slipped past the hostess station and wove his way through the tables and servers to the large bar situated to the left of the restaurant. He lucked into an open stool at the end and caught the bartender with the same friendly smile. A lovely Malbec appeared in front of him within seconds of the request.

That was going to be one of the things he missed about Buenos Aires when he moved on to his next temporary home —the wine. The intense dark-red wine had grown on him faster than the white Torrontés. He worried that it simply wasn't going to be as good when he ordered it outside of Argentina.

It had taken years to start drinking wine again after leaving Paris. While he and Charlie hadn't exactly downed casks of it, they'd emptied their fair share of bottles when Will had been able to cobble together some time off. The old memories had tainted the wine for too long.

Had Charlie tried the local Malbec since arriving in the city? He'd always preferred red over white.

What the fuck was he thinking?

It didn't matter what Charlie had or hadn't tried.

Will took a deep swallow of his wine and turned partially on his padded stool to stare out across the crowded restaurant. He needed to get Charlie out of his head and his thoughts focused on why he was trying to meet with Benicio in the first place.

The bastard had been dodging his calls, messages, emails, and letters for over a month now. He was trying to remain professional about this and stick to official channels, but time was running out. Allowing Benicio to avoid him and ignore him wasn't going to work any longer.

Butterflies battered his stomach, and a bead of cold sweat trickled along his spine. He wasn't the confrontational type.

He didn't have trouble standing up for himself or defending himself when someone was acting like a jackass, but this problem with Benicio was more complicated, and he was technically a bystander butting in where he didn't belong.

Yet, there was no way he was backing down. He'd made a promise, and he was sticking to it.

He was nearly finished with his glass of wine when a large man in a dark suit appeared at his elbow. The stern figure was clearly one of Benicio's bodyguards. He'd spotted them when he'd first started following Perez. He'd taken to tracking him for a few days, trying to figure out the best time and place in which to corner him. Striking in the late evening when he was home or at the *parrilla* appeared to be the best bet, a moment when Benicio's guard was probably relaxed and he might be more willing to talk.

"Dr. Monroe?" the man said in a voice that was more like a growl.

"Yes, I'm him," Will replied quickly, hoping he sounded confident rather than nervous.

"*Señor* Perez will see you now," the bodyguard announced. He turned and led the way through the restaurant, leaving Will to scurry after him, dodging servers and customers along the way.

They moved down a short hall off the main dining room, and his heart gave an awkward lurch when they entered the chaotic kitchen filled with steam, open flames, and shouting cooks. Was the office really through the kitchen? That seemed strange but not completely impossible. It was just that Perez looked the type to have a fancy office somewhere in the building, away from the noise and rush of people.

At the far end of the kitchen, the large man shoved a door that opened to the dark night pierced only by a harsh streetlight. The second he stopped walking to argue that he was not going to be brushed off by Perez yet again, a strong hand wrapped his right biceps from behind and shoved him forward.

Will gasped and tried to dig his heels in, but the smooth linoleum gave him nothing to work with. He twisted to find yet another beefy bodyguard had come up from behind him without drawing his attention. While Will would admit that he was not a small man, his five-ten stature and lean build were no match for these two as they almost too easily jerked him outside.

His cheeks burned with embarrassment as he was tossed out of the restaurant and into the filthy alley at the rear of the building. Never in his life had he been ejected from a place. He stumbled a few steps to keep from falling on his face. With his balance restored, he whipped around to shout at the bastards before they slammed the door shut, only to find they weren't just tossing him out. No, they had joined him out there.

Fuck.

Will held up his open hands in front of him to ward off the two men. "Look. I'm not trying to start any trouble. I wanted a five-minute conversation with *Señor* Perez. There is no reason to resort to violence."

"*Señor* Perez has made it abundantly clear that he has no interest in talking to you now or ever," the first bodyguard grumbled. "You have ignored polite refusals. He doesn't see any reason to continue being polite with you."

Will's heart sped up, and his eyes frantically searched for a means of escape. The far end was blocked by a high chain link fence that he wasn't so sure he could scale prior to being caught. The second bodyguard blocked his escape in the other direction, standing between him and the sidewalk.

He backpedaled, trying to get past the bodyguard and closer to the street. If he was lucky, he might be able to sneak by the other behemoth. His brain was still stuck in a state of denial, believing he could talk his way out of this, when the first punch sailed through the air. Ducking to his left, he evaded the fist that was aimed at his jaw. He didn't move fast enough to escape the punch to his gut.

All the air rushed out of his body as pain exploded throughout his abdomen. He bent over, trying to shield that part from further injury while desperately sucking more air into his lungs. He was utterly unprepared for the next hit whipping his head about and slamming him into the nearby brick wall.

Time slowed as several more hits rained down on his face and body until everything became a blur of pain. In a final act of desperation that he wasn't overly proud of, Will kicked out with his right foot, nailing his attacker in the balls. The man went to his knees instantly with a long, low groan.

The other bodyguard who'd been content to watch the beating barked out an angry noise and lunged for Will. Gritting his teeth against the agony pouring through his body, Will shoved away from the wall and ducked under the other attacker's arm. He stumbled and ran through the alley to the street.

As soon as he reached the sidewalk, he turned right and kept running for another two blocks before he dared to glance behind him. But there was no one following on his heels looking to inflict more pain.

Stopping, Will leaned his shoulder on a lamppost and drew in several pained, ragged breaths. His face was throbbing, and blood trickled from his split lip. One eye was already swelling closed, and while his abdomen hurt, it didn't feel as if any of his ribs had been broken. None of it was good, but it could have been a hell of a lot worse.

This had been a warning. A fucking painful one, but a warning all the same.

There was no doubt that if Benicio Perez wanted him dead, his corpse would have been dragged out of that alley tonight.

If he continued on this course, there was a damn good

chance he was going to end up with a bullet in the back of his head.

Did this mean he was going to stop?

Fuck, no.

It meant he needed to be smarter about this. The direct approach was not going to work. He had to come up with something else. Preferably after everything stopped hurting.

3

CHARLIE SANDS

Pacing. He was freaking pacing.

Even when Soren's cover had been blown and he was surrounded by Russian agents out for blood, he'd been calm, confident Soren could talk or fight his way out.

But one tiny glimpse of someone who might be Will Monroe and he was a mess. Forty-eight hours had passed since that moment on the street in front of the gallery, and Charlie was sure he'd never relax again.

He shoved both hands into his thick hair and pulled, trying to get his brain to cooperate. It wasn't Will. There was no way in hell that it was Will.

What the fuck would he be doing in Buenos Aires in the first place?

They hadn't seen each other in years. Will should have a successful practice set up somewhere in the US with a cute little husband, a mortgage, and a healthy chunk of medical school debt.

But that guy looked just like the Will he remembered. Well, he was older. Even in the split second he'd seen him, Charlie could pick out the new lines around his mouth and eyes that made the other man seem harder and colder. It was one of the things causing him to doubt himself. Those eyes. They weren't the eyes he remembered from Paris. Every time Will had lifted those beautiful ocean-blue eyes to him, they'd held such hope and optimistic determination.

That man wasn't Will. Couldn't have been.

And even if it was, what did it matter? He was probably in Buenos Aires on vacation with his boyfriend or husband. Their paths would not cross again.

Kairo shuffled through the living room, heading toward the kitchen. His expression was zombielike, his eyes appearing bleary from staring at the computer screen for too long.

"Please tell me there's some coffee made," Kairo mumbled. His black, shoulder-length hair was tied up in a messy knot on the top of his head and his usually neat beard was a bit scruffy.

"There's about half a pot left. I think it should still be warm," Charlie automatically answered as he followed his friend. They'd decided to rent a house for a month on the edge of La Boca. It wasn't a posh or necessarily safe neighborhood, but after the locals got a good look at Edison and maybe even some dark glares from Westin, they decided to give them a wide berth.

The house itself was a quaint two-story place with four bedrooms and two baths, so they weren't constantly tripping over each other, even if the kitchen was obscenely small. But Charlie knew better than to complain. Over the years, they'd been crammed into far tinier and less luxurious accommodations and survived the experience.

He leaned his hip on the bright-blue tiled counter and crossed his arms over his chest. "Why don't you rest instead of throwing more caffeine at your body?"

Kairo sniffed at him as he grabbed the mug he'd used earlier in the day and rinsed it out. "You know I don't like sleeping while both West and Ed are in the field."

Charlie smirked at the shorter man. "I don't think they're

going to get into any trouble, considering how weak our lead currently is."

Kairo wrapped his hand around the handle of the carafe and lifted his tired amber-brown eyes to Charlie, directing an expression of utter disbelief at him. "Seriously? You don't think they could find trouble?"

"Okay, okay," Charlie conceded with a huff. "Yes, they could find trouble if they really wanted to, but they know to keep their noses clean. Besides, I can keep an eye on things while you catch up on some sleep. You're about to fall over."

Without pouring any coffee into his mug, Kairo replaced the carafe on the coffeemaker and returned his cup to the counter. "You know what? I'm taking you up on that offer. You keep an eye on those lunatics. Ed is watching Perez's house, while West has got a spot outside the restaurant. The last check-in was twenty minutes ago. Benicio Perez was at the restaurant. West said that he'd return here when Perez headed home. Ed plans to come back here by midnight so long as the house is quiet."

Charlie followed a shuffling Kairo to the workstation he'd set up on the dining room table. It held a mad scattering of papers and a couple of dirty mugs, but the man managed to do all his incredible technical work with a single laptop. The only thing more impressive was what this genius could do with his phone.

Kairo dropped into a seat, tapped a few keys, and held up a tiny earpiece to Charlie that would give him direct contact with both teammates in the field.

"I'm handing shit over to Charlie while I grab some sleep. Don't blow anything up," Kairo muttered. He had to be talking to Edison and Westin. There was a brief pause, and Kairo chuckled. "Don't worry, big guy. You know we rarely leave a town without creating one new crater."

Charlie snorted. That had to be Ed complaining about the lack of action on his part. For the demolitions expert, it

23

wasn't a party until something exploded or was at least burning.

Kairo reached up and pulled out his own earpiece and set it in the protective case for later. He gazed up at Charlie, his eyes widening slightly when he found his boss still holding the tiny earwig.

"Were you able to locate any security cameras near the art gallery?" Charlie inquired, hating the hesitance in his own voice. He hadn't told Edison or Westin that he thought he'd seen Will outside The Blue Wind two days earlier. They wouldn't get it. Or maybe they would, and he was just too chickenshit to face their teasing remarks.

A long sigh slipped from Kairo's full lips and he slumped in his chair. "There were a couple that were a good distance off, and they weren't exactly focused on the corner you indicated, so I wasn't able to pull anything incredibly clear."

"But was it Will? I want to know if I'm losing my mind."

"Oh, there's always a chance that you're losing your mind. You've always been crazy. But because of this?" Kairo paused and shrugged his shoulders. "What I can tell you is that at the time you and Ed were leaving the gallery, there was a guy standing on that particular corner who was of medium height and appeared to be between the ages of twenty-five and fifty."

"That isn't helpful at all."

Kairo flashed him a tired, crooked grin. "I never promised it would be."

"Yeah. Okay. I need to let it go. It wasn't him. It…the guy caught me off guard." Charlie scrubbed his empty hand across his face. When he dropped it to his side, he shoved the earpiece into place. It was time to move on. "My mind was a million miles away thinking about this artist and Little Shit. I wasn't expecting a blast from my past."

"Listen to that! The Boss Man has come to keep us company," Edison crowed softly.

"What blast from the past are we talking about?" West

demanded with expert precision. He would go straight to the heart of the matter he was not supposed to know about.

"None of your business," Charlie growled. His team knew far too much about his love life, and most of the time he didn't care because he engaged exclusively in flings. But Will was different, and he didn't want to discuss Will.

Kairo pitched his voice lower so it was unlikely to get picked up by the earpiece. "I could do some digging. He wouldn't be all that hard to locate in the US. I could confirm his current location to ease your mind."

Oh, that was tempting. So very tempting.

In six years, Charlie had not once caved and asked Kairo to locate his ex, though the thought had occurred to him numerous times. And it would help to settle his frazzled nerves. But this was a dark path to go down. He'd always believed that going cold turkey with Will was the best route, and he was sticking to that.

"No. Don't bother. It's fine," Charlie replied, very aware that Ed and West were hanging on his every word, dying to know what he was talking about.

"All right, then," Kairo said with a groan as he stretched his arms over his head. Joints popped, and it was on the tip of his tongue to tease the younger man about his advancing age. But none of them were twenty, stupid, and indestructible any longer.

"Shit!" West snarled the second Kairo's butt left the chair. "We got a problem."

"What kind of problem?" Charlie barked.

Beside him, Kairo whimpered softly but still dropped back into the chair and turned toward the laptop. He snagged the earpiece he'd just taken out and shoved it in place.

"Shooting at the restaurant. People are fucking pouring out of the place. It's total anarchy," West described.

"Of course he got the fun location," Edison moaned, but Charlie ignored him, his eyes locked on the computer screen as he stood behind Kairo's shoulders. Different screens flashed by him at an astounding rate. He couldn't make sense of most of it, but as long as Kairo could, that was all that mattered.

"Any guesses on the number of shooters?" Charlie inquired.

"Well, it sounded like just one, but it escalated to at least four shooters damn fast. How do you want to handle it?"

"The calls have started coming in to the police," Kairo confirmed.

"They're going to have trouble getting close," West countered in his usual calm, cold tone. "We've got people still running out of the restaurant and stopping traffic in every direction. I'm not seeing any blood yet, so this might not be an indiscriminate shooter."

"Kairo, keep tabs on the cops. We need to know when they're within a couple of blocks of West's location. Ed, you're on the move. I need you ready to support West—" Charlie barked out orders over the clatter of keystrokes.

"I've got eyes on the shooters," West interrupted. "Two have emerged from the building and are on foot. Three bodyguards have also hit the street and opened fire. Should I provide cover? Intercept? Shit! One is down."

"Cover and intercept," Charlie shouted before the other could be lost.

"On it."

Charlie raced to grab his phone and keys from where he'd left them on the coffee table in the living room. He didn't know who these people were or what kind of beef they might have with Benicio Perez, but they might be able to provide some valuable information. If not, they could always hand them over to the local authorities when they were done with their interrogation. They had no interest in getting involved in a turf war or drug war or whatever the fuck Perez was into. They needed to make sure Little Shit and his family didn't have anything to do with Thiago Vergara.

He jumped into one of the two rental cars they'd reserved and sped across town. He might have memorized the route to the restaurant after spotting the possible Will thanks to driving it at least three times a day for the last two days, as if he might spot the man again. No such luck. But it did mean that he didn't need some navigation app giving orders. His attention was on the updates he was regularly receiving from West and Kairo. Ed was currently bitching about being stuck in traffic.

Being in La Boca gave Charlie an advantage over Ed since San Telmo was slightly north of him while Recoleta was significantly north of West's location. Their clever sniper managed to fend off Perez's bodyguards without giving away his hiding spot and give the surviving troublemaker some breathing room to escape.

"New problem," West announced to the group.

Charlie swallowed a curse. Of course there was another problem. "What's up?"

"My new friend took a bullet to the abdomen. Doesn't look good. We need a doctor."

Charlie sighed heavily. The four of them could patch up most of the basic wounds and set bones on the fly, but digging bullets out of organs was tricky business. Their chance to get information was shrinking by the second. "Hospital then."

"He says he's got someone who can handle it. No hospital. He'll give directions, but I don't think he can handle being on the back of the bike with me."

"We didn't rent a motorcycle, West," Charlie bit out as evenly as he could manage.

"I *borrowed* it."

"I've got your location. I can give Charlie turn-by-turn directions to you. He's only six blocks away," Kairo interjected before Charlie could snap and demand the obvious question of why he didn't "borrow" a car instead. They needed to get this job done quickly. The first signs of boredom among his crew always manifested as restlessness and petty crimes because they had the skills to get away with them.

Charlie followed Kairo's direction to West's location while also getting updates on the approach of the cops to the area. Kairo might have also been playing with the traffic lights on the way, creating a few more traffic jams to slow up the police while opening up avenues to Charlie.

After five minutes, he drove behind a strip mall where most of the shops were already closed for the night. He flashed his lights twice, and West stepped out from where he was hiding behind a dumpster. They stopped for a moment to toss a too-pale, bleeding man into the back seat, then raced off.

"Who are you? Why are you helping me?" the stranger demanded.

"We're helping you because Benicio Perez is currently on our shit list," Charlie replied, flashing his most winning smile in the rearview mirror. "Considering the little shootout you had in his restaurant, we're guessing he's on yours, too. We help you stay alive and you help us by giving over some information we need."

The man's dark eyes darted from him to West before he gave a jerky nod. "Okay, but doctor. I need to get to the doctor first."

"Not a hospital? Most docs can't dig out a bullet," West grumbled.

"No, he can. Th-there's a clinic near La Boca and the Matanza River."

"Okay. We'll take you to this clinic in La Boca," Charlie agreed just so Kairo and Edison could hear him.

"I've got you. The direction you're headed in is clear of cops," Kairo confirmed. "I'll work on getting Ed to your location as support."

The drive to the clinic was smooth, even if the area did become significantly rougher as they went farther. Definitely not the kind of neighborhood that was going to pay much attention to a guy with a gunshot wound, which was helpful for them.

When they reached the small, single-story building with bars over the windows, their nearly unconscious guest demanded that they go around to the rear. He was expected. Charlie wasn't exactly sure how that was possible, but he didn't ask questions. The guy had lost a lot of blood in the past several minutes despite West's efforts to staunch the bleeding. If this man didn't get some help soon, he wasn't going to be able to give them anything that resembled answers.

Charlie threw the car into park and turned off the engine. "Run inside and warn the doc. I'll bring him in."

"Got it," West agreed as he jumped from the back seat.

Charlie climbed out from behind the wheel and took West's place. Helping the smaller man out of the car was more or less carrying his bloody, unconscious ass. Luckily, he was relatively short, barely topping five five, and incredibly slender. Not much weight to manage even if it was dead weight.

He slipped inside the building to find stained, broken tiles on the floor and white walls that had yellowed with age under the bright overhead lights. West stepped out from one of the rooms closest to the rear entrance and his expression was strange. His mouth was hanging open and his eyes were wide, as though he'd seen a ghost.

"What?" Charlie snapped.

"Ummm…maybe you should let me take it from here. You can wait in the car or something," West said in a low voice.

"What? Don't be fucking ridiculous," Charlie snarled as he continued down the hall, trying not to let the dying man smear blood on the walls. West backed into the room as

Charlie entered. "Doc, I—" Words left him. All thought left him.

The doctor standing in the center of the room with a scowl on his face was William Monroe. His ex.

"It had to fucking be you," Will grumbled. He exhaled loudly and waved to the examination table, then turned to snag a set of gloves. "Put him on the table before he dies!"

West had to step forward and take the man's other arm to snap Charlie from his paralysis. He'd been right. He had seen Will on that street corner two days ago.

And now he was standing in a clinic where Will worked.

A clinic in a bad neighborhood in Buenos Aires.

A clinic where the shooter said the doc expected him.

"What the fuck is going on?" Charlie exploded.

"You think *now* is a good time for talking?" Will snapped at him as he moved to draw over a tray filled with instruments. "Get him on the table and get your asses out of here if you're not going to help."

As much as he wanted to argue—and he *really* wanted to argue—Will had a point. The guy was dying and didn't have much time left if the doctor didn't start working on him. He and West hefted the smaller man onto the table as the sound of squealing tires reached them.

"Doc, how many people do you have in the building with you?" West demanded.

"It's just me. The last nurse left thirty minutes ago. What—"

"You work on saving his life. We'll cover you," Charlie bit out.

"You were followed?" Will shrieked.

Charlie took an absurd amount of pleasure in smirking at his ex. "Come on. Now's not the time, right?"

With the look Will gave him, Charlie was lucky he didn't end up with a scalpel embedded in his forehead.

Charlie ran out behind West, closing the door to the room

as he left. Will needed to work as quickly as possible if they were going to get out of this alive and remain out of jail. He followed West down the hall to the rear door and peeked out. One car could be seen near their rental with at least two occupants.

"I got the back. You check the front," West instructed.

Charlie nodded and jogged along the corridor. "Kairo, we've got guests. You got eyes on us?"

"There are no fucking cameras in your area that I can find. I'm blind!" Kairo shouted in his ear, sounding as if he were on the edge of panic.

"Ed?"

"Still three minutes out," the man growled.

Charlie reached the waiting room that was lined with hard plastic chairs and silently swore at the wall of windows. Yeah, they were covered in bars, but those weren't going to stop the bullets. Was it too much to hope that Will also had bulletproof glass on the windows?

He glanced out to see another car stop in front and three men climb out with weapons in hand. "Three in the front. Two in the rear. Approach with caution." He paused and licked his lips. "Also, Will is here. He's currently digging the slug out of our new friend's gut. We need to keep him safe and buy him time to work."

"Oh fuck," Kairo groaned. Yeah, that was pretty much how Charlie was feeling, but he couldn't think about it.

"Wait! When you say Will, you don't mean *your* Will, right?" Ed demanded.

Charlie cringed. "He's not *my* Will, but yes, Dr. Will Monroe is fucking here and up to his elbows in some guy's guts."

He pulled the Smith & Wesson from the holster at the small of his back and popped the clip out of habit to check it before slapping it in place and chambering a round. Keeping low so his shadow didn't move across the windows as he crossed to the far wall, Charlie edged up to the wall and pressed his shoulder into it while gazing out across the parking lot. He had just slipped into position when bullets flew through the windows into the lobby. Glass sprayed in every direction, and Charlie swore under his breath. These assholes weren't even going to make any demands first. Didn't care if there were innocent people inside the building.

The only good thing was that they didn't seem to be expert marksmen since they weren't hitting shit and were blowing through their ammo like it was water. The second at least two of them clicked empty, Charlie leaned out from his hiding spot and fired through the broken glass. One man dropped with a head shot, but the other guy moved at the last second, taking the bullet in the shoulder.

The uninjured gunman ducked behind their car and shouted at him. He couldn't make it all out, but it was mostly cursing. Apparently they weren't expecting poor Doc Monroe to return fire.

"One down, two left in the front," Charlie reported.

"One down, one left," West added. "No. My mistake. Two down. Rear is clear for now."

"Parked. Entering on foot," Edison stated. "Five hundred yards and closing."

A whisper of footsteps along the hall warned him that West was moving to the front to help him. Thanks to the positioning of the building, no one could approach by car without passing the front first.

"Two hiding behind the sedan. Ed is nearly here," Charlie murmured.

"Got it. I can provide a distraction when Ed is in position. You go check on Doc Will."

Charlie grunted and shoved away from the wall. He wasn't exactly in a huge hurry to see his ex when he was in this mood, but he needed to know Will was okay.

When he reached the door, he dragged in a deep breath

and released it. He could do this. Will wasn't the type to start throwing scalpels and syringes like lawn darts even if he appeared to be incredibly pissed to see Charlie.

He pushed the door slowly open and stuck his head in. Will was fiercely concentrating on the man on his table. A pale-blue mask covered the lower half of his face while a cap covered his hair, but there was enough of his face showing to see the significant bruising around one eye and peeking out of the mask. Had that been there when he'd seen him two days ago? Even in the dark, he would have noticed that Will was hurt. What had happened?

The surgeon glanced up for a second and then returned his attention to his work. "The damage wasn't as bad as I was expecting. Just a few stitches. I'm closing now. He will need to go to an actual hospital for blood and a shit-ton of antibiotics."

"We'll handle it."

"Put on a mask if you're staying in here!" Will snapped.

Charlie nearly growled at the angry man, but he restrained himself. He spotted a box of surgical masks near the entrance and quickly pulled one on before stepping fully into the room. "How much longer?"

"Five minutes."

"Cops have finally been called," Kairo chimed in. Almost at the same time, he heard more gunfire at the front of the building.

"All the targets are down. I'll let Ed in," West informed them.

"No! Tell him to bring his car around the back. We need to get his guy to the hospital and the doctor somewhere safe," Charlie countered.

"What? I'm not going anywhere with you!" Will shouted, but it was merely white noise and Charlie ignored him.

"Kairo, do what you can to slow the cops." Charlie turned

his attention to Will. "You've got two minutes, and then we're out of here even if I have to knock your ass out."

Charlie marched out of the room to find West. They needed to make more plans to cover for Will and to buy them some time even after the police arrived. Luckily, this was a normal part of their job.

What wasn't normal was finding his ex in the middle of this mess.

That didn't matter. He was not letting Will Monroe out of his sight until he knew what the hell was going on.

4

WILL MONROE

GETTING IN THE CAR WITH CHARLIE SEEMED THE LESSER OF two evils, but only by a hair. He had no interest in sticking around the clinic to explain to the police why those men had shot up the place or how they came to suddenly be dead.

But then, he was hoping to avoid any questions from Charlie.

Luckily, they weren't speaking at all as Charlie drove them to the other end of La Boca while his patient and clinic were left in the capable hands of Edison and Westin.

He glanced over at his companion, and his hands tightly gripping the steering wheel as though he had something to be pissed about. Charlie and his friends were the ones sticking their noses into his affairs. He didn't ask for them to interfere.

He wasn't blind to the fact that Francisco probably wouldn't have made it back to the clinic without their help, though. The man had a fighting chance at surviving, thanks to their actions. It was just a shame about Santino. How had things escalated to the point of a shooting in a restaurant? What a fucking mess!

He closed his eyes and leaned his head against the window. God, he was exhausted to the bone, and parts of him still ached from the beating he'd suffered two days ago. He should just pass out, but he was abuzz with nervous energy, and his stomach twisted into knots that might never be untied.

And now he was stuck in a car with Charlie.

Avoiding him in a city the size of Buenos Aires should have been easy. But no. Charlie walked into his clinic with a man who had been shot.

The more disturbing thing was that he wasn't all that surprised.

Part of him had always felt that Charlie's story of being an IT team leader was bullshit. Both Kairo and Soren could talk convincingly about it. Edison wasn't bad either. It was just that West looked more at ease with a gun in his hand than a computer. And Charlie. *Ugh.* The guy had a love-hate relationship with his phone. How was he supposed to manage a computer, let alone a team of so-called computer geeks?

There had been nights in Paris when his restless brain had searched for alternative jobs for what Charlie did. Drug dealer. Mob boss. Spy. Serial killer. As time went by, the ideas grew more and more twisted and insane, but Charlie's kindness and warmth toward him never wavered. Charlie had always made him feel treasured, precious. No matter if they'd bickered and shouted at each other, not once had Will felt unsafe with this man.

Even with the mad fantasies haunting him, Will had kept his mouth shut. He'd been terrified of rocking the boat, afraid that if he opened his mouth and asked questions, Charlie would decide he wasn't worth the trouble.

In the end, that was exactly what Charlie had decided. Stupid him for thinking they could have a future together. Stupid him for thinking that Charlie might actually love him.

Idiot. Fool.

The only person Charlie loved was himself.

Even after so many years, their last night was so clear in his mind—as if it had been burned into his memory.

· · ·

36

SIX YEARS AGO

Nerves twisted his stomach into knots as he headed back to his apartment in the ninth *arrondissement*. The hospital where he was completing his residency had just offered him a permanent position. That was on top of the offers he'd already gotten from hospitals back in the States.

Everything was neatly coming together after years of hard work. The plan had always been to return home after he completed his training, but the urge to cross the ocean and see his family again seemed to have dwindled.

And it was all thanks to Charlie.

What should have been a wonderful thing was twisting him up inside. He needed to decide soon what his next step was going to be, but he couldn't without discussing it with his lover first. Would he even be willing to talk about something like that with him?

Charlie never spoke about the future. He refused to even commit to plans for the weekend. It was always a shrug and a noncommittal "Let's see how things go."

He returned home to find Charlie cooking an amazing dinner in his kitchen, which allowed him to buy a little time, to figure out the right words. For now, he was happy to just fall into his arms and pretend that the world they'd carved out for themselves could continue indefinitely.

They sipped wine and chatted about nothing important after dinner, simply enjoying each other's company.

Will lay with his back against Charlie's chest, while his lover had his bare feet propped up on the coffee table. Music was playing, soft and low. And Will finally had the courage to open his mouth.

"The hospital offered me a job after I finish my residency," Will blurted out. He gulped down the rest of the wine in his glass to keep from blurting out anything else in his sudden panic. He could feel Charlie stiffen under him.

"That's awesome! Congrats!" Charlie said. His tone

sounded genuine, but there was something underlying that he couldn't quite put his finger on. Wariness? Regret? Fear?

No, it was fine. He was just reading his own nerves into it.

"Are you going to accept? I didn't know you were thinking of staying here."

Honesty. Honesty. Honesty. Will mentally repeated the word to himself as he sat up and placed his empty glass on the table. Holding on to his smile, he turned to face Charlie on the sofa, bringing up one bent knee to rest on the cushion between them.

"I'm not sure anymore," he started slowly. He rested his left elbow on the back cushion inches from Charlie's hand and threaded his fingers through his hair, pushing it from his eyes. "I wasn't, originally. This was getting the chance to study under Dr. Gauvin and expand my skills in a new city." Will paused and flashed a wide grin at Charlie. "But living in Paris has been more enjoyable than I was expecting. I don't find myself in a huge rush to return to Portland."

"Oh."

That was *not* reassuring at all. Tightness was spreading through his chest, squeezing his heart and lungs. This was not a heart attack. Heartbreak, maybe. But he wasn't having a heart attack.

Will clenched his molars together and fought to control his expression. They needed to talk this through. Maybe Charlie didn't understand that he wasn't just talking about the city.

"But we've had a lot of fun this past year, as well," Will pressed, hating the strangled tone that was wrapping around his words. "Why should that end, right? I was thinking that I could take the job offer for this hospital, and we could continue…"

Charlie turned to glare at the coffee table in front of him before Will even finished speaking. "Will, you know my posting in Paris is temporary."

"Sure. But—"

"I'll be finishing up here in the next month. Our next job is lined up for Vienna."

It was on the tip of his tongue to boldly state that he'd follow Charlie to Austria. It wasn't a big deal. He'd go wherever Charlie went. He was a doctor now. The world was always in desperate need of another doctor. As long as they got to stay together.

But the words didn't come out because that wasn't what Charlie wanted to hear. Charlie didn't want him to go along to Vienna or anywhere else.

"We always said this was only about having fun while we were in the same city," Charlie continued through Will's choked silence.

"Yeah, I know. Just another piece of ass," Will snarled. He shoved to his feet and stalked to the kitchen. They'd already finished the last bottle of wine, but he knew he had to have something else, something strong in the apartment. There was no fucking way he was getting through this night sober.

Charlie followed close on his heels. "Will, don't. You know it's not like that."

He snorted. "Oh, please. You made it very clear that first night that you were going to fuck my brains out and not call the next day."

Except he had.

Charlie called every day after the first night. They saw each other several times a week. They slept wrapped in each other more often than not. Will couldn't imagine where he'd gotten the crazy idea that he meant something to this asshole.

He started opening and closing cabinets loudly while he searched for any kind of alcohol. Wasted. He needed to be wasted. He wasn't expected to report to the hospital until late morning. If he began drinking now, he would have enough time to sober up. His body would be wrecked by the hangover and Charlie, but he'd be conscious.

"Will, listen, I never know where I'm going to be one day

JOCELYNN DRAKE

to the next. You can't live your life waiting for me to return to you, never knowing when I might be back. That's a shit life, and you deserve better than that," Charlie argued.

Shoving away from the counter, he whirled to face Charlie, part of him hating that the man had four inches on him so that he was forced to look up. "It never occurred to you that I might be willing to go with you? Maybe I want to see more of the world and help as many people as I can, regardless of what country I'm in. Maybe it's enough to do my job and be with you. Ever consider that?"

"Maybe that's not enough for me."

"No. What you mean is that I'm not enough for you. Fine. Whatever," Will said, each word growing more clipped until he felt like he was breaking them off with his teeth. "Get out of here. I need to get some sleep for work tomorrow."

And that was it. Charlie left, softly closing the door behind him.

No big explosion. No shouting and throwing dishes. He didn't even get to toss Charlie's clothes out the window to the streets below, because he never left anything at Will's apartment despite constantly staying there.

It wasn't the quiet that bothered him. It was that Charlie didn't even try to fight for him, for what they had.

PRESENT DAY

Now, he was stuck in a car with Charlie, heading to only God knew where, and eventually they would have to talk to each other. He hated to admit that curiosity was chewing on him. How in the world did Charlie end up in the middle of this? Could Charlie have some business with Benicio Perez or the Perez family?

That would be bad. The Perez family was nothing but trouble for all of Argentina.

It was on the tip of his tongue to warn Charlie about

40

dealing with the Perez family, but then he clearly remembered the ease with which Charlie, Westin, and Edison moved with those guns. Charlie had mentioned Kairo's name as they were moving about the clinic. The other man must have been supporting them remotely.

What the fuck is going on?

Thankfully, Charlie pulled up to a quaint two-story house in a quiet neighborhood before they had to start talking to each other. Charlie killed the engine and got out of the car, leaving Will to follow. With a sigh released between clenched teeth, Will climbed out and trudged up to the house.

As he stepped inside, Kairo's smiling and slightly shocked face immediately greeted him.

"Holy shit! Doc Will, it is you. I know Charlie said it was you, but I couldn't wrap my brain around it," Kairo shouted.

"Good to see you," Will murmured, sticking his hand out.

The man snorted, batted it away, and pulled Will into a tight hug. Kairo had always struck him as being too nice to be stuck with this group of delinquents—but then, nothing seemed to ruffle Kairo's feathers.

Kairo released him from the hug, only to hold him by the shoulders. "That being said, how the fuck did you get mixed up in this crazy shit?"

"Yeah, Doc Will, how did you get pulled into the center of a shooting?" Charlie drawled from where he stood glaring at him from the middle of the living room. His arms were folded over his chest and his biceps were straining the long-sleeved, blue cotton shirt he wore. The stupid part of Will's brain might have sighed a little. Charlie had always looked so good in blue. All shades of blue.

Why did time have to be so kind to this man? It was like he'd magically grown hotter for every year that passed. It was terribly unfair. Will was quite sure his new wrinkles and sprinkling of gray hair only made him appear older, not more attractive.

"I'm not in the middle of a shooting," Will countered stiffly. "In case you didn't notice, I work at a free health clinic. That means that I see all manner of injuries and illnesses. If I ask too many questions, people who need me won't come in out of fear. It's more important to me to save lives than to pry into their private lives."

"And do those injuries include bullet holes?" Charlie growled.

"Occasionally."

Charlie narrowed his eyes on him. He knew that look. He was treading on very thin ice, but that didn't explain why his heart skipped a beat and his mouth suddenly grew dry. It was nothing. So, his ex was hot. Big deal. He was also a domineering, lying asshole.

"What the fuck, Will?" Charlie exploded, throwing his arms up in the air.

Behind him, he heard Kairo's footsteps hurry down the hall to another part of the house. *Coward.* Trying to get out of the line of fire and leaving Will on his own. He hadn't seen Charlie lose his temper often when they'd been dating, but when he had, it was a scattershot method. Anyone who was within eyesight stood a chance of getting hit even if they hadn't caused the problem in the first place.

Will crossed his arms over his chest, closing himself off to his former lover. "What would you like to discuss, Charlie? Why I'm in Buenos Aires? Does that mean you're willing to talk about why you and your friends are here? Or how about why you, West, and Ed are so adept at using guns? Almost with a kind of military precision. Has the IT business gotten that cutthroat?"

Watching Charlie deflate in front of his eyes was a high he'd never felt before in his life. Charlie was an expert at deflection and evasion, but the man knew he was fucking trapped this time.

"We're not talking about me—"

"We're never talking about you!" Will snarled. "And you

know what? We're not talking about me, either. You gave up the right to have any interest in my life years ago."

"What did you expect me to do? Just drop off your patient and walk away?"

"Yeah, I did."

Charlie threw up his hands again and paced across the room, moving with ease around a low coffee table and past a heavily padded armchair. "Are you fucking kidding me? You can't be this stupid." When he turned back, he pointed at Will. "If we hadn't stayed, you *and* your patient would have been shot dead. You get that, right?"

Yeah, he got it.

Will balled his hands into fists at his side and drew in a deep breath. He needed to get a handle on his emotions. Shouting hurtful things at Charlie was utter nonsense. They weren't dating, didn't mean anything to each other. Charlie, West, and Edison had helped him escape as well as helped to save Francisco's life. He couldn't forget that.

"You're right. I'm sorry." His voice grew calmer and steadier with every word that he spoke. "Thank you. You and your friends risked your lives today to protect me and my patient. I'm very grateful for that. Can you tell me if Ed and West got Francisco safely to the hospital?"

"They just dropped him off at the ER. They hung back long enough to make sure that he was taken care of," Kairo called out from the next room, proving that he was hanging on their every word. "And Charlie, you might want to take your earpiece out."

Charlie rolled his eyes and snarled curses under his breath as he dug something tiny out of his ear. Will assumed they were all wearing one, so it was very likely that Westin and Edison heard at least Charlie's half of their argument.

He marched into the next room. Will followed him part of the way so that he could see Charlie cross to where Kairo was sitting behind a laptop. His ex handed the other man something and stormed toward the living room. His temper didn't appear to have been placated by Will's words of gratitude.

"What's going on with you? Why are you even here? You should be back in the States with your practice and-and a husband," Charlie stammered, his anger simmering in his voice. "How are you mixed up in this kind of mess?"

"Don't worry about it. Our lives went in vastly different directions. I've got it under control."

Lies. Big, nasty, smelly lies.

Nothing was under control.

But Charlie didn't need to know that. It felt like everything was spiraling out of his control with each passing day, but he refused to give up. He could still figure this out.

Charlie closed the distance between them and grabbed his chin with his thumb and forefinger, tilting his head up so that the overhead light illuminated the bruises on his face. "Is this what control looks like?"

Will jerked his chin out of Charlie's grasp and smacked his hand away with his right, but his former lover caught his wrist to inspect his battered and healing knuckles.

"What the hell is going on, Will?" Charlie pressed, his voice softening for the first time since meeting in the clinic.

Hell, no.

Charlie was not allowed to use that voice. It was already creating cracks in the armor wrapped around him. Everything inside of him was crying out to spill the entire story to Charlie. He'd been fumbling in the dark for months now, and it wasn't just his life on the line. Francisco could have been killed tonight. Santino was dead. But he couldn't stop. Not now. Time was running out, and if something wasn't done soon, they'd lose their chance.

Sure, Charlie was his asshole ex, fantastic at driving him crazy, and too bossy for anyone to tolerate, but Will couldn't deny that Charlie was also a born problem solver. The man could peer straight through all the chaos, see the perfect solution, and lay out the steps required to accomplish exactly what needed to be done.

But he couldn't drag Charlie into this. Wouldn't do it.

"Look," Will started only to stop again. He took a step backward and held up both of his hands to ward Charlie from drawing any closer. The distance helped to clear his head and put steel into his spine. "I appreciate the concern, but really, I've got this. Thank you for risking your lives to save Francisco and to protect me. But right now, all I want is to return home and try to sleep for an hour before the cops are banging on my door."

"You're not leaving," Charlie growled, once again becoming an immovable mountain.

"What?" Will shrieked when he could get the gears in his brain turning.

"Actually, you do need to stay," Kairo interjected, stopping Charlie from throwing more fuel on the fire that was building in Will's temper. The sweet man slipped into the room and came to stand between Will and Charlie. He even gave the taller man a shove, putting more distance between Charlie and Will. "You were the last one to leave the clinic, right?"

Will nodded.

"Then you can easily say that you went over to the house of some old friends from your days in Paris," Kairo stopped on a wince as if belatedly realizing that he was stepping on a sensitive area, but quickly pushed on. "You hang out here for the rest of the night. Ed and West are already grabbing some takeout. You turn off your phone and crash here. Tomorrow, you head to the clinic and act surprised like the rest of the world. Plus, you'll have four guys to support your story." Kairo placed a hand on Will's shoulder and offered up a kind smile. "You need some plausible deniability, Doc Will. This option keeps the cops from digging too deeply into your life."

It sounded good. Really good. Just one night of not having

to worry. It bought him some time to mentally work on his story for the police. They'd been called to the clinic several times in the past for break-ins. People hit the place searching for drugs they could abuse or sell, but he'd learned long ago to keep very little on hand. It also didn't hurt that the clinic's neighbors were on the lookout for potential thieves. They couldn't afford to allow service to stop at the clinic. They had too few other options.

"Okay. Thanks," Will agreed with a nod, refusing to even direct his gaze at Charlie.

"Excellent! Everything will work out. Don't you worry," Kairo replied.

Will wasn't convinced of that in the least, but at least he had a safe place to spend the night.

Edison and Westin arrived a few minutes later, heavily laden with food. The delicious smell stirred a disgruntled growl from his stomach. He couldn't remember the last time he'd eaten. The clinic had been slammed all day, which was pretty damn normal. He usually took a break in the afternoon to cram a sandwich into his system, but he couldn't recall even doing that.

Conversation around the table was awkward as they dug into the food. Charlie wasn't talking. Westin never talked. And Will refused to talk about what he'd been doing over the past decade, mostly because he didn't want Charlie to know anything about his life.

That left Kairo and Edison to hold the conversation together with a patchwork of crazy stories about weird things that happened in places they'd visited over the years. But as he listened, Will could tell there was so much they were censoring. Huge chunks of their lives that he wasn't supposed to know about. And these were the people he was supposed to be trusting with his life. Including the man he'd given his heart to.

He was a fucking idiot.

As soon as the food was eaten and cleared away, Will escaped to the bathroom to shower. He couldn't get away fast enough. The *milanesa* sandwich and *provoleta* were sitting heavy on his stomach, mixing with the anxiety he couldn't shed after spending the past couple of hours with his ex. Kairo kindly loaned him a spare change of clothes since he was still trapped in his dirty scrubs from the clinic.

For several minutes, Will was simply content to stand under the lukewarm water as it hammered on the top of his head, letting it slowly wash away the miasma of dark thoughts and fears clouding his mind. Little by little, the worst of it sluiced off his too-slender frame and went down the drain.

When he exited the bathroom, he was feeling a bit more in control of his mind and emotions. At least, until he found Charlie leaning against the opposite wall, his arms folded across his chest and a neutral expression on his face.

Will carefully slid out of the doorway and motioned to the bathroom behind him. "It's all yours. Even left you some hot water."

"Come with me," Charlie grumbled.

Will sighed. "I'm not in the mood to argue with you anymore."

"Then don't. Come on."

Rolling his eyes at Charlie's back, Will followed him down the hall and into one of the bedrooms. He needed to only draw in a deep breath to know this was the bedroom Charlie was using. Hints of his cologne and something that was just Charlie lingered in the air. His heart immediately sped up and a tingle started to spread throughout his body. How long had it been since he'd been alone in a bedroom with his man?

He opened his mouth to state that he was not sharing a room with him, but Charlie spoke before he could get the words out.

"You'll sleep in here tonight. I'm taking the couch."

Will closed his mouth and had to reorder his thoughts

after that unexpected announcement. "You don't have to do that. The couch is fine with me," he replied, aiming for civil and polite.

The couch would be perfect. He couldn't imagine being able to sleep when every time he rolled over, he was wrapped in the too-familiar scent of his former lover.

"You look like you could really use a good night's sleep, Doc Will. Take the bed." Charlie's voice had dipped low and felt like a pair of strong arms wrapping around his soul. He wanted to lean into that and let go of everything for a while. Forget the rest of the world for five or six hours. That was all he needed.

But the price of leaning on Charlie was far too high. He'd never be able to rebound from that.

Charlie crowded close, and Will swallowed hard. He was trapped between the queen-sized bed and his former lover with no way of escape unless he was willing to run across the mattress. Not the most graceful exit, but he was considering it if it meant keeping the remains of his heart intact.

"Besides," Charlie continued in that same low, soothing voice, "if I let you take the couch, I won't be able to do this."

A metallic click echoed through the room, jolting Will from the spell Charlie was weaving. He glanced down to see that Charlie had snapped a handcuff on his right wrist.

"What the—" he started but didn't get the rest out as Charlie jerked the other handcuff over to the headboard and closed it around one of the wooden spindles, effectively locking him to the fucking bed.

"This way, we can all sleep in peace without worrying about you escaping and doing something stupid," Charlie said, his tone hardening.

"You fucking asshole! You can't do this! You can't keep me prisoner here!" Will shouted at the top of his lungs. He jerked on the handcuff several times, but it just loudly rattled against the wooden frame, not budging an inch.

"You have no idea how much of an asshole I can be," Charlie threatened. He leaned forward so that the tips of their noses were nearly touching. His breathing burst between his parted lips in rough pants as if he'd recently returned from a run.

"Trust me, you gave me an excellent crash course in how selfish and cold you can be."

Charlie's expression twisted up in a bitter smile and he lifted one hand to cup Will's jaw. Will flinched at the incredibly gentle contact, demanding his body not react to the heat and blissful familiarity of his touch. Everything about Charlie called back to memories of happier times. He wanted to pull away and run, but Charlie had him trapped.

"What does it say about you?" Charlie whispered. "As much as you hate me right now, we both know that I can make you melt in my arms." Charlie's large thumb moved across his chin and swept along the bottom edge of his lip. Will clenched his teeth to keep his mouth shut. "I know all the ways to make you shout my name. To make you mine."

It was true. As angry as he was at Charlie, he could feel a hundred little fires lighting across his body while his blood rushed to his cock, steadily filling it with a throbbing ache. Too much time had passed since he'd last been with someone and with just a touch from Charlie, the deep, smooth voice sliding into his ear worked to knock through his carefully erected defenses. His former lover knew his body better than anyone else. Charlie could deliver on all his promises and more.

Will swallowed hard and forced his eyes up to Charlie's liquid dark-brown ones. "Congrats. You know how to make me hate myself even more where you're concerned. Is that a natural gift or something you learned as an IT Team Lead?"

Pain flashed across Charlie's face in an instant, and then it was gone. He dropped his hand from Will's face and took a couple of steps away, giving them both the breathing room they needed.

"Get some sleep, Doc," Charlie bit out before leaving the room.

Only when the door was closed behind Charlie did Will collapse on the edge of the bed. His entire body was trembling while his neglected dick ached. Charlie was right. If the man had kissed him, he'd have caved completely. He would have let Charlie turn him inside out to escape from the horror and pain of the past few months.

But he'd wake up the next day and regret everything.

He needed to get as far away from Charlie as soon as possible. He couldn't let Charlie break him again.

5

CHARLIE SANDS

Charlie managed to get two steps away from the bedroom before he had to stop and brace one hand against the wall for support.

What the hell was he doing?

Every emotion was boiling up and swirling together in his chest to become a toxic concoction threatening to poison him and Will.

He was completely out of control. Every word out of his mouth was designed to either piss Will off or hurt him. Why? What was the point?

He'd defused plenty of hostile situations without a single casualty. He'd run into way too many men he'd slept with who were pissed that he wouldn't stretch their one-night stand into something more. Each and every one of those he'd managed to defuse with relative ease.

Well, his common sense had died the second he set eyes on Will Monroe.

And there was no way of resurrecting it if Will was going to keep putting himself in harm's way. It wasn't hard to guess how those bruises had appeared on his face. The doctor had gotten his ass handed to him and was probably lucky to still be alive.

If Will thought he was going to be allowed out of Charlie's sight now, he was out of his damn mind.

Except Charlie had no right to barge into Will's life now, even if he was in danger. Will could do whatever he wanted with his life. Charlie had no say.

And how the hell was he supposed to explain to the rest of his team that he was now thoroughly distracted by whatever was going on with Will? That was not the reason for them being in Buenos Aires in the first place. They had an entirely different job to take care of.

Cursing himself and Will, he continued down the stairs to the first floor, where his friends were sitting in the living room, sipping beers. At least, he didn't have to worry about Will until morning. That might be just enough time to either come up with a solution for Will's problem or to cauterize the remains of his heart so he couldn't care about his ex's life being in danger.

"Did you tuck your boy in and give him a good-night kiss?" Ed called when he entered the room.

Well, first there was a good chance he was going to kill Ed. Then he might figure out his Will problem.

West lifted his left foot and kicked Edison in the knee. "Asshole."

"Seriously, a little tact," Kairo chastised.

"Charlie knows I'm joking," Ed countered, waving his beer bottle at Charlie.

Clenching his teeth against a sigh, Charlie dropped into the empty armchair while Kairo sat in one of the chairs dragged in from the dining room. Westin and Ed dominated the floral-patterned couch.

"After you dropped off that Francisco guy, did you spot anything interesting?" Charlie asked. If they could talk about the problems ahead of them, he could possibly forget about the bigger problem on the second floor.

"Nothing," West replied with a shake of his head.

"We took a pass by the neighborhood with the clinic, but the cops had it all locked down pretty good," Ed added. "You gonna tell Doc Will that we're the ones who cleared out his drugs to make it appear like a robbery?"

"Tomorrow. We still need to find a viable way to get those drugs back into the clinic without it raising any suspicions." Charlie rubbed his bearded jaw. Ed and West left the bodies and cleaned up from Will's impromptu surgery so no one would be able to tell the doctor or his patient had been there at the time. With just a few minutes of tinkering, his guys had made it look like warring gangs had fought over the drugs in the clinic after it had been closed for the day. There was nothing to put Will at the scene during the shooting.

"Did Francisco volunteer anything about what happened at the restaurant?" Kairo leaned forward and rested his elbows on his knees. "What started the shooting? Was he there for Benicio Perez or someone else?"

Ed shook his head. "The dude was out of it. What he did mutter was slurred and gibberish. My Spanish isn't that good."

"Don't know if Will drugged him that deeply or if it was from the blood loss," West stated. "We couldn't get anything useful."

Charlie glanced over at Kairo. "See if you can hack into the hospital records. Keep an eye on this Francisco. Make sure we know when he's released. If he's got dirt on Perez, I want it, too."

Kairo grinned at him. "You'd think he would be willing to cough up that much to his rescuers."

"We'll probably have to move fast. Will wouldn't have half-assed patching him up," Edison interjected. "Unless the guy gets some infection, he'll probably be released in a day or two at most."

"Not to be a dick—" West started, but Kairo was quick to interrupt.

"But you're so good at it."

"Do we have anything to keep us following Little Shit around?" West continued as if Kairo hadn't spoken. "And I mean anything solid linked to Thiago Vergara. Sure, things got crazy at his restaurant, but we're not even sure if any of this is related to Perez. Some other big-shot asshole could have been eating there."

"No," Charlie bit out, hating to even admit it, but there was no avoiding the truth. "We've got nothing other than the fact that he's an utter asshole and has some bad opinions about Thiago Vergara. All the same, Benicio Perez wouldn't have even been born yet when Vergara disappeared."

"True, but he's definitely into some shady shit," Edison added. He leaned forward and placed his empty beer bottle on the table. "That's got to count for something. His family could have helped to move those Vergara paintings through the black market after the artist was kidnapped."

"Or they could be common thugs running drugs and an extortion racket. Nothing to do with why we're here," Charlie countered. He lifted his hands to his companions. "We came here for a very specific job—to solve the mystery of where the Vergara paintings came from and how they ended up in the custody of Ehren's uncle. We can put that on the back burner to take down the Perez family, but you know that could turn into a much bigger mess than we're currently equipped to handle."

"Not to mention, we ain't getting reimbursed for either job," West pointed out.

They weren't hurting for cash to fund their little adventures after they'd gotten handsomely paid in Amsterdam by

Soren and his new boyfriend, but it wasn't like they could blow it endlessly on whatever caught their fancy.

"I say we follow up on the last lead that we have—Francisco," Charlie suggested.

Kairo tilted his head to look at Charlie, sending a lock of hair across his eyes. He blew at it until it finally moved. "And if it doesn't pan out, what? We're just walking away? What about Doc Will? You think he's gonna be safe? We don't know if he's mixed up in dangerous shit, or if he's an innocent bystander."

"*Doc Will* made it very clear that he doesn't want us anywhere near his business," Charlie sneered.

"I think the more accurate statement would be that he doesn't want *you* near his business," West smirked.

"And here I thought we were a package deal. You guys set to become a trio so you can protect Will?"

Edison held his hands up. "Geez, Charlie. Don't get your panties in a bunch. Nobody's talking about ditching you."

"Even if Will is way cuter than you," West said—because one of them had to throw gasoline onto the fire. West had zero interest in Will, but the sniper was excellent at finding the perfect spot to hit for optimal damage.

Charlie narrowed his eyes on the man, and West held his gaze without blinking. There was no one cooler than West. "You done?"

"No, I can keep going. You think Will is single? Or has he found himself a hot Latin *papi* to take care of him?"

Charlie was out of his chair before West finished speaking, and he wasn't even aware of it. Both Ed and Kairo caught him as he tried to take a step toward his old friend. West didn't move a muscle except to widen his grin.

"Enough. Let it go," Kairo murmured.

"You know West is being a dick because he hasn't gotten to shoot enough people recently," Edison added.

Yeah, he knew that. West got restless and he lashed out at the people that mattered most to him rather than dealing with his own issues. Charlie usually didn't mind being his target. It was just that West rarely ever mentioned Will. It was the most tender spot, the one that Charlie couldn't remain rational about.

"We're not leaving," West announced in a voice closer to his normal grumble. "Even if Benicio Perez and the Perez family have nothing to do with Thiago Vergara, we've got to be sure that whoever that Francisco decided to piss off at the restaurant doesn't decide to strike out at Monroe because he saved that guy's life. Doc Will might hate your guts, but we still see him as a friend. We look out for our friends."

Some of the tightness eased in Charlie's chest so that he could breathe a bit easier. He hadn't even noticed it until now. He took a step backward, and his friends released him so he could flop into the armchair.

"He doesn't want our help," Charlie growled.

Edison snorted. "When the hell has that ever stopped us?"

"Besides, it's not like Doc Will knows what we're capable of. He'll never even see us," Kairo reassured him. "Just some quiet digging. Maybe a couple of security cameras on the clinic and hidden at his apartment to keep an eye on him. Nothing major."

When it came to Kairo, the concept of privacy was always a flexible, fluid thing that moved to suit his needs. Charlie wasn't a fan of invading Will's privacy, particularly without his knowledge, but a little surveillance would help him sleep at night and keep Will alive. That was a win-win in his book.

"We stay. We dig. Some surveillance," Charlie agreed. He turned his gaze on Kairo and pointed at his reconnaissance specialist. "No cameras *in* his apartment or house."

"Spoilsport," Kairo muttered.

"Just until we confirm Perez isn't involved in our mystery and we know that Will is safe."

There was a chorus of agreement. It felt like it was almost too easy, too eager, but he did not want to think about it.

"I'm getting a beer. Anyone want another?" Charlie asked as he shoved to his feet. He looked over his shoulder to see West shake his head.

"Nah. I'm heading to bed. That was enough fun for me," Ed murmured, stretching his massive arms over his head.

Charlie couldn't say he was surprised Kairo followed him into the kitchen. He grabbed a beer out of the fridge and held it out to the other man, who took it with a grin. Charlie snagged one for himself and shut the door.

Leaning against the counter, he twisted off the cap and tipped his beer toward Kairo. "All right, you got me alone. Spit it out."

"You're not over Will."

Charlie sighed. At least Kairo didn't beat around the bush. "And?"

Was there any point in denying it? He'd slept with plenty of guys over the years and run into more than enough of them later. Not one of them caused even a flicker of emotion in him other than a faint feeling of amusement or annoyance.

But Will…he was so different.

Will was the one he'd *dated*. Will was the one he'd practically lived with for a year. Will was the one he'd bothered to memorize hundreds of little things about, because when it came to Will, everything fascinated him. He knew Will liked hot black tea or white tea with strawberries. Never green tea. He knew that even when Will was in the grumpiest of moods, all he needed to do was massage the man's arch with the right amount of pressure and Will was moaning like they were filming a porno. His former lover was a tactile creature who loved to touch soft things as a way of calming his nerves. He loved being held. He would burrow so close as if he wanted to climb right inside of Charlie's chest. And Charlie had loved that, too. Holding Will's slim body in his arms so that there was no separating them.

Will was the only one he'd seriously considered turning his entire life upside-down for just so he didn't have to walk away from him.

Yet in the end, he hadn't. He'd kept his job because he thought it was the thing that defined him. He'd walked away so Will could have a shot at a better, happier life than what he could offer.

"We all get why things ended badly in Paris," Kairo said as he removed the cap from his beer. "But we're not in the CIA anymore. We can date now and actually be ourselves. Come on! *Soren* of all people is in a serious relationship now."

"With an assassin," Charlie pointed out.

Kairo scoffed as if that was the least of Soren's problems. "Alexei is a total sweetheart. He's good for Soren, and we both know he'd do anything to keep his boyfriend safe."

Alexei doing *anything* was part of what gave Charlie nightmares about that man.

"Think about it," Kairo continued, bumping his arm against Charlie's. "Soren. The guy who fell apart when his boyfriend got killed because of a job. He found his bearings again, and now he's happy."

Charlie rolled his eyes. "I get it. If someone as hopeless as Soren could find someone, there's a chance for even me."

"I don't know. I think you might be in worse shape than Soren."

That earned a glare, to which Kairo grinned broadly.

"I'm saying the guy who was your fucking everything— whether you want to admit it or not—is right here. It's like a sign from the heavens or fate or something. Some higher power is putting a second chance in your lap." Kairo pointed at him with his beer, his expression turning frighteningly serious. "That shit does not happen in real life."

"That sounds wonderful. Very Hallmark," Charlie

mocked, and Kairo did not seem amused. "But even if I lost my mind and took your advice, you seem to be forgetting one very important thing—Will hates my guts."

Kairo snorted. "Details."

"That's a big fucking detail."

"The fact that he hates you so much probably means that he's not over you, either. You might be able to fix things between you. Get your second chance."

"And what?" Charlie held out his hands in front of him. "What the hell do I have to offer? What's changed from Paris?"

"A lot has fucking changed, and you know it. You've changed, even if you don't want to believe it." Kairo paused and took a deep drink of his beer. "You can do anything with your life now. Besides, it seems pretty obvious that Will isn't all settled down as some cute country doctor. You don't know what he wants anymore." Kairo snorted. "The scariest thing for you might be discovering that you don't love him now because he has changed so much."

Lovely. Kairo just had to think of something that hadn't occurred to him.

Could Will have changed that much?

He was definitely colder and harder than he remembered, but was it possible for the core of who Will was to really change?

"I've got a suggestion you're going to hate," Kairo started.

"What?"

"Call your brother."

"Fuck off."

Kairo smiled at him as if he'd expected that response. "Call your brother. At least when you disagree with him, you can tell yourself you know more than a goddamn professional." Kairo drained the last of his beer and tossed the bottle into the paper bag for recycling. "Night."

Charlie glared at his own barely-touched beer and sighed.

His younger brother, Stephen, was a psychiatrist. Yes, he specialized in pediatric psychiatry, but he still knew his shit—not that he'd ever say that where his brother could hear him. Stephen would probably have some very logical and comforting things to say.

He'd also have many things to say that Charlie wasn't ready to hear.

It was tempting to call Stephen, but he couldn't.

Even if he didn't want to let go of Will, did he have any right to try to insert himself back into his former lover's life?

Maybe it was better to let this second chance slip through his fingers. Will was better off without him.

6

WILL MONROE

Will wasn't proud to admit it, but he slept.

Too many days of running on too little sleep had left him ragged and exhausted. He should have been up worrying about Francisco or at least mourning Santino. How could things have gone so wrong?

He needed to escape.

The police and the clinic needed to be dealt with.

He also had patients who relied on him to make regular house calls.

But he sat on the bed and leaned against the pillows for a minute. It wasn't even a comfortable bed. The mattress was too soft and lumpy. He closed his burning eyes for only a second, the too-familiar scent of Charlie wrapping about him.

The next thing he knew, faint gray light was creeping around the edges of the curtains. He blinked and tried to rub his eyes with his right hand but couldn't. He was handcuffed to the bed.

Fuck. Charlie.

The chaos.

Charlie and his friends were in Buenos Aires.

Francisco and Santino.

He needed to get out of there now so he could deal with his life. Preferably *without* Charlie.

Will sat up and slung his legs off the edge of the bed. He jerked at the handcuff holding him in place. The metal rattled against the wood, and he flinched. He needed to be quiet. A visitor right now would not help his escape.

He quickly searched the top of the nightstand but found nothing of use. Just the lamp, a plastic cup of water, and a lighter. He wasn't going to try to set the bed on fire. The drawer didn't offer much more help besides a pad of paper and a pen. It was as if Charlie didn't trust him.

No! The pen!

He snatched it up with his left and bit the pen clip with his teeth, pulling it free before placing the pen on the nightstand. Lying flat on his stomach, he worked the slender piece of metal into the keyhole. Picking handcuffs wasn't all that hard. He needed to get the catch.

So, maybe he'd briefly dated this guy who happened to be mildly kinky.

And maybe he'd also happened to be enormously forgetful.

Forgetful about things like where he put the key or about unlocking Will prior to leaving for his shift at the hospital.

The relationship had been utterly forgettable, but Will had picked up one useful skill, at least.

Within a couple of minutes, Will was free of the cuffs and rubbing the sore skin on his wrist. He was half tempted to take the cuffs with him. No telling if they might come in handy, but he tossed the idea aside. It was better if he didn't have anything in his life to remind him of Charlie. Especially handcuffs.

Will patted his body, trying to figure out what was missing. His phone was downstairs on Kairo's spare charger, and his shoes were by the front door. Scrubs? *Shit.* His scrubs were probably in the wash. Ed had offered to toss them in. Never mind. He owed Kairo a T-shirt and sweat pants. He had enough scrubs to get by for now.

Very slowly, he eased the bedroom door open, trying not to make any noise. The house was deathly silent. Not even the sound of cars on the street permeated the building. The world was still asleep. If he could sneak a few blocks away from the house, he could call a cab to pick him up.

But he didn't get that far.

Standing against the wall opposite his door was Edison. The tall, broad-shouldered Black man grinned, and Will swore under his breath. So much for a sneaky escape. He thought he'd been so quiet.

Ed lifted one hand and motioned for Will to step into the bedroom he'd just left, making room for him to follow.

Will dropped onto the edge of the bed and sighed as Ed closed the door behind him.

"Leaving without saying good-bye?" Ed asked in a teasing whisper.

"I need to get home and back to the clinic. You don't need to be dragged into this shit anymore."

"And what kind of shit are you dealing with?"

Will lowered his gaze to the floor. "Don't worry about it."

"I can't help it. You and Charlie split a long time ago, but I still consider us friends. I want to help you."

This was what he expected from Edison. Some people would look at Edison and just see a huge, muscular man and call him scary. Will stared into that man's eyes and wondered how his frame managed to hold in such an enormous heart. The guy wanted to help everyone he met, but Will refused to let him get involved. He was no fool. Ed and Charlie were a package deal. There was no way Ed could help without Charlie following right behind him, and Will wanted to get as far from Charlie as humanly possible.

"I know you do, and I greatly appreciate it, but really, I've got this under control. Don't worry about me." Will gazed up and flashed him the most confident smile he could muster. It must not have been much, because Ed didn't appear convinced.

He straightened his shoulders and sat up. "If this is about Francisco, you don't need to worry. The guy lives in the neighborhood near the clinic. He's been in the clinic to see me several times. I'm sure that's why he had you bring him to me. I'm not in the middle of whatever mess he's found himself in."

The worried scowl eased a bit, and he propped his hands on his hips. Will's heart fluttered in his chest. The skepticism lingered in his eyes.

"Is that kind of insanity normal at the clinic?" Ed inquired, his brows meeting over his nose.

"Shootings? No. But I have seen more than a few patients who were shot or stabbed." Will paused and heaved a heavy sigh. He shoved his hand through his messy hair. "That neighborhood isn't the best and doesn't get much help in the way of government funding or police protection. I've made it my policy not to ask questions, just help people. If I started asking questions and reporting every bullet wound to the police, those people would stop coming in, and they'd be dying in some back alley."

"I get it. I get it. I guess we're all surprised to find you here in the first place. We thought you'd be in the States."

Will forced a smirk. "And instead, Charlie and West walk in to hand me a patient with a bullet wound in Buenos Aires."

"Yeah, something like that."

Will shrugged. "Being out of the country made me realize that I could go anywhere with my training, and there are plenty of places that are in desperate need of doctors. I've been traveling." He paused and huffed a tired laugh. "A lot. I've been traveling a lot."

"You been here long?"

Will shook his head. "Nope. About five months. Another doctor I met in Thailand and kept in contact with moved here a few years earlier. He needed to return to the States for a family emergency. He emailed and asked if I could take over the clinic while a more permanent replacement was lined up. I'm not supposed to be here much longer."

Edison grunted as if he were thinking over what Will had told him, while Will's caffeine-deprived brain scrambled to think of something he could tell this man to convince him to let him sneak out of this house.

"I know things are tense between you and Charlie, but the rest of us are just looking out for your well-being. We're not trying to make this hard on you," Ed commented.

"I know, and I'm sorry everyone else has to suffer because Charlie and I can't act like adults when we're in the same room together."

Edison snorted. "Honestly, I thought it was going to be worse. At the very least, I figured weapons would be drawn or half the house would be on fire when West and I got back."

"Kairo was brave enough to act as a referee." Will smiled.

"I'll help you avoid Charlie and get out of here, but I want you to promise me something."

Will's heart skipped and sped up. "I...I can't promise anything, Ed, but I can try my best."

That seemed to be enough for the big man because he gave a short nod. "Stay away from Benicio Perez."

Will tried to swallow, but his mouth and throat were suddenly dry. That...there was no way he could stay away from Perez. He hoped to avoid the man, but there was something he needed to do first, and it very much involved the Perez family.

"Please, Will. I don't know what Francisco and his friend were doing in that restaurant, and we're more than happy to pull it out of Francisco after he's healed. But just in case, I wanted to warn you to stay away from Perez. We're not sure what he's into, but all signs point to Perez being a very bad man."

Fuck! This was getting complicated.

It was on the tip of his tongue to ask yet again what the hell they were all into and why they were in Argentina in the first place, but he really wasn't in the mood for another lie or deflection. Part of him also didn't want the answer to that question because he was afraid he might start to worry about all of them.

"The world is filled with bad people. You learn to avoid them," Will replied, trying not to sound as bitter as he felt.

It was hard some days when he was constantly worried about funding for the clinic or whether there were enough hours in the day to see everyone who needed him or why good people had to remain trapped in bad relationships—including bad governments.

"Yeah, I know. Just do me a favor and try to avoid Perez."

Will smirked. "Unless he walks into my clinic, I think it's very unlikely that our paths are going to cross." That was as close to the truth as he could get. If he was lucky, his business with Perez would be concluded very soon.

"I guess that'll have to do." Edison reached behind him and quietly opened the door. He leaned into the hallway and picked something up. When he turned back, he held out Will's worn sneakers with his cell phone sticking out of one of the shoes. "Get these on. Charlie is out like a light on the couch. I can drive you home or to the clinic. Whichever you prefer."

Will leaped off the bed and snatched up the shoes. "Thank you so much."

"No problem. You and Charlie going another round isn't helping anyone."

That was the truth.

As silently as he could manage, he crept down the stairs

behind Edison—who moved too damn quiet for a man his size —and out the front door. The sun was still brightening the sky when they slipped into the rental car parked on the street. Will didn't relax in the front seat and draw a full breath until they turned the corner. His brain kept screaming that Charlie was going to rush out the front door and stop his escape, but it never happened.

Charlie hadn't stirred from where he was stretched out on the couch, one arm thrown across his eyes as if he were trying to block out the world or just the sight of Will sneaking away from him.

Yeah, he wished they could be civil toward each other. He wished they could shelve all their old feelings and chat like friends. Maybe that would happen after a few years, but not right now when things were chaos and emotions were running high. If they'd met when people weren't shooting them and someone was in danger of bleeding out, they might have been able to chat over drinks while Will pretended that a part of him wasn't dying.

Will closed his eyes and leaned his head against the window as Edison drove them to the clinic. After all these years, Will could admit to himself that he'd believed Charlie was *the one*. He'd expected it to be difficult in the early years, but he'd always thought they'd find a way to build a life together. They'd been so happy in Paris. It seemed only natural that they'd be able to add to it, make it more permanent while staying in Paris or eventually moving to the States.

He hated that the old pain still aching in his chest was related to his own self-loathing. How could he have been so stupid? Clearly so much of what he had with Charlie had been one-sided. Yes, Charlie was happy when they were together, but the guy had never seen their relationship as a chance at something more. Will had been someone to pass the time with and that was it. He felt like a fucking idiot.

Will closed his eyes and gave in to the urge, telling himself that it would be his only chance. After he got out of the car, he'd never see any of them again. "Can I ask you something? How have you been…the past six years?"

"Are you asking about all of us? Or just Charlie?" Ed's voice turned sly and slightly teasing.

Will's eyes snapped open and he glared at his companion. "All of you, of course."

"We've been good. The usual crazy adventures and mischief."

A soft snort escaped him. "Usual crazy adventures. I get the feeling that your definition and the rest of the world's definition would greatly differ."

"But Charlie? Would you feel better if I said he's been miserable without you?"

"No! Of course not!" Will snapped. He shifted in his seat and crossed his arms over his chest. "Well…maybe a little miserable would be nice."

Ed's laughter filled the car, helping Will to relax. "Then maybe he's been a little miserable."

A muffled chuckle escaped Will. He'd take that. He didn't want Charlie miserable any more than Charlie wanted him to be miserable. But the petty side of him felt a bit better to think that just maybe Charlie had been hurt over their parting too.

"Before I forget, we got your drugs," Edison blurted out when they were a few blocks from the clinic.

Will jerked upright and his head snapped around to stare at the other man. "I'm sorry. What?"

"We thought it might help to throw any suspicion off you if we made it look like it was a robbery that broke down into a gang war," Edison continued. "Sorry, but we smashed into your pharmacy area and stole pretty much everything you had on hand. West and I will sneak it back in once the cops stop watching and the place is secure."

"How long do you think that will take?" Will inquired,

finally remembering to power on his phone. They'd turned it off as West and Ed had arrived with the food so Will could easily deny that he knew anything about what was happening.

"Judging by the neighborhood, probably a day or two."

Will winced when his phone wildly vibrated in his hand as countless voice mail and text notifications rolled in. Yeah, shit had gotten crazy last night, but what was anyone expecting him to do? Chase the people who broke in and shot up the place? He was a doctor. Not the police.

They could have thought he'd been kidnapped, though. *Shit*. He hadn't considered that.

"This will be the first break-in since I've been there, but my predecessor mentioned that it used to happen quite frequently, forcing the clinic to remain closed until supplies could be replaced. A lot of the people in the area engage in… illegal activities. He said that when their families couldn't be treated due to the break-ins, they stopped."

Edison chuckled. "The criminals started policing themselves when they were all being hurt."

"Pretty much. There aren't a lot of other alternatives. The hospitals will take them, but more questions are asked, forms filled out, and police notified. Everyone appreciates our 'no questions' policy."

Edison stopped the car not far from the clinic and shifted it into park. There was plenty of police tape surrounding the building, and one squad car was parked outside. At least the dead bodies had been cleared away. Will's heart sank to see the poor building pockmarked with bullet holes and broken windows. It was going to take weeks to get the glass replaced because they would need to spend what little money they had on getting doors and locks replaced first. How long were they going to need to stay closed? How many people were going to go without the help they needed?

He swallowed a frustrated sigh. It could be worse. Francisco could be dead. He could be dead right now. Then he wouldn't be able to help anyone.

"Do you want me to walk up to the clinic with you?" Edison offered.

Will was so very tempted to take him up on that offer, but he preferred to keep Ed and all the guys out of this mess if at all possible. "No, I got this. Thanks, though, for everything." He reached for the door handle but Ed stopped him.

His friend shifted in his seat as he dug a piece of paper out of his pocket. He handed it over and Will's heart locked up to see Charlie's name along with a phone number.

"Before you tear it up," Ed quickly said with a crooked grin, "remember that you can use that to get ahold of all of us. Think of it as a 'just in case.' You know, just in case shit goes sideways and you need a hand. We're gonna be in Buenos Aires for a few more days at least. We've always got your back. Even if Charlie is being an ass."

Will tucked the slip of paper into the pocket of his sweats and clapped Ed on the shoulder. "I appreciate it. And I promise to keep it."

Without another word, he slid out of the car and walked briskly toward the clinic, trying to ignore the imaginary weight of the paper in his pocket. He had Charlie's number again. That night after their fight, he'd deleted all of Charlie's contact information. It also helped that Charlie had never reached out to him. That night, it had felt like he'd cut off a limb, but it had been for the best, giving him his best shot at recovering rather than clinging to false hope.

He would keep the number, as he'd told Edison, but he had no intention of ever using it. Charlie, Ed, Kairo, and Westin would all be out of his life in the blink of an eye. It was better to not get used to them being around.

His footsteps stumbled on the sidewalk and he pressed a hand to his chest against the sudden ache there. In his life for less than twenty-four hours and the idea of losing them made it hard to breathe.

No, it was better if he never saw them after today. He had his own life to lead.

And Charlie had his. The two paths didn't cross anymore.

7

CHARLIE SANDS

THE MUSIC WAS LOUD AND ANNOYING.

Which was a first.

The music was never loud and annoying. The same way the eye candy was never boring. But both were true tonight.

Edison had generously offered to take him out to get drunk and/or laid. Most likely, he'd drawn the short straw of their companions and was forced to occupy their leader, giving Kairo and Westin a night of peace and quiet.

It had been more than forty-eight hours since Will left the house, and Charlie was turning into more of a bear. His mind drifted to Will over and over again, no matter how hard he tried to forget about him. Edison mentioned that he'd passed along Charlie's phone number just in case Will ran into any more trouble, but he had yet to hear a single peep from him. Not that he expected Will to contact him. Well, other than to tell Charlie to rot in hell.

He was worried.

He had good reason to worry!

Will was in the middle of something he shouldn't be, and Charlie was willing to bet it had something to do with Benicio Perez. Nothing good could possibly come of that.

Will had trained for years to become a surgeon. His only desire in life was to help sick people.

A smile played through Charlie's mind. Will also wanted great sex and to be held when he slept. Outside of work, those were his ex's favorite things in all the world. Charlie would never call himself a cuddler. The second everyone was satisfied, he was pulling on his pants and making a beeline for the door.

But that changed his first night with Will.

Oh, they'd gone into it knowing exactly what it was—a one-night stand.

The sex was amazing. So good in fact, that Charlie hadn't been able to get his legs to work to climb out of the bed. It meant Will could take the perfect opportunity to pull Charlie's arm around his waist and up against his chest, wrapping Charlie's larger body across him like a blanket.

"You wanna do this again before breakfast?" Will had asked as he yawned.

Charlie's brain had struggled to form the words needed to remind his companion that he wasn't staying the night. It had been too busy melting down over how perfectly Will's long, slender body fit with his own. As if they were made to lay that way.

The next thing he knew, Will's breathing had evened out into sleep and Charlie had followed right behind him. When he woke the next morning, it was to Will straddling his hips while gently kissing him awake. They'd had sex prior to breakfast and then in the shower after breakfast.

After that, it was like he never really left Will's place. He'd gone to work, done his job, but part of his soul had left with Will as he worked at the hospital. Only when they were together in Will's apartment had he felt like he was whole.

A feeling he'd not had since they'd split up.

He needed to get his head out of his ass. There was no

getting Will back. The man had his own life, and Charlie had his. They were moving in separate directions.

"Oh, how about that one?" Edison's low, deep voice rumbled through his ear, breaking through the endless swirl of thoughts about the good doctor.

He looked up, scanning the bar he'd largely forgotten about. There was no need to point the guy out. The same one had been very directly staring at him for the past thirty minutes, clearly expecting Charlie to approach him.

The man was appealing in all the usual ways for his type. Yes, he had a type—young, short, cute, with a bubbly personality. Outgoing free spirits who liked to be bossed around in bed but not tied down in a relationship were his bread and butter.

No emotional baggage.

No tomorrow.

No fuss.

Sure, he'd had a few clingers who'd decided afterward that they didn't want the party to end with just one night, but they'd been easy to brush off with a gentle smile and a wink.

His life was perfect. Adventure. Excitement. Good friends. And his bed was never empty.

Why the fuck would he want to complicate his life with his ex?

Will wasn't short, cute, or bubbly. He definitely wasn't a free spirit. Will was nearly the same height as him; dangerously sexy in a smooth, polished sort of way; and possessed a sharp, dry humor that reminded him of a fine wine. Will was the steady, calm dependable type you built a life with. And he certainly wasn't someone who could ever be brushed off with a smile and a wink.

He was the opposite of what Charlie wanted in every way, and yet he needed the man like he was oxygen.

Edison's low laugh reminded him that he wasn't with Will

but sitting in a bar with his old friend, trying to forget about Will.

"I guess he got tired of waiting for you," Edison teased.

Charlie blinked the world into focus to see a short, curvy man with lush lips and huge dark eyes strutting toward him. That mouth was formed into a perfect pout. The guy had the act down, and yeah, Charlie felt like he should be eating it up right now. All he wanted to do was wearily sigh.

"What's wrong with you? You just gonna stare at me all night?" the stranger demanded in an angry voice, but it was undercut by the little smile that kept sneaking out as he spoke.

Charlie smirked and purposefully looked away as he reached for his beer and took a long drink before turning his attention to his new friend. The fact was, he had no idea he'd been looking in his direction. He'd been so lost in thought about Will that he'd not paid attention to his surroundings.

"You could at least buy me a drink if you're going to appreciate all of this," the young man continued, sweeping one hand along his body from the top of his head to his dick.

"Except you've already been reimbursed," Charlie countered with one arched brow. "You've had a *very* long stare at me. I think we're even."

"I'd like an even longer examination without the clothes," he murmured.

Ed snickered next to him. Charlie grinned at his friend, his mood improving slightly. Maybe he really did need a distraction. Something to take his mind off Will.

Fuck.

"I'm gonna get another. You want?" Ed asked, holding up his empty beer bottle.

Charlie shook his head. He didn't want another drink, and as he turned his attention toward the man who smiled broadly at him, he realized he didn't what was being offered. He wanted only one person, and that wasn't going to change so long as they were in the same city. He needed to get the hell out of Buenos Aires and fast.

"Thanks, but not tonight," Charlie said to the stranger. That stopped Ed dead in his tracks while the other guy stared at him with his mouth hanging open.

"What?" he squawked.

"Serious?" Ed asked.

Charlie ignored the twink, keeping his full attention locked on Ed. "Yeah, I've had enough for tonight. I was thinking of heading back."

Ed gave a shrug and shoved his hand into his pocket, digging out his keys. "Let's roll."

The twink marched away in an angry snit, muttering insults under his breath, but Charlie ignored him, feeling all the more that he'd made the right decision. He was not in the mood. "You can stay if you want. I can catch a taxi."

His friend made a face and motioned for him to accompany him. "We both know I dragged you here because you needed to get out of the house."

Yeah, he knew that.

With a final pat to make sure that his wallet and phone were in his pockets, Charlie followed Edison out of the bar that was steadily growing more crowded. They wove their way through the crowd of revelers. A few made a passing grab at him or Edison, trying to convince them to stay or have a drink, but they both kept moving.

When they stepped out onto the sidewalk, Charlie tipped his head up to the sky and dragged in a deep, cleansing breath. The air was crisp and cool. Not enough to leave behind a frost, but enough to nip at the sweat that clung to his skin after the hot interior of the bar.

"Charlie Sands calling it a night early and alone. Now I know shit is bad," Edison teased, as they turned and walked along the sidewalk toward the car. Ed had opted for a trendy bar that was popular with both locals and gay tourists in a busy part of town. Usually loud and busy was just the ticket for pulling Charlie out of a funk, but not tonight.

"Have you thought about calling him?" Ed asked when they'd gone more than a block in silence.

Charlie snorted. He'd been expecting that. Edison might have given Will Charlie's number, but Kairo had also been sure to grab Will's cell number while the phone had been on the charger. He also knew that Kairo had tapped into the GPS chip in Will's phone, using it to track the man. Just in case there was trouble, of course. If he wanted to know exactly where Will was, all he had to do was text Kairo. The information would be at his fingertips in a minute.

"Thought about it? Of course I have," Charlie snapped. There was no point in denying it. They all knew exactly what his problem was. Or rather, who. "But what's the point? Will can't stand to be in the same room as me. Our lives have gone in separate directions. He's doing his thing, and I'm doing mine."

"Except doing your thing is about having fun and sleeping with little cuties you pick up in bars. Right now, you ain't having fun, and you're not even picking up twinks."

Charlie glared at Edison, who smirked at him because the man knew he was right. "You think I need to be sleeping with anything that moves?"

Ed rolled his eyes. "It's not my place to judge who you sleep with. My point is that you're miserable. You're back to being the guy we knew those last days in Paris. It took you a year to climb out of that headspace."

They paused at a street corner, waiting for the light to turn in their favor. Cars raced by and the buildings around them were ablaze with neon lights. Music and laughter poured from every business. Buenos Aires was his kind of town. Something was always happening. People were filled with a need to indulge in good food, good wine, and good company. He *should* be happy here.

But he was being a melancholy ass pining for someone who didn't want him anymore.

"I'll get over it," Charlie muttered as he started across the street with the change of the light.

"Without even trying?"

"What are you talking about?" he snapped.

Edison groaned and threw up his arms as if Charlie was being intentionally dense about this. "Man! It's different now. Talk to him. Tell him what we were doing in Paris. Why you couldn't stay with him."

"God! You and Kairo are like a pair of meddling spinster sisters. And then what? Try again? Did he give you any indication that he might consider giving me a second chance? Because from where I was standing, I'm pretty sure he wouldn't piss on me if I was on fire. And you know what? He'd be right."

"Maybe so, but the Charlie I know wouldn't let that stop him. The Charlie I know fights for what he wants."

Yeah, Edison was right. Any other time, for any other reason, Charlie would be right in there fighting for what he wanted.

But everything was different when it came to Will. He'd already lost him once, hurt the man who'd been the center of his universe. If he tried and failed, it would truly be over. There would be no more shots, no more chances. And just thinking that there was zero chance of seeing Will again made his chest tighten until he couldn't draw a breath. He'd gotten used to the idea once, but he couldn't do it now. Not when the memory of the man was so fresh. He'd heard his voice just two days ago. They'd stood in the same room, breathed the same air.

And to not have a chance at that again…

It felt like it was going to kill him.

He and Ed didn't talk on the ride to the house. When they got back, they found Kairo tinkering with his computer while

West was stretched out on the couch, reading a novel. Shock was etched across both their faces when he and Ed strolled into the house. They'd returned earlier than anyone had expected. Charlie managed a small wave and headed up to his room for a shower to clear his head.

As he stood under the spray, adjusting the temperature, a smile formed on his lips as his mind easily conjured up Will's voice complaining that Charlie liked the water too cold. All his precious bits were going to freeze.

To which Charlie would wrap his arms tightly around Will, his hands sliding down over his slick body while he promised to keep all of Will's precious bits warm. Will's laughter would echo off the tiles and fill the tiny room before it was swallowed up by their kisses.

Charlie grabbed the soap and lathered up his hands, trying to scrub away the old memories, but almost as soon as those happy ones swirled down the drain, a new one bubbled up. A rare tender one that he couldn't help clinging to.

His hands slowed on his body and his eyes drifted shut.

Charlie was waiting in Will's apartment when he shuffled through the door. He'd been at the hospital for thirty hours. His man was drained and pale. It was more than needing food and sleep. It was as if all the hope and joy had been sucked from his soul.

Charlie ushered his lover to the shower and carefully stripped him. After getting the temperature to exactly where Will liked it, they stepped inside. He took his time washing every inch of him, massaging away tension from muscles until Will leaned nearly all of his weight on him. His fingers drifted between the cheeks of Will's ass, and his lover moaned against his throat. He hadn't meant for any of his touches to be particularly sexual. He was just trying to offer comfort.

But Will turned those wide, lost eyes on him and pushed back into his hand. "Make me forget everything, Charlie. Please."

And right then, nothing had been more important to him in all of his life. He kissed Will as if their lives depended on it. Their tongues tangled slowly while their wet bodies moved together, seeking that delicious fric-

tion. He blindly grabbed the conditioner and used it to loosen Will's tight body while never breaking off the kiss that stretched on and on.

When Will was panting and desperate, Charlie turned him toward the tile and pressed inside of him. It was the one and only time in his life he'd been bare with anyone. Both he and Will were religious about protection. He'd stopped sleeping with anyone else long ago, and he knew Will wasn't straying, but they'd never given up the condoms. Until now.

Nothing had ever felt so good.

Nor had he ever felt so close to another person.

Will's cries of ecstasy were still ringing in his ears years later. They lost themselves in that moment that Charlie wished would never end. Will was his completely. Only his.

But too soon, Will's body tightened and he shouted Charlie's name as he came on the white tile. Charlie followed right behind him, filling his lover's body.

Charlie's eyes jolted open and he was startled to find himself hard and alone in the shower. Swearing at himself, he turned the water to cold and rinsed off the soap.

He was losing his mind.

This couldn't continue.

He was clinging to a ghost.

Yes, they had great memories together, but they'd been apart for six years. They'd both changed. Even if he could convince Will to give him a second chance, were they even compatible any longer?

There was only one way to find out.

If he was going to lose Will forever, he'd rather know that he'd at least tried to win him back. This bullshit of holding on to a memory wasn't going to cut it. He wanted the man who looked at him with fire in his eyes.

He wanted to taste that fire.

And so much more.

8

WILL MONROE

WILL SHOVED HIS HANDS DEEPER INTO THE POCKETS OF HIS thick jacket and ducked his head closer to his collar to block the rush of wind. The burger he'd grabbed at the tiny restaurant for a late dinner was sitting greasy and heavy in his stomach, filling him with regret. It had tasted good, and he'd been craving something that reminded him of home.

Home.

Wasn't that a funny concept?

He'd returned to the States a handful of times after finishing his residency but never stayed for more than a few weeks at most. He'd visit with family and old friends. Each and every one of them would beg him to stay, set down roots, remind him that doctors were desperately needed there, too.

But then a new request or assignment would come in, and he'd grab his bag as he headed for his next flight abroad. As soon as he'd sit in that cramped chair, something would loosen in his chest. He could take a deep breath and his heart would give an excited skip, thoughts of being lost and empty fading away. He'd have purpose again. Direction.

A voice in the back of his head would whisper that he was running, but he usually managed to ignore it.

Until he saw Charlie.

That damn voice had grown louder since Charlie reappeared in his life.

Was that all he'd been doing for the past six years? Running and hiding in foreign countries, spending all his time up to his elbows in blood, death, and desperation so he didn't have to think about how his heart had been broken?

Yes, he'd done some good over the past several years. Saved lives. Strengthened communities.

But if that was true, why did he feel so empty inside?

It was his own fault. He couldn't even blame it on Charlie. He was the one who hadn't done anything about moving on. Yes, he'd faked dating in the past few years, but he'd known deep down that his heart wasn't in it. He'd done it out of loneliness, or it was something he'd felt like he was supposed to be doing. It had never been because he'd truly felt something for the other person.

Will let a sigh slip between his lips. He needed to get his head on straight. To do something about his life—something about his personal life, at least. It was time to let go of this old anger and frustration. To fucking move on.

Seeing Charlie only served as a brutal wake-up call for himself.

Charlie had moved on with his life. Charlie was probably happy and didn't have an ounce of regret about their past. He likely regarded their past as a good memory and continued doing whatever he wanted.

And that was what Will needed to figure out.

He and Charlie had spent a great year together. They'd laughed and had fun. Then it had ended.

Besides, it had been five days since they'd last seen each other. It was likely Charlie and the rest of his crew had left Buenos Aires. He was never going to see him again.

Another cold, bitter wind swept along the street, cutting through his clothes as if he were wearing nothing at all. Will tried to huddle into his jacket farther. He should have grabbed something heavier, but the walk from his rental house to the restaurant was only a few blocks. He hadn't thought he'd be outside that long.

As he turned the corner and headed down the block, his steps slowed as he saw a man lingering outside of his house. There was also a car parked near his house with what looked to be a couple of people inside of it. Not good. This did not feel good.

The rental was a small, single-story place with some large old trees out front, offering shade from the summer heat and too much cover for potential intruders. He lived in the house alone. There was no reason for anyone to be lingering near his place.

With his heart lodged in his throat, he stopped and very carefully turned around, trying to make sure his sneakers didn't make a sound on the sidewalk. Luckily, the street wasn't incredibly well lit. The thick shadows offered him some cover.

He watched over his shoulder to make sure they hadn't spotted him yet as he slipped his cell phone from his back pocket. But who was he going to call? The cops? They didn't feel like they would be the biggest help.

Charlie?

No, he was just thinking that Charlie and the others had left town. He couldn't—

His phone lit up in his hand, flashing Charlie's name across it as the call came in. Thank God his phone was kept on silent. And that he'd bothered to program Charlie's number into his phone. He'd cursed himself a thousand times for doing it in the first place, but now it seemed to be paying off.

Will answered the call with a swipe of his thumb and picked up his pace.

"Don't go home!" Charlie shouted before Will could say anything.

He winced and glanced over his shoulder at the house, but it was too late. Someone had spotted him. One of the men shouted and pointed in his direction. The two men standing outside his house started running down the street while a car engine roared to life.

Fuck!

Will ran, holding the phone pressed to his ear. "Too late. I've been spotted," he replied. He wanted to know how the hell Charlie knew that someone was waiting for him at his house, but that was a question for when his life wasn't in danger.

"I'm already on my way," Charlie stated, his voice hard and surprisingly calm. "West and Ed are also moving to back us up."

Charlie made this sound like a damn military operation. Will was so in over his head. He was a fucking doctor. Not some soldier.

"Charlie," he said and turned sharply onto another street. He just needed to break their line of sight, right? Then he could hide from them. "Charlie, I can't do this. I-I don't know—"

"How many are there?" Charlie interrupted.

"Four, I think. Two, two are on foot. Two in a car. But maybe more. I don't know." It was fucking hard to run with a phone pressed to his ear. He needed to hang up and find a place to hide. Or maybe find someplace busy. Lots of people. They wouldn't try to grab him or kill him in front of a crowd, right?

"What street are you on?"

"I-I don't know." He kept running, catching a glimpse of a street name on a sign. He read it off as he passed it and Charlie immediately repeated it.

"Good. I'm not far. You still run every day, right?"

"Yeah. But—"

"You keep moving. Don't stop. I'll be right there. You

shout out when you pass a cross street. I'll tell you when to turn."

Behind him, gunshots rang out, shattering the silence of the night and rising about the beating of his heart in his ears. His footsteps stumbled and he instinctively ducked his head. Every muscle in his body tensed, expecting to feel the tear of bullets as they ripped through his flesh.

Somehow he kept his feet moving, driven by the sound of pounding footsteps behind him and the squeal of tires. They were getting closer.

"Charlie!"

"I heard it. You keep moving!" Charlie shouted. "A moving target is harder to hit. They aren't going to get you."

"Please, Charlie. I can't do this," he panted. Panic was squeezing his lungs, making it impossible to drag in a breath. He shouldn't be winded after only a few blocks, but his heart was racing, he was light-headed, and his leg muscles were trembling. He didn't want to be shot. He didn't want to die. Not like this. Not—

"Baby, I won't let them touch you. I swear it. You just need to get to me. One more block," Charlie bargained. "At the next corner, turn left. I'll be waiting."

"Okay. Okay. I can do it."

Just one more block.

Tightening his fingers around his phone, Will pushed himself, digging deep for a little more energy. Charlie wouldn't lie to him. He wouldn't abandon him.

Each slap of his feet on the pavement sent a shockwave up his legs while the cold air was razor sharp on his throat. He ignored it all. Even tried to block out the sound of the men shouting at him. As he reached the corner and turned, more shots were fired. He yelped when something whizzed by his ear, but he kept running.

At the end of the next block, another car sat at the corner in the muddy yellow lamplight. He stumbled and slowed. Was this the other car chasing him? Had they gotten ahead of him? Trapped him?

"It's me! It's me! Don't stop!" Charlie shouted in his ear. The passenger side door swung open, and he spotted Charlie's face grimly lit in the dome light.

A sob of relief nearly broke from Will's throat and he pushed on. As he reached the car, he dove inside, his head and shoulders slamming into Charlie's sturdy frame. The car lurched forward in a growl and screech of tires. The door slammed shut under the force of the vehicle racing away.

Will couldn't bring himself to even sit up properly in the car. He dropped the phone and tightly wrapped his hands in Charlie's shirt and jacket while keeping his face pressed against his shoulder. Terrified cries finally erupted from him.

"I know, baby. I've got you now. No one is going to touch you. I promise."

Charlie shifted his body and a strong arm was suddenly wrapped around Will as best he could from that awkward position. For several minutes, Will stayed like that. Not moving. Not wanting to even think. He soaked in the reassuring scent and feel of Charlie. Safe. With Charlie, he always felt safe. *Fuck logic.*

"While I want nothing in the world more than to keep you right here, I need you to put your seat belt on," Charlie said so very sweetly after they'd gone a few blocks.

The panic had ebbed enough that he could think about the fact that he was clinging to his ex-boyfriend like he meant to never let him go. He needed to pull his shit together. He was alive and unharmed. Charlie seemed to know what he was doing.

He pried loose a trembling hand and pulled himself upright in the passenger seat.

Charlie immediately stretched out his right hand and placed it on top of Will's head. "Keep your head down."

"What?"

"We're still being followed."

Will's heart lurched to the top of his throat. He ducked and twisted to look out the rear window. There were car lights behind them, but how could Charlie tell if they were being followed?

"We can't go to your place," Will argued. There was no way he was willing to put the others in danger because of his mess. He grabbed the seat belt and jerked on it a couple of times until the damn thing finally released enough slack to allow him to click it in place. This whole thing was such a clusterfuck.

"Don't worry. We'll take care of our problem first," Charlie reassured him, his hand slipping away to join the other on the wheel.

"How? I—"

"You got our location?" Charlie started. His voice tone was different from what he'd been using. Colder and harder. All business and no comfort. Was he talking to the other guys? The last time they'd seen each other, Charlie had been wearing an earpiece that connected him to West and Edison.

"What the hell is going on? Who the fuck are you?" Will demanded.

Charlie glanced at him briefly and then snapped his gaze to the road. "Later."

"I'm serious. There's no way you're IT techs. That's bullshit." Anger and confusion bubbled up in his chest, filling his words. It felt better to let the irritation consume him. At least, it was better than the fear and panic.

"If I tell you, are you going to tell us what the hell you've gotten yourself into?" Charlie growled.

Okay. So, that might be a very fair point. If Charlie and his friends were risking their lives to help him, they deserved to know exactly why someone very much wanted him silenced permanently.

"Maybe. How did you know there were people waiting outside of my place?"

"Kairo put a couple of surveillance cameras outside your house," Charlie stated.

"You have cameras on my house!"

His ex appeared completely unrepentant about it. He reached over without looking and placed his large hand on Will's head, pushing it down. This time, it didn't slide off but came to rest on the back of his neck. Strong fingers kneaded tense muscles, and Will felt his eyes drifting shut. He knew he needed to bat Charlie's hand away, to make him stop, but it felt so damn good and it was helping to keep the panic at bay.

"Only on the outside." He made it all sound so reasonable when Will was pretty sure he needed to snap at the man. "I had a feeling this wasn't over."

Will chewed on his tongue. He wanted to argue and shout about the invasion of his privacy and how he didn't need Charlie spying on him, but it was very obvious that he did.

Charlie turned the wheel sharply to the left, flinging Will's body into him.

"Are they in place?" Charlie asked, his voice once again changing as he spoke to whoever else was listening to them.

"What's going on?" Will demanded.

"Next turn. Light. Light. Light!" Charlie continued with increasing urgency. Will looked up to see the light change from red to green just in time for them to race through the intersection. Charlie snorted and cursed under his breath. Were… were they controlling the traffic lights? How was this even possible? Who were they?

After another block, Charlie turned the car sharply to the right. Tires barked and squealed, complaining about the rough treatment. Will braced one hand on the dashboard to keep from getting flung about the car.

More tire shrieks echoed behind them from the other car, followed by a loud bang. Will jerked around to see the car wildly fishtail before flipping onto its side with an angry metallic crash.

"Nicely done," Charlie rumbled.

"What the fuck?" Will whispered.

"We're good now," Charlie continued. "I'm bringing him to the house. We're about ten minutes out." As he spoke, Charlie squeezed the back of his neck, massaging flesh and muscle as if this were all the most natural thing in the world.

But it wasn't. None of this was normal or natural. It was insane. He was in a goddamn action movie, not real life.

Gritting his teeth, he pulled out of Charlie's grasp and leaned on the car door, trying to put as much room between them as he could manage in the sedan. Unfortunately, the only way to get a comfortable amount of space was to get out of the car completely, and that wasn't an option.

"I want to know what's going on. How did that car flip? Why did you put cameras outside of my place? How do you even know how to do that? Just-just…what the fuck, Charlie?" With each demand, his voice rose in volume and pitch. The panic was returning, and it sucked. Normally he was calm and in control, but he was so damn far out of his comfort zone that some hysterics seemed in order.

"West put a bullet in one of the rear tires as they turned, flipped the car. Kairo is a genius with surveillance tech and hacking. And the rest, we'll talk about later. *After* you tell me what you're doing that is getting you chased and nearly killed."

Will crossed his arms over his chest and glared out the windshield. None of his world made sense any longer. Yes, he'd gotten himself into some of this mess, but it felt like it had all gotten worse with the appearance of Charlie in his life. Even if the man did save his ass. *Twice.*

"I thought you were gone already," Will murmured in the silence that had settled over the car. "Ed said you were staying only a few more days."

His former lover grunted softly. "Not yet. I didn't want to leave until I was sure you were safe."

Will wanted to say that he didn't need anyone looking out for him, but that would have been the most ridiculous lie he'd ever told. Right up there with the ones he told himself every day, such as that he was fine and happy. That he didn't need Charlie's smug smirk to make his heart beat faster or the feel of his hands on his skin to feel alive.

Will leaned his head on the window and closed his eyes. He tightened his arms across his chest, trying to hold in some of his body heat. Now that he wasn't terrified and running for his life, he could feel the cold air biting at his skin.

"Thank you," he whispered.

A laugh lifted from Charlie, sounding as though he was surprised that Will would even say those two words to him. "Anytime," Charlie murmured.

Will squeezed his eyes shut harder against the shaft of pain that cut across his heart. He didn't believe that at all, but he wished it were true. He wished a lot of things were true when it came to Charlie.

But there was only one truth that mattered: Charlie didn't love him enough to keep him.

9

CHARLIE SANDS

Will was okay.

Charlie was not.

In fact, he wasn't sure he'd ever feel okay again.

Someone had gone after Will. They'd meant to take him, probably intended to kill him. That was not fucking okay.

Charlie had managed to keep his shit together while he was driving with Will. The attackers needed to be handled, and his ex needed his calm strength to gather his own scattered emotions.

But as they pulled up to the rental house, with Kairo in his ear, reassuring him that West and Ed were on their way back, his anger was rising. How could Will be taking these chances with his life? What the fuck was so important to him that he'd take risks like this?

Oh, he didn't doubt that it was for a good cause. Will was a natural-born, save-the-world crusader. It was part of the reason they got along so well. But Will's type of crusading was supposed to be in the hospital or making sure kids were vaccinated.

He was *not* supposed to be chased by people who meant to kill him.

Charlie slammed out of the car and marched up to the front door with Will trailing behind him. As he stepped inside, he pulled the earwig out and handed it over to Kairo, who was still working behind his computer.

"You got any information on the people after Will?" Charlie demanded.

"Facial recognition has been a bust. It's too dark outside of Will's place to get a clean image of any of his stalkers. I'm working on pulling the plate from the car using any cameras you might have passed."

"So, you've got nothing," Charlie grumbled.

Kairo gave him an annoyed look. "I'm saying that I'm working on it, asshole. I might have been busy keeping everyone's butts out of trouble a couple of minutes ago. Why don't you ask Doc Will if he recognized any of them? That could make this entire process go a lot faster."

That was the thing. He was trying to avoid talking to Will for a few minutes in order to get a handle on his emotions.

But Will wasn't going to give him that chance.

"What the fuck, Charlie?" Will shouted at him as he came through the living room to stand at the edge of the dining room where Kairo had set up his workstation. "I want to know what's going on. Who are you people? And don't give me any more of that IT bullshit. We both know that's a lie."

"We're the people that saved your ass!" Charlie roared. What hopes he had of getting his temper under control evaporated before his eyes. He marched toward Will, and to the man's credit, he backpedaled only a couple of steps prior to catching himself. "My bigger concern is what a doctor is doing getting chased and shot at in the middle of the night."

"I don't see how it's any of your business. This is my life. Not yours!" Will snarled.

"It's my business when my people are put in danger—"

"I didn't ask you to get involved!"

"Are you serious right now?" Charlie took a step forward,

crowding Will so that he was forced to tilt his head upward, the light glittering in his fathomless blue eyes. "Do you think that I'd let you put your life in danger? That I'd just walk away when I know you're going to get yourself killed?"

"Let me?" Will repeated, his voice jumping several octaves.

"Oh fuck," Edison moaned from the doorway. Apparently, he and Westin had returned, though Charlie hadn't heard it over their shouting.

"It's better they get it out of their systems," Westin muttered. From the corner of his eye, he could see his two friends bypass the living room and continue down the hall to the kitchen. They might not be in the room, but they'd be able to hear everything. Hell, the entire block could hear their shouting.

"You don't get to make any decisions regarding my life," Will continued the second both Ed and West were out of sight.

"I do if you're going to throw it away on stupid, dangerous shit."

"You have no say—"

"Listen very carefully to me, William," Charlie said between clenched teeth. "If you don't start telling me who the hell wants you dead, I'm going to set Kairo loose. In twenty-four hours, he will be able to tell me everything you've done with your life since the last time we saw each other in Paris. Every life you've saved, every person you've fucked, I'll know it."

Will's eyes widened and he sucked in a harsh breath. He placed both of his hands against Charlie's chest and shoved. Charlie rocked back, but he caught Will's left wrist. Maybe it was the soft catch he heard in Will's breathing when skin met skin. Maybe he was just beyond sensible thought at that point.

As he shifted to even footing, Charlie jerked Will into him. He captured Will's mouth in a brutal kiss that tried to take everything from the man who was at long last in his arms. For two seconds, Will stood absolutely frozen. Charlie nearly pulled away.

And then Will moaned.

Nothing had ever sounded so fucking good.

The kiss went from angry to desperate in a flash. Charlie thrust his tongue into Will's mouth and Will caressed it with his own while the fingers of his free hand twisted in Charlie's shirt, pulling him even closer. Charlie cupped the side of Will's face, his fingers sliding through silken brownish hair that had been kissed by the sun with little blond streaks.

Will. He was finally holding his sweet Will. Tasting him. Devouring all his whimpers and cries of pleasure.

He'd thought he'd never have this again.

All the blood in his body had left his brain. He was so light-headed he could freaking fly. Will tasted exactly the same, kissed the same. It was as if nothing had changed. They'd skipped back in time to that tiny apartment in Paris where they'd laughed and made love on every possible surface.

Will ripped his mouth away and shoved hard, breaking free. Charlie was so shocked he released him, causing him to stumble. His heart stopped at the look of gut-twisting pain that flashed across Will's features for a second before the anger returned. He never saw the fist coming until it collided with his jaw, whipping his head to the side.

"Don't fucking touch me!" Will snarled. "You don't get to touch me. Do you have any idea how long it took me to get over you?"

Charlie staggered to the right, holding his aching jaw. The brief pleasure he'd tasted was now blood tinged and throbbing, but it was nothing compared to the pain in his chest.

"Fuck! My hand!" Will hissed and paced the opposite direction in the living room as he held his right hand in his left.

"I'll get the ice!" Kairo called out from the next room. His chair scraped across the wood floor and feet raced toward the kitchen.

"And the fucking booze," Edison added.

Yeah, they needed it.

Charlie straightened to stare at Will's back. His shoulders were hunched inward and he was cradling his hand to his chest. His entire body was tensed as if he were waiting for some new attack, and that hurt more than his jaw.

"I never did," Charlie whispered.

"What?" Will whipped around, his eyes narrowed and his lips pressed into a hard, unforgiving line.

"I never got over you," Charlie repeated. Will's gaze darted away, but not before Charlie saw the surprise that filled his eyes. "But you're right. I'm sorry. I shouldn't have kissed you. Losing my temper and being scared aren't excuses. I'm sorry, Will."

Will gave a jerky nod and swallowed hard. "Okay. Thank you." He sounded surprised that Charlie had even apologized. His shoulders drooped a little and he started to relax by tiny measures.

Everything in him ached to cross the room and wrap Will up in his arms, to say or do anything to make that pain on his face go away, but Will was correct. He didn't have that right any longer. Will wasn't his to protect and comfort.

They stood in a heavy, awkward silence for more than a minute before Kairo rushed in. He tossed a bag of ice at Charlie and handed another wrapped in a dish towel to Will. Edison and West moseyed into the room after him with bottles of beer in their hands.

"Well, now that we finally got that out of the way, maybe we can talk about this shit like adults," West drawled as he dropped onto the arm of the couch.

Will's gaze slid over to Charlie for a second. It quickly darted away again, and he settled on one of the couch cushions. Kairo took the center cushion next to Will while Charlie fell into the armchair. Edison remained standing, his shoulder propped against the doorway, sipping his beer and grinning as though he were watching the world's most interesting soap opera.

"It's kind of a long story, and insane," Will started slowly. With the ice balanced on his right hand in his lap, he lifted the beer to his lips and took a long swallow.

Charlie set his own beer on a side table and held the ice to his jaw, but he didn't feel the pain or the cold. His eyes were locked on Will, inspecting every inch of him in a new light. The rose-colored glasses of Paris had been ripped away, and he was faced with someone he wasn't sure he knew any longer.

Will's features had grown leaner and harder with time. Though he was only thirty-seven years old, there were definite flecks of gray mixed into his shaggy brown hair that fell in front of his eyes every time he looked down. And those eyes, they were colder and weary—two things he would never have said about Will's eyes when he'd known him in Paris.

Even his lips seemed thinner and harder, but amazingly they still felt exactly the same when they kissed. He didn't exactly understand the physics of that, but he wasn't complaining.

"It's okay. We like long, crazy stories," Ed urged.

"I don't want you to think I'm not grateful for all that you've done for me. I know you've saved my life twice now. I appreciate it, but—"

"Stuff the appreciation, Will," West cut him off. "Regardless of whether Charlie is an asshole, you know we'd always help you. Why don't you stop stalling and just spill it already?"

Will directed a dark look at West, but there was a twist to his mouth as if he was also fighting a smirk. That was West, though. Cold, no-nonsense, and annoying as hell, but a person always knew where they stood with him. Most people wanted to strangle him. Will was one of the few Charlie had met who found West amusing.

"I came here five months ago at the request of a friend who needed to leave for a family emergency," Will started with a sigh. "The agreement was that I would be the main doctor who worked at the clinic and I would take over a handful of hospice patients he had." He paused and shrugged one shoulder. "The clinic work is similar to what I've seen in other places that I've worked. Nothing too out of the ordinary. Same with the hospice patients. All have terminal cancer, and my job is largely to keep them as comfortable as I can in between visits with the oncologist."

"None of this is sounding all that crazy," Kairo teased lightly.

Will took another swallow of his beer, finishing it off, and Charlie felt his body bracing for the crazy that would inevitably fall from Will's lips.

"One of the cancer patients doesn't have any family left, so I've found myself spending more time with him. It was just idle chatting at first. Something to keep the loneliness at bay." Will glared at his beer bottle. "But then he told me about his wife, who passed away ten years ago." He paused and looked up at Charlie. "You know about *Los Desaparecidos?*"

Charlie nodded. "The estimated thirty thousand people the military dictatorship made disappear during the late seventies and early eighties."

"Along with more than five hundred children who were either kidnapped or born to imprisoned mothers," Will added.

"Fuck me," Kairo whispered in horror.

"Kids? They took kids?" Ed demanded.

A bitter smirk twisted up Will's lips. "Do you think they just released the woman they kidnapped after they discovered they were pregnant?" He shook his head. "No, they were allowed to give birth and then were likely executed. The babies were raised by military families or given up for adoption, with most of the families knowing where those babies were coming from."

"How does your patient's wife fit into this? Was she one of the kids?" Charlie asked softly.

Will shook his head. "No, the wife's sister and brother-in-law both disappeared. The sister was six months pregnant at the time. Remains for both were located several years ago, but his wife died searching for any clue as to what happened to the baby."

West leaned forward, his head cocked to the side. "And what? You somehow linked this baby to Benicio Perez?" West's lips twisted into a smirk. "Yeah, we talked to Francisco and found out he was there trying to meet with Perez. You think he's related to your patient's dead wife."

Edison snorted. "No fucking way. That baby would have to be in his fifties by now. Benicio looks like he's thirty at most."

West flipped him off. "Fine. Then his dad."

"Actually, we think that Benicio Perez's mom is my patient's niece," Will cut in, stopping their bickering before it could escalate any further. "She knew her sister was having a girl. Not a boy. And yes, we estimate her age to be fifty-four, making her the right age to be Benicio Perez's mother." He sighed and placed his empty bottle on the coffee table. "Carlos is dying. It's his final wish—to complete his wife's search for the truth. But the only way to confirm what happened to the missing baby is to get a DNA sample from Benicio Perez."

"I'm gonna take a stab in the dark—Perez said no," Charlie guessed.

That earned him a glare, but it didn't feel like all of Will's ire was directed at him. Some of that anger was saved for Benicio himself.

"That's an understatement. Benicio Perez is the son of Lorenzo Perez, a powerful right-wing member of the Chamber of Deputies, but he's got aspirations for the presidency. He's part of the new movement to whitewash history and even erase claims that *Los Desaparecidos* even happened. It's disgusting."

"Particularly if it turns out that he married one of the children stolen in that era," Charlie grumbled.

"Exactly. Benicio is following in the footsteps of his father with the same ideas. They can't afford to have any possible links to *Los Desaparecidos*, even if it is entirely by accident."

"Did you contact Benicio? Tell him about your suspicions?" Kairo inquired.

Will nodded, and Charlie's stomach sank. "I did. I tried to appeal to his respect for history and the truth. I tried to appeal to his sense of compassion for a dying man. I even promised to keep the results a secret. Only my friend and I would know the truth. He flatly refused me."

West snorted. "Did you try underhanded methods to get his DNA?"

"Yes. Sort of. A week ago I tried to surprise him at his restaurant. I thought we could talk face-to-face. If he refused, I hope to sneak a bit of DNA from a water bottle or a glass." Will made a sound of disgust. "He simply sent his bodyguards to beat me up in the alley."

"And that's why you looked like you'd had the shit knocked out of you when we saw you at the clinic," Charlie cut in.

Will didn't meet his gaze. Just nodded. "Santino and Francisco are old friends of my patient. They volunteered to meet with Benicio at his restaurant." He dropped his head back against the cushions of the couch and squeezed his eyes shut. "I still don't know what the hell happened that night. Why were either of them armed? It's not like I need a pint of blood to run the test. Saliva or even a hair follicle will work."

"So, you're determined to get the truth for this dying friend of yours," Charlie stated.

Will's eyes flashed open, filled with fiery determination. Charlie nearly smiled. That was the Will he knew from Paris. No one and nothing ever stood in this man's way when he set his mind to something. Not exhaustion. Not lack of knowledge. And apparently, not even bullets.

"Carlos is dying and if I can answer this one question for him, he can pass away with a modicum of peace. He accepts that their research might be wrong, and that Benicio might not be his grandnephew, but not knowing is eating away at him."

Edison chuckled darkly and pointed his beer bottle at Will. "And wouldn't it be sweet to tell that asshole that his mother is a member of the group that he and his father are trying so desperately to erase?"

"It wasn't about that in the beginning," Will started and then scoffed. "But yeah, after how much he's fought me. After what happened to Santino and Francisco, I would love to see his family taken down a few pegs."

"All right." Charlie removed the bag of ice from his jaw and dropped it on the table. He picked up his beer and lifted it in salute to Will. "We're in."

"What?" Will cried, but Charlie ignored him and turned his attention to his three friends.

"I'm assuming you don't mind a change of plans," he said, lifting one brow.

West offered his usual indifferent shrug, while Kairo and Ed were decidedly more enthusiastic.

"Oh, he definitely sounds like the type of asshole who needs to be squashed. I'm down for it," Edison agreed.

"Appears to be more interesting than our last job. That was going nowhere fast," Kairo added.

It was a shame they wouldn't be able to tell Stephen and Ehren how those paintings ended up in Yusuf Badem's collection, but answering this question and protecting Will was currently more important.

"Wait! You're not in. You can't help me on this!" Will argued. "I've put your lives in danger enough. I just need to find a way to be sneakier about this. That's all. I will figure this out."

Charlie leaned forward, bracing both of his hands on his knees as he looked Will in the eyes. "We've got this. We know sneaky. We're former CIA."

10

WILL MONROE

CIA.

Charlie said they were CIA.

Why was he shocked? He shouldn't be shocked at all. Something had always told him that the IT story was utter bullshit. Yes, they could all talk tech mumbo jumbo, leaving Will completely confused, but that didn't mean anything. He was regularly confused by the apps on his phone.

No, it was something else. A gut feeling.

But CIA?

Oh, it had crossed his mind along with a lot of other crazy ideas, but none of them had truly been possible.

"Are you shitting me? This is a joke, right? You're making fun of me because I got myself into this mess."

"No. It's not a joke," Charlie answered calmly.

Will lurched to his feet and paced to the other side of the room. He was facing a painting of a sailboat as it glided into a bay, but it barely registered. His brain was a scrambled mess of broken thoughts.

CIA would explain why they so easily handled the threat at the clinic.

And his pursuers tonight.

"CIA?" he demanded, turning to face the four sets of eyes closely watching him.

"Former," Kairo emphasized. "But yeah."

Will's gaze snapped over to Charlie alone. "Even in Paris?"

Charlie's lips turned into a frown and he gave a single, curt nod.

He lurched a step in Charlie's direction as rage and pain swelled up. He tried to ball his right hand into a fist when a different kind of pain caught his breath, reminding him that he'd hit Charlie once already tonight.

"I have no problem with you hitting me again," Charlie began and nodded at Will's hand, "but you're liable to break something if you do. You need both of your hands, Will."

"But Paris…"

If he'd known…

If Charlie had told him…

If Charlie…

A thousand what-ifs were suddenly swirling through his brain, threatening to choke him. But it didn't matter anymore. That was six years ago, and there was no changing what happened between them. If he started thinking about it, if any of what Charlie did made sense to him now, it would break him.

Will stepped backward and lifted both hands in the air. "Fine. Whatever. Paris is the least of my problems right now," he declared, ignoring the fact that his voice was thick and choked. The past had no place in the present. He had a friend who had a dying wish that needed completing, and Benicio Perez very likely wanted him dead. Those were much bigger problems than his broken heart.

"Will, come sit down. We'll figure this out," Kairo beckoned sweetly, patting the empty cushion next to him.

He didn't argue. Some rational part of his brain recognized that he likely didn't look too sane or steady at that moment. He crossed the room and returned to his seat. Kairo grabbed the ice pack he'd made, and placed it back on Will's hand with a smile.

"There's not too much we can tell you," Charlie said. When Will dared to glance at him again, it was to find Charlie staring at his own hands.

"Was it all of you?" he ventured when he could pull himself together enough. He was beginning to think maybe he shouldn't have punched Charlie. He should have kissed him longer. Charlie wasn't the type to string someone along. He was proud of his fuck-them-and-leave-them-happy policy. Dating couldn't have been an option for Charlie's occupation, and yet, with Will, he—

No! No thinking like that.

He couldn't or he'd shatter.

"Us four plus Soren," Charlie confirmed. "Soren was the field agent, while we were largely support for him. We operated in Western Europe, based in London and Paris most of the time."

"But shit went sideways a couple of years after you left Paris," Edison grumbled. "We were burned."

Will's eyes snapped from one person to another, his heart stumbling to see the same angry and hurt expressions on all their faces. "Burned?"

"The Company disavowed any knowledge of us," Kairo answered.

"Like being fired, but messier because the Company doesn't help get you out of the shit storm you might be stuck in at the time," West elaborated.

"Damn," Will breathed, his gaze darting over to Charlie.

His former lover offered him a half smile that did nothing for the sadness in his eyes. "It's okay. Part of it was our fault. Part theirs. We're better off now."

"Definitely," Edison chortled. "Charlie is slightly more

tolerable now that we don't have to answer to idiot bosses in the States."

"Or worry about politics," Kairo added with a sigh.

"I don't understand. What are you doing now?"

"We're mercenaries. We take the jobs we want. We help people who need it," Charlie replied, staring straight at Will.

He forced a chuckle that came out a little choked. It was a night of overwhelming insanity, and he was well past his limit of what he could deal with. "I hate to break it to you guys, but I'm not one of those rich doctors. A lot of what I do is volunteer. I'm given a stipend that's enough to cover basic living expenses, or my wages go toward paying off my student loans."

Edison snorted. "Shit, Doc Will. We'll give you our friends and family discount."

"You've already made this entire trip more entertaining. That's payment enough," West murmured.

"Will—"

"Don't," Will said more sharply than he meant, but he couldn't hear whatever was going to come out of Charlie's mouth next. He could handle bossy Charlie, but not sweet, heartfelt Charlie. "I need to think. I...I can't wrap my head around everything." It wasn't just that they were former-CIA-turned-mercenaries. It was also the lies and life they'd lived before that. The could-have-beens trying to sneak into his thoughts that he was fiercely fighting.

"How about another beer, then?" Charlie asked with a small smile.

Will returned it. "Yeah. That would be good." Not that he was looking to get drunk—though it was fucking tempting. But a beer sounded like a better idea than trying to deal with everything in front of him.

After Charlie grabbed everyone another round of beers, the guys took turns regaling Will with stories of the insanity they'd gone through since gaining their freedom from the

CIA. This time around, it was obvious that there was a lot less censoring going on. They weren't intentionally trying to hide anything from him, but rather, truly including him in their world. It made it a little easier to forget, to put some distance between himself and the thoughts he was trying to avoid.

"There's one thing I don't get," Will interjected as he was nursing his third beer. "I thought Soren was part of your group, but he's not in any of your stories. He's not a mercenary, too?"

The room grew silent and all the eyes shifted to Charlie, who sighed heavily as he lounged in his chair. His fingers picked at the label on the empty beer bottle balanced on his flat stomach.

"Soren and I had a falling out after we were burned. It wasn't just that he felt betrayed by the Company. Someone he cared about was killed while we were on that job. Not his fault. The guy was in the wrong place at the wrong time, but Soren always felt responsible." Charlie paused and huffed. "We both said a lot of shit we shouldn't have."

"I can't imagine you doing that," Will teased softly.

Charlie rolled his eyes, but one corner of his mouth quirked upward. "Yeah, yeah. Anyway, Soren struck out on his own and became a cat burglar because the idiot is addicted to thrills and danger."

"Not unlike you guys," Will pointed out. "But are you still not talking?"

Kairo snickered. "No, Charlie and Soren kissed and made up a while ago."

"Soren still prefers to fly solo," West added, which Will found surprising. Of the men he'd met in Paris, Westin St. James always struck him as the most independent of the group. If anyone was going to go solo, he'd have expected it to be West. And yet, here he was.

"Though we did help him out a few months ago in Amsterdam. The man still knows how to find trouble."

"Right now, his trouble is a short, sassy twink who is likely to get him killed." Ed laughed.

"Or just kill him," West muttered.

Will's gaze bounced around the room, trying to follow the undercurrent of what they were really saying. "What?"

"Soren has fallen head over heels for a guy who's a very dangerous assassin," Charlie filled in.

Kairo tossed in, "He also comes from a family of dangerous assassins. Soren now has some very scary in-laws."

Will stared at Kairo for a second and then looked back over at Charlie, wondering if he was actually drunk now. "Is this real? Any of it? None of this feels real anymore."

Charlie's smile softened, and his eyes took on a sad cast that tugged at Will's heart. He'd always hated when Charlie watched him like that, as if there were some dark shadow falling across him that Will couldn't touch, couldn't dispel. "It's real."

Will opened his mouth to say something, not that he was entirely sure what it was, but Charlie stopped the words by suddenly shoving to his feet.

"It's late. You should get some rest. We can figure out next steps tomorrow. We can meet to come up with a plan of attack on how to handle Benicio and get the DNA sample Will needs," Charlie announced.

"Whoa! Whoa!" Will shouted, lurching awkwardly to his feet. *Fuck.* He was tired. Definitely not drunk. Just fucking exhausted. His mind was clearing by the second as adrenaline and irritation got his synapses firing again. "I didn't say you were helping me. Or that I'm staying here. Or—"

"Or what? Where are you going to go? A hotel? With no one to watch your back? Or your house? You think it's not being watched now?" Charlie made a dismissive noise and plucked the beer bottle out of Will's hand. He placed it on the coffee table and grabbed Will's shoulder, deftly steering him toward the stairs and the second-floor bedrooms.

"But—"

"Sleep," Charlie growled, cutting him off. "We all need sleep. Kairo has plenty of security on this place, but I'm sure no one has found us yet. Let's get a good night's sleep, and then we can tackle your problem fresh tomorrow."

"Have you always been so fucking bossy?" Will snarled as Charlie continued to pinch, poke, push, and prod him through the room and up the stairs as if he were some wayward child fighting his bedtime. Will was not arguing that he wasn't sleepy. He was fucking exhausted. His problem was sleeping under the same roof as Charlie freaking Sands yet again.

Especially after learning what he had about the man's past.

When they reached Charlie's bedroom, Will moved to the far side, trying to put as much space between them as possible, but even that didn't help. They were alone, and it was as though the air crackled between them. It didn't matter that Charlie wasn't looking at him, seeming to pretend he wasn't there. Will knew better.

His former lover moved over to a dresser and slid out the top drawer. He dug around in it for a couple of seconds before pulling out a gray T-shirt and a pair of basketball shorts.

"Here. To sleep in," Charlie said, tossing them on the end of the bed. It wasn't a big deal until Charlie lifted narrowed eyes to him and added, "I'd rather see you in that than borrow more clothes from Kairo."

Something holding him together suddenly started to melt. When they were dating, Charlie had never displayed an ounce of possessiveness or jealousy. He'd been confident to the point of almost appearing indifferent.

But that one grumpy statement was doing dangerous things to Will's exhausted brain.

Charlie couldn't possibly mean that he wanted Will in his clothes as a mark of ownership. As if he wanted Will wrapped in him alone, wanted him cloaked in his scent to ward off any who might think they had a chance at stealing Will from him.

He wasn't Charlie's, even if his body could still recall how it felt to be completely owned by him.

"Whatever. It's not necessary," Will bit out while stomping on old memories that were adding a flush to his skin.

Charlie grinned. "What are you gonna do? Sleep naked in my bed?"

The burning across his cheeks stretched to the tips of his ears while the little remaining blood not in his face plunged to his groin. "No! I'm not sleeping in here. I can crash on the couch."

Charlie's smile never wavered. "I can't handcuff you to the couch."

"You're not handcuffing me, period!"

"You can't be trusted. You escaped with Ed the last time."

"Where the hell am I gonna go?"

The more infuriated Will became, the more Charlie's amusement seemed to grow, but how could he keep calm? His entire world felt like it had been flipped inside out. He was a doctor, and yet people were trying to kill him because they wanted to keep the truth suppressed. The man who'd owned and shattered his heart was standing in front of him, telling him that he'd once worked for the CIA but was now a mercenary.

And in the midst of all this chaos, there was only one thing he was sure of. Only one thing that he wanted.

With a snarl of frustration, Will marched the three steps that separated them and grabbed Charlie's face with both hands. His former lover didn't resist as Will pulled him forward, their lips crashing together. The kiss was just as hard and violent as their first one downstairs, but Charlie moaned and his mouth opened, welcoming Will inside. Their lips softened and the kiss slowed to a gentle exploration without losing the biting edge of desperation.

JOCELYNN DRAKE

After all this time, how could his kiss be the same? The same hunger, the same need. Kissing Charlie was like coming home.

It wasn't real. It was all a lie.

But he was so fucking tired, he didn't want to think about any of that now. Later, when the sun was up and he was stronger.

With the night wrapping them up and his heart aching, Will wanted to pretend for a short time that this was real and that he could have this man.

Will broke off the kiss only because he needed to come up for air. He pulled away from Charlie and stared up at eyes so dark they were nearly black, cringing a little. "Is this where you punch me as payback?"

"No." Charlie kissed him like he never planned to stop.

11

CHARLIE SANDS

CHARLIE REFUSED TO LET THIS BE A MISTAKE. WILL WAS kissing him, clinging to him as if he needed Charlie more than air. He was not going to disappoint him a second time.

The twinge of pain in his jaw was a good reminder to proceed with caution. The sweet man in his arms was more than capable enough of protecting himself.

Tilting his head to the side, he deepened the kiss while wrapping his arms around Will's slender frame. Too slender. Why was Will so skinny?

No!

Later.

He'd worry over the man's well-being and health later. Right now was about making him feel so very good.

Will pressed his body into Charlie's with a happy whimper, sending the previous thought fluttering off with the wind. They fit so perfectly. Will was made to be in his arms, and that was where he was going to stay from now on.

Pressing his hands into Will's back, he slowly ran them down, molding their bodies together. A delicious moan rose from Will's throat. He lifted his mouth and tipped his face toward the ceiling, offering Charlie his fragile throat. So much perfection in a single, stubborn package.

He slipped his fingers under the edge of Will's shirt and ran them up, sliding across smooth, warm skin. Another wonderful noise escaped Will and he thrust his hips forward, rubbing his hard cock against Charlie's thigh. Blood rushed to his own dick, leaving him almost light-headed. Little voices were urging him to rip off Will's clothes and toss him onto the bed, to bend him over and take him hard and fast. He wanted to be buried so fucking deep inside of Will that they could never be separated.

But he was going to take this man slowly. He was going to savor every second of this.

Will wouldn't know he was stuck with Charlie until it was too damn late.

With one hand pressed to the middle of Will's back, he slipped the other down to knead an ass cheek while shifting a thigh between Will's legs. As he expected, Will thrust harder into him as a shiver ran through his body.

"Charlie," he moaned. "You're going to make me come."

Dipping his head, he nipped at Will's full bottom lip and then licked across to the corner of his mouth. "That can be arranged. Is that what you want? You want me to make you come, baby?"

Another shiver ran through Will's body, and he blinked open exquisite ocean-blue eyes. God, how had he forgotten what it was like to stare into those eyes? It was like being swept out to sea, surrounded by nothing but that endless blue.

"Sex. It's just sex. You can do—"

Charlie stopped whatever he was going to say with another deep kiss that left Will's hips driving into him. The words were probably something mean that he'd regret later. He didn't care. He deserved all of Will's prickles, barbs, and distrust. There was no fixing the past, but he could make his former lover feel good right now. He could start something fresh and new today.

Fingers pulled and plucked at his shirt until they finally moved beneath the edge to glide across his chest. He gripped Will a little tighter as a thrill ran through him. It wasn't simply the joy of being touched and caressed—it was that Will was doing it. He knew these hands as well as he knew his own. And these hands knew his body so fucking thoroughly.

"Fuck me, Charlie. Oh God, just fuck me," Will groaned into his mouth.

With a smirk, he ripped Will's shirt over his head and tossed it aside before grabbing his own and repeating the motion. They came together in a wash of hot skin on skin. Greedy fingers tugged at the zipper and button of his jeans and Charlie grinned into the next hungry kiss. An endless stream of noises were escaping Will as he writhed against him, the hair on Charlie's chest rubbing hard nipples and smooth skin.

Fingers suddenly slipped into his pants and wrapped his cock, shattering the smug hold on his control.

Will chuckled as he stroked him. "Dead of winter, Charlie, and you're still walking around commando."

"It's not that cold," Charlie grunted through clenched teeth. How the hell had the tables gotten turned so quickly?

"I guess it's good that not everything has changed," Will murmured into his collarbone.

"No, not everything."

The soft melancholy of Will's words was enough to help Charlie surface above the rush of need that attempted to swamp him. He worked Will's pants open and shoved them past his lover's hips. Digging his fingers into Will's ass, he lifted the man onto the tips of his toes. Will released him and grabbed his shoulders for balance as Charlie rubbed their cocks together.

"Yes! That. I can come like this," Will shouted, thrusting

himself forward.

Charlie snorted and nibbled on Will's jaw. "Do you really think I'm going to let that happen?"

Will moved so he could look Charlie in the eye, a wonderful smirk forming on his puffy lips. "If you think you're going to fuck me, you better get to it. It's been too long. Not gonna take much for me to come. Hate to leave you hanging."

Oh, that taunt. Will still knew how to push all his buttons, and he loved nothing more than a challenge.

Clothes came off in a whirlwind. They were tossed carelessly about the room, but the only thing Charlie cared about was the surprised laugh that jumped from Will as he was shoved backward onto the mattress. He landed with a bounce and Charlie followed him, kissing his way across his chest. He paused long enough to worship each nipple until Will was panting and writhing beneath him. Will shoved his hands into Charlie's hair and twisted, trying to force him lower faster, but Charlie refused to be rushed. He'd not tasted this skin in so damn long.

"Charlie!" Will snarled.

"Don't rush me. I've waited six years to do this," Charlie argued. He let his hot breath dance across damp flesh.

"You—" Will started, but the words were lost to a whimper as Charlie licked across the head of Will's dick. Will was probably going to remind him that it had been Charlie's decision to let them both suffer, and he didn't want to hear it. Not right now.

He slowly took more and more of Will into his mouth, loving the feel of that silky skin, the weight of him on his tongue. He cradled Will's hips in both hands, controlling his thrusts when he tried to speed him up. It drove Will crazy to be trapped, and it allowed Charlie the chance to savor this moment.

"Charlie!" Will shouted in a trembling voice. "If you're going to fuck me, you need to stop. So...so close."

Slowly, he let Will's dick slip from his mouth and he stared up that beautiful body stretched out in his bed. Will's face was flushed and his lips were parted in one desperate pant after another while those wide, pupil-blown eyes watched him with such need. No one had ever looked so enticing, so perfect to him in all of his life.

"How do you—"

"On my stomach. I-I want to be on my stomach," Will said, cutting him off.

It wasn't a surprise even if Will had always preferred to be on his back with his legs on Charlie's shoulders. When they were dating, he said he liked to watch Charlie's face as he slid into him. But he got it. That position was too personal, and Will had already stated that this was just sex.

Charlie was only too happy to prove to him that it was never just sex between them.

"Roll over," he directed with a pat on Will's hip. "I'll get the supplies."

The bed squeaked as Charlie crossed to his duffle bag and Will quickly rolled over onto his hands and knees, that beautiful ass in the air begging for him.

It took a moment to dig out a condom and a small bottle of lube. He was always prepared, but he'd never expected that he'd be using this with Will when he packed it for this trip. He kneeled in the center of the bed behind Will, shoving the twisted blankets aside. Frozen for a heartbeat, he stopped to appreciate the elegant curves of his body. The way his spine dipped and rose to meet with strong shoulders. The sweet roundness of his ass and the way his balls were tucked so tightly against his body while his dick curved toward his stomach. Everything about Will was utter perfection.

With ease, he rolled on the condom and tossed the wrapper to the floor. He flicked open the cap for the bottle of lube but stopped. He reached out and smoothed a hand up one thick thigh to the curve of his ass.

"Quit fucking teasing," Will snarled, his voice partially muffled from where his face was pressed into the pillows.

"You said this was just sex. What if I don't get another chance to fuck you?" Charlie taunted.

"You're not," Will snapped, even as he pressed harder against Charlie's hand, his body seeking more contact as it trembled.

"Then I need to memorize and appreciate all of you now."

Will lifted up enough to glare at Charlie over his shoulder. "If you don't get your dick inside of me right now, I'm going to jerk off and go to sleep."

Charlie grinned at him while moving his hand between Will's legs to sweep up his balls and across his dick. A long, low moan fell from Will's lips and he swore the man's eyes rolled into his head. "That could be fun too. I seem to recall watching you jerk off in the bathroom while you watched me shower."

"Charlie!" But this time, his name was more of a pleading whine than a demand.

He removed his hand from Will's body and squeezed some lube onto his fingers. As much as he hated to admit it, Will was right. His own control was starting to wear thin. It would be fun to watch Will jerk off while nestled among the pillows, his head thrown back in a cry of pure ecstasy, but right now, he needed inside of him.

A hiss slipped between Will's teeth as Charlie pressed a slick finger into his body. Incredible heat gripped him, chipping away at his hold on his own orgasm. So fucking tight.

"Slow," Will whispered brokenly and Charlie won back some of his control.

He reached out with his other hand and slid it up Will's sweat-damp spine as he worked to stretch his hole. "As slow as you need, baby. Just relax. Let me take care of you."

Even after all this time, he still knew Will, knew his body.

This wasn't solely tension and fear making him tight. No one had touched his lover in so long. There was no question that others had followed him after they went their separate ways, but he was the first in a while and right now, Will belonged to him. If he had any say in the matter, Will would belong to him alone from now on. There would be no one else.

Charlie slowly worked him, adding lube until Will begged for more as he pushed backward, impaling himself on Charlie's finger.

When he finally worked his way up to three, Will was nearly sobbing into his pillow with desperate need and Charlie was right there with him. He paused long enough to smear lube onto his condom-covered dick before rubbing the head across that stretched hole.

"Charlie, please, dearest," Will pleaded and Charlie nearly shattered. No one had called him that in six years. He'd thought he'd never hear it again. The silly endearment had started as a joke, but there was something about the way Will said it, especially in the throes of passion, that melted all of Charlie.

He pressed the head past the outer muscles and they both moaned with relief. Gripping Will's hips tightly with both hands, he inched deeper with each thrust while Will's cries of pleasure grew louder and louder. It wasn't a matter of everyone in the house hearing him. No, the entire neighborhood was going to hear William Monroe coming very soon, and Charlie didn't care. The only thing that mattered was making Will happy.

When he was fully seated within his body, Charlie leaned forward, pressing a series of openmouthed kisses along Will's spine until he reached his neck. His perfect lover tilted his head to the side, offering him access to bite down on the tendons that ran along his neck and shoulder.

"Fuck," Will whispered roughly. "You feel…you feel…"

"What, baby? Tell me," Charlie growled in his ear.

"So good. I'm so…so full." His words were slightly slurred as if he were drunk on pleasure.

Still leaning over Will, Charlie punched his hips forward, forcing himself even deeper. Just short thrusts that left Will whimpering and chanting his name, as if it were a prayer for release. He wanted to thrust hard and deep, drive them both screaming to the edge of oblivion, but this was heaven and he didn't want it to ever end.

A hiss of pain escaped Will, and Charlie froze.

"Too much?" Charlie asked.

"No," Will grumbled. "It's my hand." He shifted his weight to his left hand and lifted his right to carefully flex it out to the side. It was the hand he'd slugged Charlie with. Not surprisingly, it was still tender and giving him trouble.

With a grin, Charlie wrapped his arms around Will's chest and pulled him up so that he was seated in Charlie's lap, his ass impaled on his cock. "Then, how about this?" Charlie murmured.

"Oh fuck," Will moaned, each word breathless as if Charlie had pushed all the air out of his lungs. "So deep. Fuck, you're so deep."

Charlie might not be able to thrust hard and long, but he remained completely wrapped in Will this way. Keeping one arm across Will's chest to hold him in place, Charlie gripped Will's dick in his other, stroking him in time to his thrusts.

Will's shouts grew louder, and he reached behind him to grab the back of Charlie's neck with his left hand. He writhed and shifted, trying to fuck himself on Charlie's dick while thrusting into his hand. The friction and slide of their bodies, each desperate pant from Will, were all building to fray Charlie's control. He wanted to come so badly, but he needed to feel Will explode first.

"You close, baby?"

"Yes! Yes!"

"Come for me," Charlie gritted out. "Show me how much you like this thick dick inside you."

"Char—" His name was lost to a fractured shout. Will's ass tightened around him, squeezing him so perfectly while hot cum covered his hand as he stroked Will through his orgasm. It was enough to tip Charlie over the edge. He moaned loudly as he thrust again and again into his lover, filling the condom, while his fingers dug into Will's shoulder, pulling him even closer. His vision faded and the world seemed to break apart for several heartbeats.

Yeah, he could die like this. There would never be a more perfect moment. He could happily die this very second, and that would be just fine.

But he didn't die.

His brain booted up and he discovered that the next moment was nearly as good as the last. Will was leaning his completely relaxed, sweaty body on Charlie's. Every muscle was loose, and he was utterly vulnerable in his arms.

Will Monroe was in his arms.

"I think I'm dead," Will mumbled and Charlie grinned against his shoulder. Even after six years, their minds were still in sync at times, though he suspected that Will would hate to know that tidbit. The grumpy man was due to surface any second, but Charlie felt more confident now in dealing with him. This was not over. *They* were not over.

Kairo was right. He'd been handed a precious second chance, and he was not going to blow it. He just had a feeling that the hard part was going to be convincing Will to take another chance on him.

"Let me take care of this and clean us up," Charlie murmured. He was loath to release Will, but he needed to handle the condom and get Will settled before he fell asleep where he was. His lover grunted softly as Charlie carefully pulled free of his body. He removed the condom and tied it off while Will flopped facedown on the bed.

Some things didn't change. After a good orgasm, Will was always a lifeless lump. Charlie could set his watch by the man. In about three minutes, he was going to be snoring, asleep in whatever awkward position he fell into.

He started toward the door and Will made a scoffing noise.

"Seriously?" Will demanded.

"What? I'm going to get a damp cloth. I'll be right back."

"Yeah, but…" His words stopped, but his eyes pointedly swept Charlie's very naked body. To which, Charlie smirked at the man. Did Will think the guys hadn't seen him naked? Or was he in denial about the fact that everyone in the house knew what they'd been doing?

Will huffed and rolled over. "Whatever."

With a snorted laugh, Charlie slipped out of the room and crossed the hall to the bathroom. He disposed of the condom and quickly cleaned himself with cold water while waiting for it to warm enough for Will. He returned to the bedroom— after having not met a single soul in the hallway—with a damp cloth for Will.

To his surprise, the good doctor was still awake, though his eyes remained shut and his face turned away from the door. He gently cleaned the dried cum from his dick and stomach, then tossed the towel aside. Only when he stretched out in the open space next to Will did he feel the other man stiffen before he shifted onto his side, putting his back to Charlie.

As he pulled the covers up over both of their bodies, he waited to hear Will say that he wasn't allowed to sleep in the bed with him or to remind him that he was supposed to be sleeping on the couch. But those words didn't come.

"This was just sex," Will grumbled instead.

"Mmhm," Charlie hummed, knowing that he didn't sound convinced in the least. He reached across Will and turned off the lamp on the bedside table, blanketing the room in blessed darkness.

"I'm serious, Charlie."

"I know you are, baby," Charlie replied as he settled his head on his own pillow. He threw his right arm across Will's waist and pulled the man backward into his body. Again, he expected Will to fight him, but his slender body relaxed into him as if it knew this was exactly where he was supposed to be.

"And you can stop calling me 'baby' now."

"Maybe in the morning," Charlie murmured. He didn't mean that either. Will might not realize it yet, but he was firmly in Charlie's clutches now and he was not letting go.

He didn't know what this meant for his life going forward, whether he would be giving up his life as a mercenary and running around the world with his three closest friends, but he'd do it for the man in his arms. He needed Will, and every minute they were together further convinced him that Will needed him just as badly.

The one problem he saw ahead of them was proving to Will that he was worthy of a second chance, that he could be trusted. That he could be everything that Will needed in his life.

As much as he hated the idea, his friends might be right. He needed to get some advice from his brother. Stephen might be an annoying worrywart, but at least he usually skipped over the "I told you so" parts and got right to the useful advice. Not that Charlie generally took it, but for Will, he would at least try.

Closing his eyes, he rubbed his nose against Will's soft hair and listened to his slow, even breathing. This was the only man he'd ever truly slept with. The only man he'd held through the night and awoken to hooded looks and beautiful smiles. He wasn't expecting that tomorrow, but he had to believe they'd get there one day. Will was his, and he was going to keep him right here in his arms for the rest of their lives.

Please, let me keep him…

12

WILL MONROE

NEVER IN HIS LIFE HAD HE BEEN SO EAGER OR SO RELUCTANT to get out of bed. He woke with his cheek pressed to Charlie's chest, the man's heart a steady thump under his ear. His leg was stretched across Charlie's waist while Charlie's morning wood poked his thigh. His own was pressed to Charlie's hip, begging for attention.

Naturally, his sleepy brain conjured up countless memories of Charlie rolling toward him and taking their cocks together in his massive hand. He would stroke them in such a slow, lazy manner, as if they could spend all day in bed. No pleading, cursing, or urging on his part would speed him up. Charlie just brought them perfectly to completion and then had to practically carry him to the shower, because his body demanded sleep.

No. No. No.

He needed to get out of the bed.

It was bad enough that he'd suffered one weak moment and begged Charlie to fuck his brains out—which he'd done with his usual bone-melting skill. He was not going to succumb to the temptation of stringing this out to more than a one-time thing.

Very carefully, he braced his right forearm on the mattress and pushed up, sliding out from under the arm Charlie had across his shoulders. It was another matter trying to free his legs of the tangle of covers without falling onto the floor, but he managed without any cursing. His body was sore, and he hated to admit that it was the kind of well-worn, well-fucked sore.

Sex was *never* a problem for him and Charlie. They had meshed perfectly together from the very first night, and it got better every night after that.

But they hadn't seen each other in six years. People changed. Things should have been awkward and uncomfortable last night.

It hadn't been. Not for a second.

He refused to look any deeper into it. They'd had sex. That was it. Nothing more. Exactly as he'd told Charlie multiple times last night.

Just. Sex.

As his feet hit the cold wood floor, strong fingers wrapped his wrist, trapping him next to the bed. Will whipped his head around to see dark, bleary eyes blinking him into focus. His hair was mussed and his beard was a little scruffy from sleep, but Charlie still managed to appear ridiculously sexy and it wasn't fair. Will had no doubt that his hair was standing up in every direction, and he probably had red creases on his face from where he'd slept on blankets or Charlie. He was pretty sure he never woke up as sexy as Charlie.

"Where are you going?" Charlie demanded in a rough voice, which, of course, was also sexy.

"To piss and shower," Will answered, clinging to his grumpiness, because if he didn't, he'd be crawling into bed again.

Charlie grunted and tugged on his arm, pulling him closer. "Later. Come back to bed. It's early."

Will jerked his arm, but Charlie didn't release him. "No, I have work. I can't lie in bed with you all day."

Charlie narrowed his eyes and the hand holding his wrist tightened a tiny bit. "What work?"

"It's Thursday, right? I've got a hospice patient I need to check on today. The visit usually takes an hour."

"The clinic?"

"Still closed. Will be for at least a week. By then, my replacement is expected in town. I just have to keep up with a handful of hospice and at-home visits. Nothing major." Charlie continued to stare at him, his fingers not loosening their hold. Will sighed and reassured him, "I'm not leaving, I promise. A shower. That's it."

"Do you need anything from your house for your hospice visit?" Charlie's fingers relaxed but didn't release him. Instead, his thumb caressed the inside of Will's arm in a slow sweeping motion, making it hard to think.

"I-I need my bag, but if it's too dangerous, I can make do without it."

Charlie grunted and released his arm. "All of us will accompany you to your place, watch your back, and help you pack. I'll also go with you to your appointment."

Will opened his mouth to argue but shut it without saying a word. There was zero point in saying anything. Half-asleep or not, Charlie had made up his mind as to what was going to happen next. And in truth, Will didn't want to return to his house alone. If they'd been waiting for him at night, what was to stop them from trying during the light of day? Not a damn thing.

He showered quickly and pulled on the same clothes he'd worn the previous day. When he left the bathroom, he found Charlie leaning against the wall, waiting for his turn with the shower. The man moved toward him as if he meant to kiss him and Will darted away, banging his shoulder on the opposite wall. Charlie smirked at his obvious skittishness and sniffed the air.

"You smell good," Charlie murmured, continuing on to the bathroom, shutting the door behind him with a soft snick.

Will stood in the hall for a second, his cheeks burning. He'd showered with Charlie's shampoo and body wash. The house had one bathroom and one half bath. All the guys kept their shower supplies in the full bath and he'd chosen Charlie's yet again, as if he wanted to smell like him. As if he belonged to him.

Shoving the thought aside, Will continued to the first floor, where Kairo and Westin were sipping coffee in the kitchen while staring at their phones. Will mentally prepared himself for grins and teasing comments, but there was nothing.

"After we pour some more coffee into Charlie and dump Ed in the shower, we can run to your place," Kairo announced as Will took his first blessed sip.

The scent of liquid heaven did as much for his brain as the caffeine. A steady supply of coffee had gotten him through med school and his residency. Now he needed it to be human in the mornings.

"Ed still in bed?" Will inquired.

Kairo shook his head. "Morning run. He should be here any minute."

As if summoned by his name alone, the front door opened. Will leaned forward and peered down the hall to see Ed enter the house, shiny with sweat. He smiled broadly at Will and opened his mouth to say something while Will tensed, his body bracing. But before the words left his tongue, Ed's eyes widened and brow furrowed. Will looked over his shoulder to see Kairo nearly jump into his cup of coffee, his phone once again intently critical.

Will sighed loudly. "Charlie said something to you."

"No!" Kairo exclaimed, not even bothering to claim he had no idea what Will was talking about.

"Commanded," West corrected without lifting his eyes from his phone. "He *commanded* us to not tease you, and threatened our balls."

Ed snickered and headed up the stairs, wisely escaping the conversation.

"It was way too early to have my balls threatened," Kairo muttered into his mug. He then gazed up at Will and smiled. "Is there a specific time you need to do your hospice round?"

Will's brain locked up for a second. Kairo had changed the subject completely. He'd fully expected there to be comments or questions about him and Charlie, but there was nothing. They seemed willing to let it pass entirely as if it was no big deal.

But it wasn't a big deal.

It was just sex.

He was simply another of Charlie's random hookups. They'd seen plenty of them over the years and probably got used to turning a blind eye to the steady stream of people strolling out of Charlie's bedroom. He was no different. The sooner he remembered that, the easier it was going to be for all of them.

"There isn't a set time, but I always try to stop by between nine and ten in the morning. Carlos is the only one I see at the hospice center and the visit takes about an hour, but I can make it shorter if you think my presence will put anyone in danger."

West made a soft noise of dissent. "We got your back. You do your job as normal."

Kairo smiled at him. "No worries, Doc Will. We got you."

Will opened his mouth to argue or apologize for the trouble, but he shut it without saying anything. He wasn't accustomed to having people watching out for him. He'd been on his own almost entirely for the past six years. In fact, when things were going wrong, people were usually turning to him for help, protection, or advice. Besides, Charlie wasn't the type of person to do something simply because he felt obligated to do it. If Charlie didn't want to do something, he didn't. It was very likely the same for his friends. If they didn't want to help him, then they wouldn't.

But they were right there, keeping him safe, and it felt good.

"Thank you," Will said at last. "Thanks for everything."

"We're happy to help you with this," Charlie replied from the doorway. Will jumped, sloshing the hot coffee across his hand. The fucker moved like a damn cat. How had he gotten through this creaky old house without making a sound?

Charlie grabbed a dish towel as Will switched the hand holding his mug. He tried to take the towel from Charlie, but the stubborn man snatched Will's hand instead and carefully wiped off the coffee with tender care.

"How much stuff do you have at the house? Will it take long to pack?" Charlie inquired.

"Not much. It shouldn't take more than fifteen or twenty minutes to pack everything."

It took him two tries to steal his hand from Charlie. He moved to the other side of the room, as far from the coffeemaker as he could get and still be in the kitchen. It was safer to not stand next to Charlie right now.

"Okay. We'll leave after Ed gets out of the shower. We'll tackle the house before heading to the hospice. Kairo and Ed will bring your stuff back here while we're at the hospice," Charlie announced.

West lifted his eyes from his phone at last and exchanged a look with Kairo. Both men nodded and suddenly left the room without another word. A minute later, they were walking out the front door.

"Where—" Will started.

"Kairo and West are going over to your place ahead of time. Kairo said that no one went into your house overnight, but they're going to make sure no one is lingering in the area, waiting for us. Ed will ride with us."

At least they weren't going to be totally alone together in the car. Ed would be the perfect buffer. Yes, this was going to be okay. Right now, the only problem ahead of him was staying in the same house as Charlie. They were definitely not sharing the same bed again.

Buffers.

The house was full of buffers. As long as West, Ed, and Kairo were around, Charlie would behave himself and Will wouldn't be tempted.

Except the buffers refused to stay as close as he wanted.

At the house, Ed emptied the bathroom of his supplies, Kairo cleaned out the kitchen, and West patrolled the neighborhood like a stubborn specter who refused to vanish with the light of day. Charlie, on the other hand, remained attached to Will's hip, helping him to pack his belongings in the bedroom.

To make matters worse, Ed, Kairo, and West all returned to the safe house with Will's belongings while Charlie alone accompanied him to the hospice.

"Breathe, Will. I'm not going to jump your bones every time we're alone together," Charlie said with a low chuckle as they headed across town.

"I'm not worried about that," Will muttered, folding his arms tightly across his chest and glaring out the windshield.

Charlie laughed harder as he pressed the brake for the red light in front of them. "Really? So, how long have you been this jumpy? Is it an Argentina thing? Or has it been around longer than that?"

"I'm not jumpy, and even if I was, it would be because someone chased me and *shot at me* last night. It's got nothing to do with you." Will stopped and replayed both his words and tone in his head. Even if he was right, he sounded like a fucking lunatic.

"Mmhm," Charlie hummed, and Will started to contemplate murder for the first time in his life. Charlie didn't believe him. Not that Will could blame him.

"Do you like doing this?" Will asked suddenly. It was better to change the subject entirely. He didn't want to discuss why he *might* be jumpy.

"What?"

"Being a mercenary. It sounded like you've been doing it for a few years, and the stories the other guys told were crazy. Do you like doing it?"

Will had expected Charlie to immediately gush about how much he loved the excitement, travel, or insane adventures he'd gone on with his best friends. Instead, the man beside him tightened his hands on the steering wheel while a strange, tense expression filled his face. It was as if he were torn over what to say in response to that question.

A weary sigh slipped from between Will's lips and he leaned his elbow against his door. "It's okay, Charlie. You can admit to being happy while we've been apart. I get it. We didn't work out. That's life. And maybe I'm still a little bitter about it, but that's my problem, not yours. I want you to be happy, to enjoy things in life. What's the point of separating if you've been miserable the past six years? You're not the kind of guy to waste time. Neither am I."

"Then yeah, I've been happy. I've had fun," Charlie admitted slowly. "It's been good. It took us all a while to get over what happened with the Company. We did some stupid, reckless shit for a bit, but we managed to pull our heads out of our asses eventually."

Will groaned and covered his face with one hand. "Do I even want to know how many times you've been shot or stabbed because you had your head in your ass?"

Charlie's low rumble of laughter was like a hug that soothed ragged nerves. "Probably not. But I've got a few scars from those moments of poor judgment. You want to kiss them and make them better?"

"No," Will grumbled.

A large, warm hand came to rest on his left thigh. Charlie squeezed, sending a rush of butterflies into flight in his stomach. How could this man still make him feel this way after all this time? It wasn't fair.

"Don't worry. We've all gotten smarter with age. We're being shot, stabbed, and blown up a whole lot less than we used to."

"You're not helping your case," Will stated, but it was with a smirk.

It was only when they arrived at the hospice center twenty minutes later that he even realized Charlie had left his hand on his leg nearly the entire car ride. After all this time, it shouldn't feel so natural, and he needed to put some boundaries in place between them.

Charlie followed him wordlessly into the neat and clean two-story, white stone building. The interior was decorated in soft pastels and had the hushed atmosphere of a church or a library. Will warmly greeted the nurses that he passed along the way to the reception area.

"Dr. Monroe, it's good to see you," Olivia said as he stepped up to the desk. The receptionist always had a warm smile for him as she handed over the sign-in sheet. She then rose to fetch the file for his patient.

"It's good to see you, too, *Señora*. How's *Señor* Garcia doing?" he asked as he placed his name on the next available line along with who he was visiting. Doctors as well as guests all signed in as a precaution to protect the hospice's inhabitants.

"Oh, you know, complaining about the cold and his arthritis. Nothing out of the ordinary," Olivia said with a smile.

"Has he seen a doctor?"

She rolled her eyes at him as she returned to the counter

and handed over the patient file. "Don't worry about him. He prefers home herbal remedies for his arthritis." As she spoke, she pinched her thumb and forefinger together and brought them to her lips, mimicking smoking a joint.

Charlie choked on a laugh and Will grinned at her. "Yes, I've heard that can be very helpful." He looked over at Charlie. "You'll need to sign in as well if you're going to follow me past the reception area."

"I would prefer to stay with you, but I don't want to invade your patient's privacy," Charlie replied.

Oliva giggled before Will could answer. "Oh, don't worry about Carlos. That man is happy to talk to the wall. He likes new guests."

Will nodded. "It'll be fine. He won't mind."

Charlie stepped up and quickly signed his name while Will skimmed over the chart, making sure there had been no significant changes since his last visit. There were several regular doctors who made rounds at the hospice and oversaw any of Carlos's emergency needs while Will focused on his day-to-day needs and comfort.

"Everything okay?" Charlie asked as he stepped close. His chest bumped Will's shoulder, and the haunting scent of Charlie's cologne wafted past his nose. It was everything he could do not to inhale deeply. Charlie was not doing this on purpose. He was simply reading more meaning into Charlie's actions, and it was ridiculous. Charlie was overprotective by nature. It didn't mean that he still had feelings for Will or wanted anything more from him.

"Yeah, we're all good here. This should be a relatively quick visit," Will replied, leading the way along the hall to a set of wide stairs. He hurried up them as if he were being chased, while Charlie's footsteps were measured and steady.

He needed to remain calm. Everything was fine. He was still in control.

At the top of the stairs, he made a left and walked a

few doors down before stopping to wait for Charlie to catch up. Of course, the man had a smirk tilting up one corner of his mouth as if he knew how rattled Will was feeling. But that was normal. People were trying to kill him, and he'd slept with his ex. Anyone would be feeling rattled right now.

With a tug on the front of the button-down shirt he'd changed into at his house to make sure he at least appeared pulled together, he knocked on the frame since the door was already standing open. A head popped up from a mound of pillows in the center of the hospital bed and turned toward the door. Wrinkles doubled as the man grinned broadly at Will.

"Dr. Monroe! Is today your day? I completely lost track of time." Carlos cackled and waved a thin hand at him to enter the room.

"Time flies when you're having fun," Will said with a smile.

Carlos picked up the remote from where it sat on the bed next to his hip and leaned toward Will as he lowered the volume on the TV. "I've got the cute nurse keeping an eye on me today. That's enough to make any man forget what day of the week it is."

Will snorted. "As long as you behave yourself." He set his bag on a nearby nightstand and opened it. He pulled out his stethoscope and placed the ends into his ears so he could listen to Carlos's heart and lungs.

"Behave myself," Carlos scoffed. "I'm a dying man. I've got an eternity to behave myself. I need to sneak in my misbehaving now while no one wants to punish me."

Charlie chuckled from the open doorway. "You seem like the type of guy who spent his life misbehaving."

Will rolled his eyes and Carlos shifted in the bed to look toward the doorway around Will. A wide grin spread across Carlos's thin lips when he spotted Will's companion.

"You'd be right about that, but I still ain't got it out of my system," Carlos agreed with a laugh.

Will straightened when he heard that Carlos's lungs were clear and his heart's condition didn't sound as if it had worsened in the past week. Cancer might be eating away at his body, weakening it steadily, but Carlos was a fighter. He was still going strong longer than anyone would have expected.

He put the stethoscope away, picked up Carlos's wrist, and checked his pulse. "Carlos, this is a friend of mine, Charlie Sands. He's…" His voice drifted off, not quite sure what to say. He decided to leave it there and concentrate on counting.

"I'm keeping an eye on the doctor after some recent run-ins he's had," Charlie finished.

Getting the information he needed, Will released Carlos's wrist, but the older man caught his hand before he could move away. "Perez been after you?"

"It's okay, Carlos. It's nothing for you to worry about."

"Bullshit!" Carlos snarled. "You think I'm so close to death that I can't see the faded bruises on your face?"

"No, but I might have been hoping that your eyesight degraded enough with age that you'd miss them."

Carlos scoffed at him. "The rest of my body might be falling apart, but there's nothing wrong with my eyes. You sit and tell me what's happening."

"There's nothing to tell. Has there been an increase in your pain levels recently?"

"Pain is fine. Still manageable under what you've been giving me. Sleep is fine, too," Carlos snapped out before Will could ask. "I talked to Francisco. He told me about Santino."

Will sighed and gave up the fight. When Carlos was in the mood to be stubborn, there was no way around him. Plus, he couldn't deny that he needed to know what was going on. He pulled the cushioned chair on wheels closer and sat at Carlos's bedside. "I'm sorry about Santino. I haven't heard from Francisco. Is he okay?"

The old man grunted and settled against his pillows. His eyes fluttered shut and he took a few ragged breaths. Will waited. Carlos was just gathering his strength. When he seemed settled, Carlos's dark-brown eyes flicked up with startling intensity.

Carlos might be seventy-seven, but Will could clearly see that he still had the fire and passion of a guy in his twenties. The Grim Reaper would need to drag Carlos kicking and screaming from this life.

"Francisco is good. Spent only two nights in the hospital. He's gone to stay with some family in Córdoba. He says you patched him up, but that some unexpected friends grabbed him off the street." Carlos's gaze slid over to the door and narrowed on Charlie.

"I'm sorry we couldn't get there in time to help Santino," Charlie murmured.

Carlos grunted. "You're looking after the doctor now?"

"We are." There was a soft shuffle of shoes across the tile, and then a hand landed on Will's shoulder, squeezing gently. "We're not going to let anything happen to him."

Will refused to think about the weight of that hand on him, about how it felt so good and reassuring, as if he'd picked up a giant shield to protect him from the world.

"I take it that it was your wife who was searching for her lost niece," Charlie continued.

Carlos made a noise of agreement. "Emilia passed away about ten years ago. She searched for decades for that child but had no luck. About three years after she died, we finally got a lead that pointed straight at Catalina Perez, Benicio's mother. Before my wife passed, she made sure to have her DNA all...all...what's the word?"

Will twisted in his chair to gaze up at Charlie. "Emilia was part of a group of mothers and grandmothers working to locate people who were stolen as well as their children. As they aged, many had their DNA professionally taken and mapped

134

so that it could be compared later if they passed on prior to locating the family they were searching for. The information is stored away. All we need is a sample of DNA from either Catalina or her son, Benicio, to prove that they are related to Emilia's sister."

"Benicio is a real asshole, just like his father. We've had no luck with him," Carlos grumbled.

"I'm assuming Catalina has passed away," Charlie interjected.

Carlos shrugged and gave a little huff as he settled deeper into his pillows.

"Unknown," Will murmured. "No one has seen Catalina Perez in the flesh in at least five years. Some people believe she is dead. Others think her husband is keeping her locked away so she can't fuck up his chances of becoming president."

"Don't worry, sir. Will has hired the best. We will help him get to the truth and keep him safe while we're doing it," Charlie declared in a firm, authoritative voice.

Carlos stared at Charlie for a second and then looked down at Will, a smirk lifting one corner of his mouth. "You trust this guy, Dr. Monroe?"

Will sighed heavily. "Charlie and I don't see eye-to-eye on a lot of things, but I have always trusted him. If he says he can help, I believe him. We'll get what we need from Benicio."

Carlos snorted. "I may not be too keen on the idea of Benicio Perez being my great-nephew, but I'd like to at least be able to carry the truth to Emilia when I meet up with her in the next life. I gave her all the love and support I could in our years together. This was the one thing I've never been able to fix for her while she was alive."

They lingered a while longer, chatting about lighter topics, Charlie making Carlos laugh so much that Will had to give the man oxygen. Charlie was instantly contrite, but Carlos waved off his apologies. Even Will couldn't chastise him too much. Carlos was dying. There was no way around it. No avoiding it.

And Will firmly believed that it was more important to go out with a smile and a laugh than wrapped in fear and anger.

As they left the hospice, Will was sure of one thing—there was no getting rid of Charlie until he had this matter settled with Benicio Perez. The man had made a promise to Carlos, and Charlie would see it through. Will appreciated the help, but he seriously doubted his heart was going to remain intact over the next few days. He could only pray that they'd figure this out quickly.

Because how was he going to survive Charlie walking away from him a second time?

13

CHARLIE SANDS

CHARLIE WATCHED WILL CLOSELY WHEN THEY WALKED OUT OF the hospice an hour later. Carlos had redirected their conversation to happier thoughts, but Will continued to seem distracted and worried.

"Has his condition worsened faster than you anticipated? Charlie inquired as they stepped outside into the cool air. The sun was high in the bright-blue sky, chasing away the early morning bitter cold and replacing it with something that felt closer to spring.

"What?" Will's head jerked up as if Charlie had startled him from thought. "Oh. No. Based on the information I was given and the assessment from his oncologist, he's doing better than any of us would have expected. Carlos is a fighter, and he's stubborn."

Charlie stood by the driver's side door and stared at Will across the roof of the black sedan. "Then what's bothering you?"

Will's lips parted as he looked at Charlie but closed again without a sound coming out, as if he were trying to decide which version of the truth to tell him. He wanted to shake the man and demand he spit out the full and actual truth. Yet, he also didn't want to force Will. He wanted his lover to want to tell him the truth. He wanted Will to see him as someone he could lean on.

That kind of trust took time to develop, and Charlie had seriously damaged the trust between them years ago.

"I'm worried about you and the others being involved in this matter," Will finally admitted, shocking Charlie. That sounded like the truth. "After recent events, I feel like Benicio and maybe even his father are going to use more violent means to stop the potential truth from coming out."

"All the more reason for us to step in and lend a hand," Charlie countered with a smile. "We have experience in these matters where you don't. We know how to be sneaky, and we know how to deal with violence when it happens. Two things that should not be part of your repertoire, Dr. Monroe."

Will frowned at him, his expression turning from worried to annoyed. That was better. Not that he wanted Will annoyed with him, but it at least put the fire and fight back into him.

"Come on. We're going to lunch. You're picking the place since you've been here longer. I want something spicy." Charlie opened the car door and dropped inside before Will could argue with him, though he might have caught a glimpse of an annoyed look.

But when Will slipped into the passenger seat, he didn't say anything other than to give directions to a hole-in-the-wall spot about ten minutes from the hospice. Charlie stood outside the place and cocked his head to the side. "Thai?"

"You said you wanted spicy. They have spicy. Plus, I'm in the mood for kway teow. Deal with it," Will grumbled as he stepped past Charlie and pushed open the door.

They were greeted by a bell chime and a small Asian woman with a surprised smile. Charlie glanced around to find only a few other guests scattered about the place that had just ten tables. There were several potted palms near the walls, which were covered in colorful pictures of the Bangkok skyline and ornate temples lit at night.

He was about to ask Will if he came here often when a tumble of Thai fell from Will's lips as he greeted the woman with palms pressed together. She replied warmly and showed them to a table near the front window.

Charlie accepted the menu but didn't look at it. His eyes were stuck on his companion. "You speak Thai," he stated the second they were alone.

Will's wonderful lips twisted into something like an embarrassed smile. "Not really. I know enough to get by in a restaurant and through a basic physical. I can't read it worth a damn."

"You were there?"

He grunted and lifted his eyes from his menu. "For a year. I was working up north in a clinic not far from Chiang Mai."

"Did you enjoy it?"

One of Will's shoulders lifted in a small shrug as he turned his attention to the menu. It was a struggle to not sigh in frustration.

"Will, I'm sorry—"

"Don't," Will cut him off. His voice had hardened, but there was something under it. Almost a tremor. His fingers tightened on the menu until the plastic holder crinkled softly. "Just don't. I don't want to talk about our past or anything like that."

"Then can we at least be civil toward each other?" Charlie pressed in a low, calm tone. "I understand that friends might not be on the table, but acquaintances would be nice. It would make working together over the next several days much easier for everyone."

Will's hold on his menu relaxed slightly as he continued to glare at it. His jaw moved as if he were chewing on the inside of his cheek. "You're right. We can be…civil."

"Civil means polite conversation."

That got him a glare, but Charlie didn't flinch or retreat.

Will dropped his gaze first back to his menu. "I liked Thailand, particularly where I was. The people were friendly, and the scenery was beautiful. The village was rustic, but everything was always so green. It was nice to be away from everything. To forget…"

What he meant was that it was nice to forget about Charlie and the completely different life they had together in Paris. Charlie couldn't blame him. He and his team had been moved to London a short time after they separated, and Charlie had been grateful for the change in scenery. He hadn't wanted to see all the places he'd visited with Will. His heart had needed to stop expecting Will to show up around every street corner and peer out the window of every shop.

"Is this what you've been doing since your residency was completed? Traveling and volunteering?"

Will grunted. "I was with *Médecins Sans Frontières* for the first few years, working here and there in Asia and Africa. I made friends with several other doctors, who took on volunteer work and side jobs outside of the organization, but in similar regions in need. That's how I ended up here in Buenos Aires."

He paused in his story when a server approached to take their order. Will spoke with a practiced ease, as if he'd been coming to the restaurant regularly, or maybe it was just one of his favorite things to get.

When Will finished, both Will and the server regarded Charlie expectantly. Of course, he'd not even opened the menu yet.

"Can you order for me? I don't have a lot of experience with Thai food."

Will looked surprised for a moment but quickly turned his attention to the menu. Within less than a minute, he ordered several things and handed their menus over to the server with a smile. "I got you three things of varying degrees of spiciness."

"I like spicy things," Charlie replied with a grin.

Will offered up a skeptical smirk. "Yes, well, there is American spicy, and then there's Thai spicy. We'll see how you do."

"What's your favorite place you've been?"

Will shrugged, his eyes drifting to the glass of water that sat in front of him. "Probably Thailand. The food is good, and I like the pace of life there in the village. There's no great sense of urgency like there was in Paris." He winced a little as if he hadn't meant to mention the place by name.

"Have you been back to the States in the past few years?" Charlie inquired.

"For short visits, nothing more. My family keeps bugging me to return and actually stay, but…"

"But what?" Charlie rested his forearms on the table and leaned forward. Will was reclining in his chair, one hand idly holding the sweating glass with two fingers and turning it.

There was a long pause before Will snorted as if laughing at some thought that crossed his mind. "I joined *Médecins Sans Frontières* because I wanted to forget about you. I'd always heard that it was some of the hardest work I'd ever do. The areas were dangerous, supplies were always low, and the variety of problems you'd encounter would be vast. I thought I'd be too busy with patients and just surviving, that I'd not have any time to think about you."

It was on the tip of Charlie's tongue to ask if it worked, but he really didn't want to know. He didn't want Will in pain, but he also didn't want to have been forgotten.

"Most of the time, I didn't think about you. There was only the work and bone-grinding exhaustion. But after the first couple of years, I started to love it." Will glanced at him and smiled. "I love the travel. I love waking up in new places and meeting all the new people. I love learning about their culture and experiencing new things. It also doesn't hurt that I feel like I'm having a real impact on a village or a group of people. Back in the States, I'm one of thousands of doctors, lost in a crowd. I'd probably spend more time fighting with insurance companies than I would spend helping people."

"So, you plan to keep doing this for a while?"

Will grunted. "At least for a few more years. I'm not ever going to be rich this way, but I'll be happy and that's enough for me."

Warmth swelled in Charlie's chest, embracing his heart and putting a lump in his throat. He wanted to pull Will into his lap and hold this treasure, but he couldn't. Instead, he cleared his throat and held on to his smile as he said, "The world needs you, Doc Will."

Will snorted. "Doc Will. Why do you and the guys call me that? Wouldn't it be easier to just call me Doc?"

Charlie's lips twisted into a more natural grin. "Sorry, but my brother got the title of Doc first. I think Kairo started the Doc Will thing as a way of differentiating between the two of you."

Will's brow furrowed for a second and then his eyebrows lifted. "Stephen, right? Little brother?"

Charlie laughed. "He'd smack you if he heard you call him 'little,' but yeah. I think you're both about the same age. He's a child psychiatrist, but he likes to shrink my head in his spare time."

"Not surprising since you have the mentality of a child most of the time."

Charlie smiled at the playful barb. It was one of the first Will had tossed at him in a teasing tone, and he loved it. "I think it's more that Stephen has a need to be nosy and a meddler in the lives of other people—particularly his older brother. He doesn't bother with our half sister nearly as much."

"How is your family?"

Charlie shrugged. He wasn't meaning to be dismissive or closed off. It was just that he didn't talk to his family. He wasn't even sure where his father was at this point, and he talked to his half sister about once a year. Stephen was the only one he managed to keep in contact with.

"Good. I saw Stephen a few weeks ago in Turkey. It's actually why we're in Argentina now."

A low chuckle rumbled from Will and Charlie's breath caught in his chest to see the slow, warm smile spread across Will's face. It was the first one he'd seen since they'd been reunited, and it was stunning. That expression carved years off his face and zipped him back in time to when they were sitting in his tiny apartment in Paris. Will's smile was a shaft of sunlight on a dreary day. It was that first drink of cool water after crossing the desert. It was all the love and joy Charlie had experienced within his entire lifetime rolled into a single look.

And after all this time, it still succeeded in stopping his heart.

"That makes absolutely no sense whatsoever, and yet I'm not surprised with you. How are Turkey and Argentina linked? Is that where Stephen lives?"

Charlie had to mentally shake himself to focus on what Will was saying. "No, Stephen has a practice in Denver, which is where he met his new boyfriend, Ehren." Charlie paused and sighed heavily. "They've known each other a short time, but as Ed would say, they are in deep smit."

"Smit?" Will tossed his head and cackled. "I always loved Ed. He's such a romantic."

Charlie groaned. "Yes, he's not worried about my brother jumping headlong into a relationship with a guy he just met, traveling halfway across the globe, and putting himself in danger."

Will cackled this time, longer and louder this time. "Oh, my God! How did I not know you were so overprotective of your brother? He's a grown man."

"That *grown man* has never gotten himself into so much trouble before. I didn't have to be so protective of him until now. It's like he's not thinking with the brilliant brain God gave him."

Will slapped a hand over his mouth, but his face was turning red as though he was struggling not to snicker in Charlie's face.

"Oh, screw you! He could have gotten himself killed!" Charlie grumbled, crossing his arms over his chest.

After clearing his throat, Will leaned forward, placing both of his forearms on the table. "I'm sorry. I didn't realize things were that bad. Is this Ehren involved in something illegal?"

Charlie sighed. Okay, maybe he was making a bigger deal out of this than he should be. "No, definitely not. As much as I hate to admit it, Ehren is one of the sweetest people I've ever met in my life, and that's saying a lot because you know Ed. I didn't think there was anyone who would ever be nicer than Ed."

He did like Ehren. He was a good guy, and it was obvious that he deeply cared for Stephen, which was the only thing that mattered to him. Charlie just could have done without Stephen's life being put in danger.

"None of it was Ehren's fault," Charlie conceded. "Ehren's uncle died recently and left all his possessions to his nephew. Ehren didn't realize that it included an enormous collection of extremely rare art, which someone else was desperate to get their hands on."

"That put Ehren's life in danger."

"And Stephen's by extension."

"Because your brother is a meddler," Will teased.

Charlie groaned. "He's thirty-two. He should know better."

Will's smile softened and he gazed at his glass of water. "We all do stupid things for love. Even at the ripe old age of thirty-two."

"Try fifty-two."

Will's wide gaze jerked up to Charlie's face and stared at him openmouthed for a heartbeat. "Is that what you are now?"

Charlie smirked at him, trying for casual, while his heart thudded painfully in his chest. "Not bad, right?"

His companion opened his mouth and then closed it again with a shake of his head and a chuckle. "Yeah, I want to give you shit, but you know you're sexy. There's more gray than I remember, and the beard is thicker. Same eyes, though. Same smirk." Will sighed. "Looks were never your problem, Charlie, and you know it." Will cleared his throat. "But you were saying about Stephen and Ehren? I don't see how they got you here from Turkey? Or even how Stephen got from Denver to Turkey?"

Charlie appreciated Will's efforts to redirect their conversation to safer territory. He'd been about to start blurting out dangerous things like how Will needed to give him a second chance because it was obvious they still had feelings for each other. The direct approach would never work with Will. The man would shut down so damn fast.

"Ehren's family on his mother's side is Turkish. That's where his uncle was living when he died."

"Ah, and where the art collection was located," Will chimed in.

The server chose that moment to bring over a large tray heavily laden with plates and bowls of food. Their conversation was put on hold as Will thanked her and then explained all the things he'd ordered for Charlie to try.

"So, you get to…"

"Istanbul," Charlie supplied. "Long story short, we took

out the bad guys without anyone getting hurt and located the art."

"Impressive collection?"

"Mind-blowing. I don't know art, but I recognized some of these artists. This stuff belongs in museums like the Louvre. There was a Rembrandt and a Picasso. Stuff from the Renaissance. It was insane."

"No wonder someone was willing to hurt your brother's boyfriend for it," Will murmured between bites of pork and rice noodles from his *kway teow*. Will stopped and frowned. "Wait. You're not following some old Nazi-looted art treasure hunt, are you?"

"Ha. Funny. No." Charlie grunted before popping a piece of chicken into his mouth that had him immediately reaching for his water. Okay, so maybe this was next-level spicy for him.

Will chuckled and picked up something else with his chopsticks and held it out for Charlie. "Here, eat this. It will kill some of the heat."

Charlie didn't question it. He let Will feed him while trying to ignore the different kind of heat that was spreading through his chest. He doubted Will even realized what he was doing. The man was a natural caretaker. And there was no way in hell Charlie was going to stop him if Will was suddenly driven to take care of him.

Reaching out with his free hand, Will grabbed the plate with the inferno pretending to be food and moved it to the other side of the table. "I had a feeling that might be too much, but it doesn't hurt to try."

"Tell that to my tongue. It'll never be the same," Charlie complained.

"Eat your noodles. You'll love it," Will admonished with a small smile. "And tell me about this non-Nazi-related treasure hunt you're on."

Charlie gave the doctor a repressive look that only put a

smirk on Will's lips. "It's not a treasure hunt. It's actually tied to what you're doing in a way."

Will paused with a spoonful of broth halfway to his lips and blinked at Charlie. "How's that?"

"Within Ehren's new art collection, there were half a dozen paintings that no one knew who the artist was. Ehren's uncle refused to have them authenticated and was extremely secretive about them. Of course, Soren recognized them," Charlie finished with a roll of his eyes. "Turns out they were painted by an Argentine artist by the name of Thiago Vergara, who dis—"

Charlie was suddenly cut off by Will violently choking. Will dropped his spoon and chopsticks into his bowl as he coughed. Charlie jumped to his feet, trying to pull Will's arms above his head or even lift him out of his seat to begin the Heimlich maneuver, but Will batted his hands away as he coughed and gasped for air.

"I'm fine. I'm fine," Will rasped as his coughing started to subside. Charlie lingered at Will's side even as he sipped his water.

"What happened? Are you okay?"

"Yeah, fine. Sit. I'm fine." He took another sip of water and put his glass down with a shaking hand. He wiped his face with his napkin, but Charlie could still see tears glistening on the ends of his ridiculously long eyelashes. Will cleared his throat and offered Charlie a shaky smile. "I'm fine. I think I inhaled a spring onion. What were you saying about this artist?"

Charlie stared at the man across from him for another second, trying to get a read on him. His heart was still trying to descend from his throat. But Will seemed fine and had already returned to his meal as if nothing had happened.

"Thiago Vergara was an up-and-coming artist in the late seventies. He was starting to make a name for himself on the global art scene when he disappeared along with thousands of other people during that time period. Everyone believed he died with the other people. His studio was raided and all his work stolen. Since then, all of his missing paintings have been accounted for."

Will looked up at him and lifted one eyebrow. "Why do I hear an interesting 'but' coming in this story?"

Charlie smirked. Oh, the dirty things he could say, but he swallowed every last one of them. Will was smiling at him. He was relaxed. They weren't trading insults and hurtful words. He didn't want to ruin this moment and cause Will to close up on him. "Ehren's uncle was the owner of four Vergara paintings that no one has ever seen before."

"You're sure? How do you know they aren't forgeries? Fakes?"

This time it was Charlie's turn to arch an eyebrow and smirk at his lunch companion. "Do you think we'd really come all this way without first having those paintings thoroughly investigated and authenticated?"

Will shrugged. "Maybe you were also looking for an excuse to burn your tastebuds on some amazing Thai."

"The paintings are real," Charlie grumbled. "We had three different experts authenticate them. One is believed to have been painted in the eighties, but the other three…" he paused for dramatic effect, "are believed to have been painted in the last twenty years."

"So, well after Vergara was supposed to have died."

"Exactly. Interesting mystery, right?"

Will's expression scrunched up and he cocked his head to the side as he watched Charlie. "But I'm confused. You're here searching for Thiago Vergara?"

Charlie shrugged and dug into his bowl. Will did have good taste when it came to selecting Thai food. The first bite might have been too hot, but everything else was amazing. "Sure. Or just trying to find out what happened to him after he disappeared. Maybe he wasn't immediately killed, but held by one of the military generals and forced to paint for them. His paintings could have been used as a type of black-market currency. The ones in Ehren's possession are the only new ones we've found, but that doesn't mean there aren't more out there."

"Ehren hired you to find him?"

"Nope." He looked up to find Will staring at him with a dumbfounded expression. "We thought it was an interesting mystery that needed to be solved. We were between jobs at the time, and none of us had been to Buenos Aires yet."

Will shook his head and laughed. Charlie froze and watched as his entire body trembled with it. His heart tumbled over itself and skipped about his chest. He hadn't heard that sound in years, and despite everything Will had been through, it hadn't changed one bit. It was loud, free, and boisterous. People stopped eating and gazed at Will, because how could you not? No one ever sounded so happy.

He'd heard that laugh for the first time the night they'd met. It was actually after they'd had sex. Well, after they'd had sex the second time that night. Charlie had made some off-hand remark that had tickled Will just right and that laugh exploded from him, changing something inside of him forever.

"I can't believe you," Will said around a mouthful of chuckles. "You run off to Argentina because you stumble across a weird mystery. Are you the international branch of the Scooby-Doo gang?"

"The Scooby-Doo gang wishes it was us."

"Whatever," Will immediately shot back. He pointed at Charlie with his chopsticks. "Is this seriously what you and your friends do now?"

Charlie smirked. "No, not quite. This is a different kind of job for us. Usually we're infiltrating drug lords to rescue kidnap victims or unseating warlords." He shrugged. "Some-times we fuck with the alphabet soup to piss them off."

"The what?"

"Alphabet soup. CIA, SVR, MI6, Mossad. Those types of intelligence groups," he listed on his fingers.

"You're crazy," Will muttered as he returned his attention to his food.

"Maybe. We thought we'd follow this trail on a whim. You have to admit that new paintings from a dead Argentine artist showing up in Turkey is an interesting mystery."

Will shrugged one shoulder. "Maybe." His tone might be grudging, but Charlie didn't miss the small hint of a grin. "Have you found any leads?"

"Zilch."

Will's eyes jumped to his face. "You're kidding."

Charlie shook his head. "We've hit dead end after dead end. We were looking into Benicio Perez since he seems to have a particular hatred for Vergara, but it's turned up nothing. Well, almost nothing." He leaned forward over his bowl and smiled broadly at Will, loving the way the man swallowed hard at being under such intense focus. "Digging into Vergara led us to Perez, which led me to you. And your problem is exactly the kind of thing that we are used to helping with."

"Oh," Will whispered. Something about Will's wide-eyed shock had Charlie dying to crawl the rest of the way across the table and kiss those damp, parted lips. He wanted to kiss Will until he was melting underneath him. It was clear no one had been there to take care of him, to protect him, in so fucking long.

No more.

Never again.

He was not letting the adorable William Monroe out of his sight.

But for now, he straightened and turned down his smile from sharklike to mild amusement. No need to scare him away and make his job of winning Will back that much harder.

"We're happy to put the Vergara mystery on hold for now. I'm more interested in keeping you safe while we help Carlos."

To his surprise, Will didn't argue. He gave a nod and looked at his nearly empty bowl. "Thank you," he whispered.

If he wasn't utterly lost before, Charlie knew he was now. Will was never getting rid of him. He was winning this man's heart back.

14

WILL MONROE

WILL WAS HAVING A HEART ATTACK.

No, a panic attack.

It just felt like a heart attack because his heart was trying to explode in his chest and he was having trouble breathing.

Charlie was there for Thiago. *His* Thiago.

Sure, the man went by Carlos now, but he'd poured the whole story of his narrow escape and ensuing name change over a bottle of cheap whiskey neither of them should have been drinking.

Shit. Shit. Shit.

Could he really keep this from Charlie? They came all this way to find out what happened to this missing artist. What if they thought he was trapped or murdered? It was wrong to keep the truth from them. They were trustworthy, right?

But he'd promised Carlos that he'd never breathe a word of his true identity to another. Will wasn't even sure that Carlos's dead wife knew the truth.

But was it wrong to keep the truth from Charlie when he and the others were risking their lives to help him?

No. It wasn't his truth to tell. He needed to talk to Carlos first. Get his approval before he said anything.

Yes. That was the right thing to do.

Then why did he feel so guilty?

His stomach churned and tried to twist itself into an angry knot around the food he'd just eaten as they rode to the house Charlie and the others were renting. He wasn't good at keeping secrets. He didn't like it. He believed in sharing knowledge and feelings.

On the other hand, Charlie was fantastic at keeping secrets. The man was a former spy. His entire life was a secret.

Did that also mean Charlie was a liar? It was one thing to withhold the truth, but had Charlie lied to him about their life together? Had any of it been real? Or was he the only one in love and wrapped up in this temporary false bliss while Charlie was using him to pass the time between jobs?

"You okay over there?" Charlie inquired. He reached across the center console and placed his hand on Will's leg.

Will instantly twitched out of his reach, pressing his body against the car door. "Fine." He inwardly cursed himself. That did not sound "fine" in the least. "Sorry. I think lunch isn't agreeing with my stomach."

"Do you want to stop at a pharmacy?" Charlie offered, drawing his hand back to the steering wheel.

"No, it'll be okay. I think it's just the stress of the past several days."

Charlie grunted in agreement. "A lot has happened."

There was the fucking understatement of the year.

"When we get to the house, you can lie down for a little while—"

"No!" Will barked and then cringed at the harshness of his tone. He hadn't meant it to come out like that. Everything felt off balance and out of control right now. It had to be Charlie. He wasn't used to being around Charlie. Old memories and emotions were colliding with the present-day mess to confuse everything in his heart. No, in his head. "We need to work out what we're going to do next. Even though Carlos is doing well right now, his condition could worsen suddenly. I want this resolved for him before he passes."

"Will…" Charlie started softly. He reached for Will but stopped and instead dropped his hand to his lap.

"I know. I know. We could be wrong. Perez might not be related to his wife. Or Carlos could die suddenly in the night. I'm not going into this blind. I just…I need to know that I've done my best to answer this question for him and his wife." Will sighed heavily and closed his eyes against the blur of tall buildings and cars rushing by them. "And who knows? Maybe Benicio's mother is still alive, and she has no idea what her true parentage is. Maybe she'd like to know the truth."

"It's okay, Will. I get it. You don't have to explain anything to me. We're willing to do whatever it takes to get this done for you and Carlos."

"Thank you," Will murmured. Some of the tension began to unwind throughout his body. Maybe Charlie was right, and he was too tense. A nap would be nice after days of running and looking over his shoulder constantly.

"Thank you for lunch," Charlie stated. "Though I do want to know if you intentionally tried to melt my tongue."

"Of course not!" Will lurched upright in his seat and turned to glare at the driver. "Do you think I'd do that to you?"

Charlie grinned. "Yep." He glanced at Will from the corner of his eye. "You do hate me, right?"

Will's mouth fell open, and he could only stare at the man for several seconds in shock. Sure, he'd spent a lot of time really fucking pissed at Charlie, but hate him? He didn't think it had ever reached that point. If anything, he'd hated himself for ever believing Charlie felt something for him. Beyond the pain of losing Charlie, his next biggest problem was feeling like an utter fool where that man was concerned.

But had Charlie truly felt nothing for him? Or had he walked away because of his job? The CIA could have been the thing keeping them apart, and there was no way Will could have asked Charlie to leave what he loved for him. It would have been like Charlie demanding Will give up being a doctor. It just wasn't going to happen.

With a growl, Will flopped back down in his seat and crossed his arms tightly over his chest as he glared at the dashboard. Queasy stomach was now forgotten in the face of fresh Charlie irritation.

"I don't hate you," he muttered under his breath, not caring that he might sound like a petulant five-year-old. "I never hated you. I don't feel anything for you. Except maybe annoyance."

Charlie snorted, his smug smile never wavering. "I can work with annoyance."

Will wisely shut his mouth and kept it closed until they got to the house. Arguing with Charlie was starting to feel like quicksand. The more he did it, the more in trouble he found himself.

When they entered the rental house, they found Kairo, Edison, and Westin lounging about the living room. Ed and West were both on their phones while Kairo was typing away on a laptop resting on his legs.

"Any problems?" Ed asked as they strolled into the room.

"None. Everything is fine," Will answered quickly, but Charlie's next words caused his stomach to sink.

"We picked up a tail not long after we left the hospice. We had eyes on us during lunch, but I'm pretty sure I lost them on the way here."

Will spun around, his mouth falling open. "Are you shitting me? Someone was following us? Why didn't you tell me?"

"You seemed upset after we left Carlos. I didn't want to add to your stress levels. You needed a relaxing lunch."

"We could have been in danger!"

Charlie smirked at him. The expression that crossed his face made Will think the other man was sorely tempted to reach out and pat him on the head. Thankfully he didn't, or he would have drawn back a bloody stump. "That's why you have me to keep you safe."

Will lifted both of his hands toward Charlie, fingers curled as if he wanted to strangle the man. But in the end, he dropped them to his side and took a few steps away from him. "How do you put up with him? He wasn't like this in Paris," he snarled to anyone other than Charlie.

"Because you weren't in constant danger in Paris," Charlie pointed out.

"And yes, he was still very protective of you in Paris," Kairo chimed in.

He didn't want to hear this. He didn't want to know. The logical side of his brain was vainly attempting to stomp on the flutters of his heart that was trying to argue about the past and send out shoots of hope for the future.

Fuck the future.

There was no future.

There couldn't be a future.

He couldn't let himself dream about a future that couldn't possibly happen only to let himself get crushed all over again. He'd barely survived losing Charlie the first time. Did he think he was strong enough to go through that a second time?

Will scrubbed his hands over his face before turning to face the room. None of this mattered. Charlie and the others were in his life now for the sole purpose of helping Carlos. "So, do you have any ideas about how we can get some of Benicio's DNA so we can test it?"

"When you say DNA, what are we talking? Like a pint of blood?" Ed asked, rubbing one hand along his jaw. He almost sounded pleased at the idea of draining a pint, or more, from the man.

Groaning, Will dropped to the floor next to the coffee table and leaned his elbows on it. Their assistance was starting to sound more like a scary idea than the help he'd thought it would be.

"He's joking, Will," West murmured.

"You sure about that?" Ed countered.

Will lifted his head and narrowed his eyes on West and then on Ed, trying to figure out who was the serious one between them.

"He's joking," Charlie confirmed in a hard voice. "What exactly are you looking for?"

Will sighed. "It doesn't have to be much. Blood works, but so does saliva or a hair so long as it still has the follicle."

"Have you tried bribing the staff at his restaurant just to get a glass or a bottle that he drank from?" Kairo inquired.

"I've thought about it, but I'll admit that I have no idea how to go about bribing someone or how you know who to approach for something like that. What's more, how would I know what they bring me was actually used by Benicio? They could take my money and just drink from the bottle themselves. I would never know." Will threw up his hands in frustration. "I'll be using what contacts I have to rush this DNA test through the system, and it will still be expensive. I can't afford to run the test multiple times. Carlos and I can accept if Benicio isn't a match, but I don't want to have doubts about the source material."

"No, that makes total sense," Charlie agreed. He leaned his shoulder against the entrance of the living room and shoved his hands into the pockets of his jeans. "If we go through the route of pulling the DNA from something he ate or drank from, we will be the ones collecting the item. We'll be positive he was the only one to use it."

"From what we've seen of his schedule, our two best opportunities are either the restaurant or his home," Kairo started. "He frequently visits his father at his offices, but the security is much tighter there. It would require a longer surveillance of that area than we've had so far. We'd also need to do some digging, get blueprints, get—"

"Nope. It'll take too long," Charlie interrupted. "We need to hit Benicio in the next day or two."

West tilted his head up toward Charlie, his brow furrowing. "That's not enough time for the bastard to relax his guard again."

"True, but Carlos is living on borrowed time. We need to act quickly if we're going to get him the answers he needs before his death."

Will's heart gave a happy thump at Charlie's words. He forced himself to stare at the table because otherwise, he'd smile up at his former lover as though he were some knight in shining armor. Charlie Sands was no rescuing knight.

"House or restaurant?" Ed inquired.

"Have you tried to approach Perez at his house?" Kairo asked.

Will's head popped up to see them all watching him. "The only time I tried to see him in person was at the restaurant. I'm not entirely sure where his house is besides being in the Recoleta *barrio*."

"Restaurant gives more chances of interference. Increased distractions," West said.

"Also, higher chances of innocent bystanders getting hurt," Ed added. "We already saw that with Francisco and Santino."

"No, I want to hit the house," Charlie declared. "It'll give us the chance of being sneaky or going with force without risking innocent people."

"Got it. I'll start searching for blueprints of the house as well as work on hacking into his security system." Kairo's fingers flew across the keys in a loud clatter as he spoke. "I've picked up a few new contacts since we've been in town who aren't big fans of the Perez family. They might be able to point me in some useful directions to cut down the time I need, but it'll still be at least a day. Preferably two."

"Ed and I will go on rotation for physical surveillance of the house until Kairo can get patched into Perez's system," West announced.

Will's head spun at how quickly these men were making plans and moving forward when he'd been stuck for days on what he could do to convince Benicio to help him. Of course, it was clear that their means weren't particularly legal, but right now, he didn't care. Carlos was out of time, and Benicio had sent men to kill him. He was done being nice and legal about this.

"What can I do to help?" Will asked.

"Stay here and stay out of trouble," Charlie grumbled.

"What?" Will gasped, jerking back as if Charlie had smacked him. "I can do things. I can be useful. I've lived in Buenos Aires for several months now. I know people."

Kairo lowered his feet from the table and leaned forward to place his hand on Will's tense shoulder. "We're not doubting you, but it's just safer if you keep a low profile for a while."

"Plus, Benicio and his men know you, know your face. They see you, and they know trouble is coming." Ed grinned at him and pointed at his own face. "There's a good chance they don't know our faces yet, which allows us to keep a closer eye on them without them realizing it."

Will's shoulders slumped. That made sense. If Benicio or his men spotted him, all their work was for nothing. As it was, they were going to have enough trouble trying to sneak and surprise Perez because of him.

"Don't worry. We'll have plenty for you to do," Charlie said with a smirk.

Will glared at the man. "If you're thinking I'm cooking and cleaning while you guys take all the risk, you can shove it up—"

Charlie held up both hands in front of him and chuckled. "No. I was thinking that you're going to be sitting with Kairo and telling him everything you know about Perez. You're also going to be listing all the various ways we can get a viable DNA sample off Perez without requiring direct confrontation." He paused and narrowed his gaze on Ed. "Or a blood withdrawal."

Ed snorted. "If anyone deserves to forcibly donate a pint or two, it's this asshole."

Will nodded. "I can do that."

Charlie turned his dark look on Will, all the joking and teasing gone from his expression. "And you will stay safe."

It was on the tip of his tongue to argue that his safety was not Charlie's primary concern. His priority was supposed to be helping Carlos. That was the job he and the others had been hired for. But considering that they'd saved his life twice already and he wasn't exactly sure how he was going to pay them for all this work, it didn't seem like a good time to argue.

The arguing would come later.

15

CHARLIE SANDS

CHARLIE TRUDGED UP THE STAIRS TO GRAB A PAIR OF SHORTS and a T-shirt to sleep in after Will mumbled something about wanting to go to bed. The day had been spent discussing plans, sharing what they'd managed to gather on Benicio Perez, and even trying to do some research on his mother. Digging up a corpse wasn't high on his list of potential plans, but if it meant keeping Will safe, he was up for a little grave robbing.

As the hour crept closer to midnight, the others quickly claimed exhaustion and shuffled off to their rooms. He appreciated their attempt to give him and Will some private time, but the doctor only followed in their example.

He grabbed some clothes out of the dresser and was turning to leave when Will appeared in the doorway wearing the same clothes Charlie had pulled out for him last night but Will never had the chance to wear. They hung on his slender frame, making the man look both younger and more fragile than he really was. Everything in him ached to tug Will into his arms and shield him from the world. Instead, he tightened his fingers on the clothes he was holding and bit his tongue for once.

"You know, you can take the bed and I'll sleep on the couch. I'm not going to disappear in the middle of the night," Will offered.

"The other option is for us to share the bed," Charlie countered with a grin. "It worked well enough last night."

"No." Will turned where he stood and took only one step out of the room before Charlie caught his arm and dragged him back inside. As soon as Will cleared the frame, he closed the door with his foot, shutting them off from the rest of the world.

He kept pulling until Will lightly crashed into his chest, the clothes in his hand dropping to the floor. Charlie lowered his head and just barely brushed his lips across the warm skin of Will's neck. A shiver ran through his lover's body.

"Don't." The single word escaped Will in a whisper, but he didn't pull away, leaving Charlie feeling conflicted. It didn't take a genius to see that Will was tempted, that he wanted the pleasure and escape Charlie was freely offering, but Charlie also didn't want Will regretting their time together. He definitely didn't want to hear Will lying to himself that this was just sex. This was so much more than simply sex, and Will needed to face that.

Charlie didn't release him, but he did lift his mouth so that it was closer to Will's ear. "I didn't ask last night…" He paused and licked his lips. He partially didn't because things had moved so damn fast he hadn't wanted to give Will a chance to say no. "But…you're not seeing anyone…"

Will shoved away from him so quickly that he nearly lost his balance in his haste to escape Charlie's hold. "Are you fucking kidding me right now? Do you really think so little of me that I would cheat on someone I was dating?" Will snarled.

"No, I…" Charlie shoved a hand through his hair and stared at the floor for a second. "Things happened so fast the other night. I didn't ask—"

"You didn't ask because you didn't care," Will shot back.

"No, I didn't. I didn't care if you were dating someone or married. I know that makes me an asshole and a dirtbag, but when it comes to you, I don't care."

"Then why ask now?"

"Because I don't want you to have any regrets when it comes to me."

Will crossed to the other side of the room, putting as much distance as he could between them while Charlie remained near the door, guarding his only exit. He wasn't going to let Will run from him.

"Charlie," he whispered on a sigh, and it felt like a knife was slicing through his heart. "I feel like regrets are all we have left."

"That's not true." Charlie surged away from the door, closing the space between them. He grabbed Will's shoulders, forcing him to turn to face him. "I don't regret our time together. Those memories are some of the best times of my life. The only thing I've regretted is walking out your apartment door that night. A hundred times I told myself to turn around, to go back."

"Why didn't you?" Will roared. He shoved Charlie hard. "Why—" he started to repeat, but the rest fell away when his voice broke. He sucked in a loud, harsh breath like he was fighting tears and violently shook his head. "No. Doesn't matter. None of it matters. It's the past."

"It does matter." He stepped close and grabbed Will's wrists, holding them gently when the smaller man attempted to shove him away. "It matters. I was selfish and greedy when we were in Paris. I knew you were getting attached, and I should have warned you. Should have walked away months before it ended to try to spare you the pain, but I couldn't let you go."

"It would have hurt no matter when you left me. Twelve months, six months, that first night. It was always going to hurt," Will confessed, cutting off another chunk of Charlie's heart.

He leaned his head forward and brushed the lightest kiss across his forehead. "I'm sorry. I have never wanted to hurt you. Our time...you...you were always my joy."

Will lifted tear-soaked eyes to him. "Tell me the truth. You owe me that. Why did you leave that night? Was it because of the CIA? Or...or was it me—"

Charlie's breath caught in his throat for a moment at the idea that Will ever thought he was the reason for Charlie's departure. He jerked him tightly into his arms and rested his cheek on the top of his head. Squeezing his eyes shut against the sudden burn of unshed tears, Charlie just held him until he could speak past the lump in his throat.

"No, baby. No. It was the CIA. Work kept us apart. I couldn't tell you, and I couldn't leave them. The lives of my team depended on me. I—" He stopped suddenly and mentally swore at himself. He wasn't being truthful with Will or himself. Releasing the love of his life, he gently pushed him back far enough to look into Will's eyes. "No, it wasn't just work. I was scared. Being with you scared the shit out of me."

Will's brow furrowed, confusion filling his bright-blue eyes. "I don't understand. Why?"

"No one had ever consumed me the way you did. I was forty-fucking-six, and you were the first person in my entire life that I loved completely. I was ready to chuck all my responsibilities, my career, everything out the window and just follow you through life like a lost puppy. It scared me. I was afraid of losing myself. Afraid of losing you. Walking away meant returning to the life that had always made me happy. It meant that I was still in control, but it was all a lie." Charlie cupped the side of Will's face and wiped away a tear with his thumb. "I regretted leaving you the second I walked out the door."

"You loved me?" his sweet Will asked in a quavering voice.

Charlie nearly laughed. Out of everything he'd said, that was what Will had heard—but then, it really was the most important part. "I loved you in Paris. I have never stopped loving you. I love you now."

Will squeezed his eyes shut and shook his head. "No." He stopped and cleared his throat. "It's enough to know that you loved me in Paris. That I wasn't alone. But you can't love me now. You don't know me. We've both changed so much in the past six years. We're not the same people."

Charlie grinned, his heart giving the first hope-filled thump in several minutes. "You're right. We don't know each other anymore. Yet, in just the past few days, I can tell you're still the same stubborn, passionate, hotheaded person with the enormous heart that I fell in love with. You're still brilliant, selfless, and determined. You won't let anyone stop you when it comes to doing what you believe is the right thing. No amount of danger or threats will stop you."

Will flushed, his eyes darting away. "Whatever. You're still an annoying, bossy asshole," he muttered under his breath.

Dropping his voice to a warm whisper, Charlie nuzzled the side of Will's head as he said, "You still can't take a compliment, baby." He lightly kissed Will's cheekbone and hands grabbed Charlie's arms. Fingers dug in and part of him tensed, expecting Will to shove him away, but he didn't. Will just hung on to him, body trembling. "Give us a second chance. Let's get to know each other. Let's see if it's at all possible for you to love me again."

A harsh laugh broke from Will's throat. "Loving you was never the problem, Charlie. It's you leaving. I can't…I can't watch you walk away from me a second time. I won't survive it."

"Not going to happen," Charlie swore. He lifted his head so that he could look Will in the eyes. "If it means giving up being a mercenary, I'll do it. The guys wouldn't be surprised in the least. They know how I feel about you. If you want, I'll follow you around the world. I'll keep you safe while you heal all the sick people you find."

Will frowned and shook his head. Fingers dug even deeper into his biceps, holding him tight as if he were afraid of him slipping away. "No. Absolutely not. You love what you do. You can't give that up for me. You'd be miserable. It would be like asking me to stop being a doctor. It's who we are."

"Then we talk about it. We figure it out together. No more secrets. No more lies." Charlie leaned in and kissed away a tear. "Together. We get to know each other again."

"Did I ever really know you?" Will whispered.

"You did." Charlie pressed another kiss to the corner of his mouth. "You didn't know my job, but no matter how hard I tried, I couldn't hide myself from you." He chuckled brokenly. "My God, baby, I think you're the only person who's ever really known me, and for some reason, you still loved me."

Will jerked in his arms and Charlie was stunned to find blazingly fierce blue eyes glaring at him. "You hurt me, but I always knew that you were a good person at heart. You're a protector. I saw it in a hundred little things you did for me. You always made sure that I was safe and cared for."

He couldn't hold back any longer. He seized Will's lips in a brutal kiss, but instead of fighting him, Will's mouth opened instantly, welcoming him inside. His tense body melted against Charlie's. Their tongues slid together, and they ate at each other as if they were starved.

With each kiss, it felt like Will was handing more of himself over to Charlie, trusting him in a way that Charlie hadn't experienced since they'd been together in Paris. It was humbling, nearly bringing Charlie to his knees. Never was he going to hurt this man again. His one and only job in this life was to protect his heart.

Will's long, nimble fingers slipped between them and plucked at the hem of his shirt, pulling it up so he could get at bare skin. His hands slid up and Charlie moaned into his mouth. Last night, Will had been needy and demanding, but content to let Charlie have all the control. Tonight, Will was the aggressor, and it was destroying what working brain cells he had left.

Clothes were torn off and left in a pile at their feet. Will's naked body against his was like embracing a dancing flame. He scorched everything he touched, and Charlie still wanted more.

His brain gave a final gasp at trying to seize control of the moment when Charlie broke off the searing kiss and gazed at Will's hooded eyes. "No regrets?"

Will graced him with a lopsided smile. "No regrets. We have some fun tonight. Tomorrow, we talk like adults."

Charlie smirked at him. "You think we could manage that? Adulting?"

"We have our moments." With a wild laugh, Will shoved Charlie toward the bed. "Lie on the bed while I find your lube."

"Top left pocket of the bag," Charlie instructed as he stretched out on the bed, his hands behind his head. He grinned to himself, enjoying the view of Will's perfect ass as he bent to dig through his duffle bag. He was definitely skinnier than he remembered. There was a scar by his left shoulder blade that had not been there when they were dating. Yes, he needed to pin Will and closely inspect every inch of his body to learn all the new changes.

But the wicked grin Will flashed him as he held up the bottle of lube and a condom made it clear that inspection was not going to happen tonight.

"What dirty thing are you thinking?" Charlie demanded, his voice barely more than a growl.

Will crawled onto the bed from the bottom and kneeled between Charlie's spread legs. He placed the bottle and condom to the side so he could slide his hands up the inside of

Charlie's thighs while licking his lips. What little blood was still operating in Charlie's brain abandoned ship and raced for his dick. Will was going to kill him, but it was the very best way to go.

"Mmm…definitely more gray than I remember," Will teased as fingers caressed his sack, sending the most wonderful tingles through his body.

"Do you mind?" Charlie asked in a choked voice. "I'm an old man now."

Will threw his head back and cackled. "You claimed to be an old man six years ago, and yet you still managed to wear me out on a nightly basis." Those deft fingers slipped up to wrap his dick and stroke him. "I don't care how old you are, Charlie Sands. You are fucking mine."

Charlie arched his back, shoulders coming up off the mattress as he thrust into Will's tight grip. "Only yours. I've only ever belonged to you." When he blinked his eyes open, the smile that greeted him on Will's lips was wicked, dirty, and so possessive, Charlie nearly came right then. This was what he wanted, what every fiber of his being ached for. To belong to Will Monroe.

"Let me inside you, baby. Need to feel your tight body wrapped around me."

Will nodded and snatched up the condom again. With ease, he rolled it down Charlie's dick, those perfect fingers teasing him every inch of the way. Grabbing the lube, he quickly smeared some along the condom. "Hold out your hands."

With both eyebrows lifted, Charlie followed his instructions and held out both hands toward him. Will laughed as he squirted the lube across all his fingers and tossed the bottle aside. He crawled up Charlie so that his knees were on either side of his hips and his forearms were braced beside Charlie's head.

"Get me ready so I can ride you," Will ordered just before he snagged his mouth in an almost bruising kiss.

Yes, this was starting to feel like evil payback. The best torture. Will's favorite position might be lying on the bed with his legs on Charlie's shoulders, but Charlie's was definitely Will riding him.

Charlie rubbed his fingers together for a second, spreading the lube as best he could prior to slipping one hand between their bodies to grasp Will's hard cock. His lover groaned into his mouth and thrust into his tight fist. At the same time, Charlie slid his fingers down the crease of his ass to tease the perfect hole.

Will nipped at his bottom lip. "Don't need to be gentle. You stretched me so good last night."

He pushed one finger slowly inside of Will, loving the way his eyes fluttered shut and his mouth went slack with pleasure. It was one of the many things he loved about this man—Will never tried to hide his reaction to Charlie. He threw all of himself into his decadent bliss. Making love to Will Monroe was an intoxicating, highly erotic experience.

"Is that what you needed, baby? You just gonna fuck yourself on my hands?" As he spoke, Will moved, pushing backward onto his finger and then forward into his fist. A high-pitched whimper left Will's throat and shot straight to Charlie's sack. He could happily come like this, watching his sweet love get exactly what he needed until he finally lost all control, his shattered voice shouting Charlie's name.

"More. Give me more," Will moaned against his lips.

Charlie added a second finger and swallowed more of Will's eager sounds as their kiss grew desperate and sloppy. He managed only a few more thrusts into that tight ass before Will was pushing his hand away and positioning the head of Charlie's cock across his stretched entrance. Will flashed him a smile that appeared half-drunk as he braced one hand on the center of Charlie's chest and slowly sat on his cock.

Will's cry of pleasure was loud enough to echo through the entire house, but neither of them cared. His lover was gorgeous in his ecstasy. It was all Charlie could do to lie perfectly still, allowing Will to slowly take him inch by glorious inch. The slick slide and incredible heat were gnawing away at his control, but he held on by his fingertips.

When he was deep within Will's tight body, Will threw his head back and gave a ragged laugh. Muscles trembled and his pale skin glistened in the overhead light. No one had ever looked so beautiful to Charlie in his entire life.

And then Will started to move. His brain shut off completely. There was only the bone-melting pleasure pouring into his body, overwhelming everything else. Every moan and whimper, that wicked grin, even the arch of Will's spine as he moved on Charlie's cock was designed to rush him toward his orgasm.

He tightened his fist on Will's cock, stroking him in time with his movements. His thumb swept lazily across the head, smearing the steady stream of pre-cum leaking from him. Within minutes, Charlie's name had become a desperate chant that left Will's lips on every breath. The fingers of his free hand dug into Will's thigh so that he could feel the trembling muscles as he got closer to his release.

"Fuck, you feel so good," Charlie snarled between clenched teeth. "Very soon, I'm coming in this ass. Making it mine. You want that, baby. You wanna feel my cum in you again?"

Will cried out and sped up, his muscles tightening around him. Lightning struck, ripping through Charlie's slender control just as he felt Will's dick swell in his fist. They both came at the same time. Will shouted and wildly bucked on top of him. Charlie thrust upward, fucking him hard through their orgasms. Dirty talk was always Will's tipping point. He just hadn't expected it to send him over the edge too.

Seconds blurred and Charlie blinked to find Will collapsed

on top of him, their arms draped over each other while cum smeared both their stomachs and chests as they panted wildly. Brain cells were sacrificed in honor of that monumental orgasm.

"Holy…holy shit," Will panted into his cheek. "Did…did we get better at that? Or…was it always that good?"

Charlie chuckled, but it was more of the breathless variety. Everything was tingling from the waist down and he was light-headed. "Yes," was all he could manage.

Will shook with laughter even though he didn't make a sound. He allowed Will to relax against him, but as soon as his breathing started to even out, Charlie smacked his ass.

"Hey!" Will cried sleepily, but he didn't move.

"Don't fall asleep."

"I'm not," Will mumbled.

Charlie snorted and smacked the other cheek. "I know you. One good orgasm and you're out like a light. We need to get cleaned up or we're going to be stuck together."

Will grumbled something unintelligible as he lifted up. He carefully removed Charlie from his body, wincing slightly. The unfortunate discomfort seemed to help wake him up. Climbing to his feet did the rest of the job as he gasped and stumbled. He looked at Charlie and flashed him a sheepish grin. "You still gonna love me if I'm not as young as I used to be?"

"Nothing could ever make me stop."

With a blush, Will turned away and headed to the door. He peeked into the hall to make sure it was empty and then hurried to the bathroom. Charlie chuckled and followed.

Fifteen minutes later, they were clean and back in bed, snuggled under the blankets in the dark. Will had his head resting on Charlie's shoulder, his fingers threaded through the hair just over his heart.

"Are you sure you can sleep like this?" Will asked softly, not sounding quite as sleepy as he had before their shower.

Charlie turned his head and pressed a kiss to Will's forehead. "This is the best way to sleep."

Will snorted. "Charlie Sands, the cuddler. The world would never believe it."

"Only because there's just one person in this world that I've cuddled." He swept his hand along Will's spine in a lazy caress, but as he brought it up again, his fingers tripped over the feel of his ribs. He returned to those ribs, his brow furrowing.

"On a scale of one to ten, how pissed would you be if I asked why you're so thin?" Charlie inquired.

Will huffed, the breath stirring some of his chest hair. "About a six and a half."

"I can work with that. Answer the question, baby."

His lover tipped his head up, and while Charlie couldn't make out his features in the darkness, he could feel the younger man's glare. "You think because you've been in my ass twice now, you get the right to ask about things like that."

"I think because you are mine and I love you more than life itself, I get to take care of you. Now, why aren't you eating properly?"

Will sighed against his chest, and to his shock, snuggled a little closer. "Until recently, my schedule was always incredibly busy and money constantly tight. I don't prioritize things like…"

"Eating. Taking care of yourself," Charlie murmured into Will's hair. He pressed another kiss to the top of his head. "That stops now, even if it means we are eating every meal together from now on."

"Charlie, you don't have time for that nonsense."

"Taking care of you is never nonsense. I just got you back. There's no way in hell I'm going to lose you to something like bad eating habits. Go to sleep."

Slowly, Will relaxed on him. Charlie listened to his breathing even out as he drifted off to sleep.

"Don't let me go," Will whispered.

Charlie smiled in the darkness, letting go of his own consciousness to follow Will into a deep, dreamless slumber. Never. He was never going to let this man go. Even if it took the rest of their lives, he'd prove to Will that he wasn't going anywhere.

16

WILL MONROE

Will felt like he was going to be sick.

He'd never been so nervous or scared in all of his life. And he'd been briefly kidnapped by gun-toting insurgents once. Not that he was ready to tell Charlie that story just yet. They were still finding their way through this fragile second chance, and he didn't think his lover's overprotective heart could take that information.

Of course, his heart wasn't doing much better when it came to watching Charlie, Edison, and West sneaking into Benicio Perez's heavily fortified compound.

That was what it was. Not a manor or an estate. Definitely not a home. It was a giant compound behind nine-foot-high stone walls, guards armed with submachine guns, and numerous security cameras blanketing every square inch of the place.

To make matters worse, Charlie and his friends had pulled this plan together over just two short days.

Two. Days.

They were practically invading a small country. This should have taken a few weeks to plan and coordinate.

"Relax, Doc Will," Kairo said in a low, soothing voice. "We've done this plenty of times before. This isn't a big deal."

Will looked down at where Kairo sat behind a console filled with top-of-the-line surveillance equipment he'd been building and programming almost nonstop for two days. He wasn't entirely sure Kairo had slept at all, but his eyes were wide and bright with excitement as if they were preparing to open gifts on Christmas morning.

"What's wrong with Will?" Charlie's hard voice filled his ear suddenly and the ball of tension in the pit of his stomach shrank a couple of millimeters.

"Nothing is wrong with Will," he snapped. Charlie knew he was in the van just a few blocks away from the compound with Kairo, and yet he was acting as if he couldn't hear him as clearly as Kairo.

"He's just lookin' a little green around the gills," Kairo teased.

"Everything is going to be fine, baby. We've done this more times than we can count," Charlie reassured him. "You just stick to your promise, and this will be over in less than twenty minutes."

"Don't worry about me. You be careful," Will murmured. He slid into the empty seat next to Kairo and focused on slowing his racing heart. The only way Charlie had agreed to even let him sit in the van with Kairo was if he swore that he would obey Kairo's every order no matter what happened to the van or the infiltration team. It had hurt to give his word, but in the end, he had no choice.

He couldn't possibly allow them to go into the compound without him nearby. Not only was this his problem in the first place, but if something happened and one of them was injured, they would need him close to administer medical care. Hell no, he was not staying back at the house.

With his hands clenched into fists in his lap, he watched the various screens in front of him. Kairo had tapped into the security system for the Perez compound and was viewing everything from their video cameras, as well as small cameras worn by each of the three men on the ground.

Smiling warmly at him, Kairo reached out and pointed to one particular square on the screen directly in front of Will and mouthed the word, *Charlie*. That was the feed from Charlie's camera, showing Will exactly what his lover was seeing as he moved. Will returned the smile as best as he could and locked his eyes on Charlie's camera.

Charlie knew what he was doing.

Charlie was going to be fine.

At least, that was what he repeated to himself over and over again in his head.

After some lengthy discussion the night before, they'd decided to go over the western wall at just after three in the morning. At that point, the evening guards would likely be halfway through their shift and would be getting tired. From what they'd seen on the interior cameras, Benicio had gone to bed more than an hour ago and should be asleep as well.

• With Kairo in control of the security systems and cameras, Charlie, West, and Ed had scaled the wall and dropped silently into the shadows on the other side. The compound itself was over five acres in the middle of the damn city, and all of it was ringed by a wall. The main entrance was guarded by a fancy iron gate and a small guard shack, while there was a second back entrance with another guard shack and a more basic gate for deliveries to the house.

The grounds of the compound resembled a small forest with lots of trees to offer cover and even a small, man-made brook that ran in front of the enormous three-story mansion. Will hated to admit it, but the place was gorgeous. He'd fully expected it to be a gaudy, over-the-top monstrosity. While it was entirely over the top, it didn't strike him as gaudy.

"We ready to rock 'n roll?" Kairo asked in a low but happy tone.

"We're locked 'n loaded. Get us to the promised land, gingerbread man," Ed replied in a rough whisper.

Will looked over at Kairo, who grinned and shrugged as if that kind of weird talk was just normal among them. It probably was. These guys had worked together for years. Even sitting in on their planning meetings had left Will's head spinning. He didn't understand half of what they were saying and even when they explained it, so much still went over his head.

But this was Charlie's world, and he was eager to understand as much of it as possible.

For now, though, the priority was getting Charlie and the others safely back to him.

"East, two hundred feet, stick to the trees. Go now!" Kairo instructed.

All at once, the three men surged forward, weaving between the trees and sticking to the shadows. There was only the faintest whisper of their clothes rubbing, but even that was barely heard above the steady wind that was cutting through the city tonight. Will prayed that worked in their favor.

"Hold," Kairo said calmly.

Will's eyes snapped to the other cameras in time to see two guards, each holding a gun with both hands, approaching the guys' position from the north and south. His heart stammered in his chest, and he couldn't draw a breath. His entire body froze as if he were crouched among the trees with Charlie and the others. Seconds ticked by so slowly. There was only the crunch of twigs and leaves underfoot as the guards crossed by the men in their path along the wall.

"All right. You're clear. Continue five hundred feet east to the edge of the light. Go...now!" Kairo instructed.

Will's heart felt like it started again and his lungs expanded. The three men in the compound didn't say a word, but they moved along the course Kairo skillfully plotted for them across the yard to the house. Kairo seemed to make it look so easy as he coordinated their trek while blotting out cameras here and there to mask their movements.

Maybe what they'd been telling him for the past few hours was the truth. They had this all under control. It was clear with every step they took that they had done this many times in the past.

Will managed a few easier breaths until the house came into view on Charlie's video screen. Crossing the yard had begun to feel like the easy part. Inside the house was more complicated. There were several guards patrolling the interior of the house. There were lots of security cameras for Kairo to handle. And then there was their ultimate goal.

Actually, they'd worked out three possible targets before Charlie, West, and Ed had even left the van.

The first and easiest was a glass Benicio had been drinking out of during the later part of the night in his office on the second floor. He'd worked at his desk, made calls, and shot off emails while drinking what looked to be scotch from a beautiful crystal tumbler. That alone should have enough DNA on it for Will to run his test.

However, if they couldn't get the tumbler for whatever reason, the backup plan was Benicio's toothbrush and/or hairbrush. Unfortunately, those would be located in the private bathroom off the master suite, where Benicio was currently sleeping.

And if things went all to hell, they were each equipped with a tranquilizer that they could give to Benicio. He would be knocked out in a matter of seconds, allowing them to swab the man's mouth directly. It would give them the best DNA sample out of all their options, but Will was hoping they'd be able to avoid a direct confrontation.

After nearly a half hour of stop-start moving across the lawn, Charlie and his friends climbed the curving stone steps to the front door. The men waited crouched under the bright lights in front of the house. They were in view of any guard who happened to walk by, but Kairo had timed it perfectly.

The man's fingers flew across the keyboard, keys clacking loudly in the silent van as he worked on hacking the biometric lock on the front door. Will squeezed his eyes shut and tried to get his heart to slow. The wind outside the van howled and buffeted the metal side for a moment before settling again. It felt like seconds stretched on into forever as he waited for Kairo to work his special brand of magic.

Just as Will's hold on his patience was cracking, Kairo hooted. Will's eyes shot open in time to see Kairo slam his index finger down on one last key. "Got it! You're unlocked. Hallway is clear for the next thirty seconds."

Will watched as Charlie opened the fucking front door. Yes, they were going in the front door. These guys had freaking balls for days.

The interior was dimly lit, but the soft golden light there bathed the foyer so that acres of white marble took on a warm, buttery glow. West crossed in front of Charlie, moving into the lead with ease and precision in his smooth move-ments. His handgun was gripped between both hands, lifted and ready as he visually swept the area for guards.

Ed moved into view next, also checking the area while Charlie silently shut the door.

A sharp, electric crack filled the van. Both Will and Kairo jerked backward in unison. One by one, the various monitors pixelated for a second and flashed off.

"Fuck! No! Fuck, no!" Kairo shouted, his fingers flying across the keys but the screens weren't coming online again. "Guys? Can you hear me? Gingerbread man to the baker? Anyone, come in!"

The scent of burnt ozone filled the air and Will struggled not to let panic consume him.

"What's going on?"

"Fuck! Shit! We've been made!" Kairo leaped out of his

seat and lunged from the front of the van to slide behind the driver's seat.

"What? What do you mean made?" Will demanded as he followed. He'd just fallen into the passenger seat when Kairo got the engine to roar to life. His friend shoved the vehicle into drive and they took off, throwing Will back against the seat.

"Made. Found out," Kairo replied sharply. He stomped on the gas, causing the tires to bark as they raced down the quiet residential street. "They were apparently watching for my hack and sent a virus. I didn't see it. It fried my equipment. The guys are in there blind. We can't talk to them, and they can't talk to us."

A million questions rushed to the forefront of his mind concerning how that was fucking possible in the first place, but none of that was important. The only thing that mattered right now was getting Charlie, West, and Ed out of there alive.

"Do they know? What are they going to do? What do we do?" Will shot out. He gripped the handle on the door to keep from being tossed out of his seat. With his free hand, he made a grab for his seat belt and fought to get it in place.

"They should figure it out pretty damn quick. This is grounds for aborting the mission completely. The plan would then be to get out of the house as fast as possible and head straight for the backup extraction point, where we are headed now."

"Yeah. Okay. Good."

That sounded smart. Prepared. Charlie and the others would hurry out of the house, dodge the guards again, get over the wall, and meet up with them. Everything was going to be fine.

"Doc? You brought your med bag, right?"

Will's stomach sank and his sweaty hand tightened on the door handle. "Yeah. I brought it," he replied tightly.

"Good. Probably gonna need it."

Fuck.

17

CHARLIE SANDS

"Fuck—"

It was the last thing he heard from Kairo, and then the earwig went silent.

Charlie flinched at the ominous *thunk* of the lock automatically sliding into place in the door behind him. He lifted his gaze to see both West and Ed glance at him with questioning looks.

"Gingerbread man? What's the situation?" Charlie demanded in the lowest whisper he could manage.

But there wasn't a single sound from their eyes in the van.

That meant just one thing—they'd been made. They had to get out of that house right now.

Charlie pivoted on the balls of his feet and made a grab for the deadbolt to slide it free, but the mechanical lock was fighting him. He was prepared to shoot the lock and force his way out when a flash of movement past the window by the door had him stopping. He gazed out and cursed under his breath. Guards were already rushing across the front lawn, moving into position to block their exit through the front.

"Through the house. Head to the exit at the rear and the

backup extraction point," Charlie gritted out between clenched teeth.

His two friends nodded without question or an ounce of hesitation. This certainly wasn't the first mission that had gone south on them. Charlie just hadn't expected it to happen this quickly.

West took the lead, a gun in his right hand while he reached down and swiftly palmed a second in his left. The sniper preferred to work unseen from a distance with a high-powered rifle, but that didn't mean he wasn't as capable on the move with a pair of handguns. Hell, Charlie had seen how lethal the man could be with just a few knives. Ruthless precision and not nearly enough concern for his own well-being.

Pounding footsteps echoed through the house as guards were already racing to their position. Charlie brought up the rear, one eye constantly turned behind them, watching for anyone who was looking to catch them unaware and pump them full of bullets.

"You thought you were going to come into my house and steal from me!" Benicio's angry voice echoed from the second floor. "You're dead! You're all dead!"

"I bet that pint of blood is sounding real good right now, huh?" Edison grumbled.

Charlie didn't answer. There wasn't a chance. Gunshots echoed off the marble across from West, and Charlie caught a blur of color from the corner of his eye. He didn't question it. Swinging around, he aimed with practiced ease and squeezed off two rounds, putting both bullets square in the guard's chest as he lifted his gun.

Yep, sneaky was now a thing of the past.

Benicio continued to shout for their deaths like a petulant three-year-old denied his favorite toy, but he was easy enough to ignore. Perez wasn't the type to actually descend the stairs to put his life in danger or bother to get his hands dirty.

"Clear," West barked, and they followed him a few feet to

the next turn in the hallway that offered them some cover from the bodyguards firing on them.

Charlie's heart thudded painfully, and his brain tried to conjure up images of Will. Had the van been discovered? Was that why the communications had been knocked out? Kairo was plenty capable of protecting himself and Will, but he was just one guy and it was clear that Perez had enough money to buy himself a private army.

"This seems like way more than the ten guards he was supposed to have on hand," Ed grumbled as he took out two more men with well-placed shots.

"He was waiting for us," West snarled.

Charlie couldn't argue with that. It was something they'd expected considering the fact that it hadn't been that long ago that Perez had made an attempt on Will's life. Unfortunately, they'd been confident they could sneak through all of Perez's precautions and get what they wanted.

"Tedious," West muttered as he shoved both of his guns into their holsters. It was their only warning.

"Shit!" Edison shouted. Charlie could just barely make out the sight of West diving forward toward a dead guard, while Ed provided cover fire.

Charlie killed one more guard at the rear and turned his attention to helping Ed fight the guards clustered in what appeared to be a large entertaining area. Fluff leaped into the air as bullets tore through the various chairs and couches that filled the long room. More bullets pockmarked the deep-red walls and tore through the paintings so that their massive frames crashed to the floor.

West hit just ahead of the dead man and came up holding his submachine gun. Bullets flew out of the weapon, peppering the air like angry bees and slicing through their attackers. The spray might have been relentless, but West was still frighteningly accurate. Men fell and didn't get up.

"Clear!" West shouted.

"Fucking madman!" Edison cackled as they followed West through the room toward a wall of glass doors that looked out across the inground pool and vast spread of green for the back lawn. From here, they had to cover only a couple of acres to reach the rear gate. Climbing the wall was an option, but they had to get rid of the guards. Otherwise, they'd be targets waiting to be cut down.

They trailed behind West as he jogged across the room. He dropped the gun he had and picked up another. He cradled it in both leather-gloved hands as if it were his favorite child. Edison took a step ahead of him and kicked the first set of double doors open.

The trio exploded into the chilly night air, welcomed by a new hail of gunfire.

A cry of pain from West cut through Charlie as he watched the sniper fall, gripping his left thigh.

"Ed! Cover!" Charlie shouted as he grabbed West's left arm to haul him to his feet. Ed stood over them, laying down enough answering fire to buy them precious seconds to get West moving again.

"It's just a scratch," West bit out. "Let's move!"

Charlie got a good grip on West and started running across the concrete and tile patio, past the pool and the scattering of remaining guards who had taken refuge behind trees. Unfortunately, with West pressed to his right side, Charlie was left to return fire with his weaker left hand. West caught on fast enough, though.

"You keep us on our feet. Let me do the shooting," West ordered between clenched teeth as he swung the gun in his free right hand around to take out a couple of guards.

Charlie didn't argue. He just kept them moving.

"Fuck! Rat bastard limp dicks!" Ed roared in pain behind him. Charlie stopped and started to turn toward the other man. He caught sight of Ed holding his left shoulder for a second. "Keep moving!" he shouted.

Charlie didn't question it. Ed was still on his feet and running in their direction. That was enough for him.

They didn't get more than a dozen steps when an explosion nearly knocked them off their feet. Charlie and West stumbled forward, regaining their balance. The shooting stopped completely. Charlie glanced back to see the rear half of the house engulfed in black smoke and flames while a huge smile spread across Ed's face.

"C-4? I thought I told you not to bring it!" Charlie bellowed, though he was laughing on the inside.

"When have you ever known me to not have a little C-4?" Edison returned. He caught up with him and West, allowing Charlie to see that the man had taken a bullet to his left shoulder. He was sweating heavily and his teeth were clenched against the pain, but he was still smiling.

"You know that shit's not Silly Putty, right?" West teased.

Ed took West's arm and slung it across his broad shoulders, taking Charlie's place despite the additional pressure placed on his injury. "That's why I call my stuff Danger Putty." He then looked over at Charlie. "You can clear the way and make sure Kairo's ass is waiting for us. We'll be right behind you."

Charlie grunted and darted ahead of his companions. The few guards that had been left fighting them at the rear of the house had either run off or were now making sure Little Shit had escaped the house that was now on fire.

As he reached the guard shack at the rear of the property, he found two guards already dead on the pavement, dark blood spreading across the pale gray and wrapping around the spent shell casings. The van was backed into the driveway with the rear doors open. Kairo stood near the doors with a gun in his right hand, his left resting on the knife hilt at his waist.

But Charlie's eyes were immediately drawn to Will's pale face illuminated by the dome light. His lover was crouched at the rear of the van, but he jumped down the second he spotted Charlie. He started to run forward, but Kairo immediately caught him, pulling him to the van. Panic flashed through Will's blue eyes, and he looked as if he were about to fight Kairo.

"In the van," Charlie called out. "West and Ed are hurt."

Will's expression hardened, but he leaped into the van as ordered and grabbed his medical kit. Kairo headed for the driver's seat. He would be ready to haul them out of there the moment they were all loaded up.

Charlie turned to see West and Ed closing in on him, appearing drained, sweaty, and bloody. West's limp was growing more pronounced, and Ed was slowing. Charlie moved to the other side of West, and he got his companions safely to the van without sustaining further injuries.

As he slammed the door shut behind them and Kairo peeled out of the neighborhood, Charlie was only more determined to crush Little Shit into the dirt.

But first, he had to convince Will not to leave him.

18

WILL MONROE

Taking care of bullet wounds while being tossed about in a speeding van was not the easiest of tasks, but Will knew better than to ask Kairo to stop or even slow down. They needed to get away from the compound before the cops arrived—or, more importantly, before Benicio got his men organized enough to come after them.

Will's heart had stopped with the explosion and only seemed to start again when he saw Charlie running toward them out of the darkness. He wanted to go directly to the man and check him over for injuries, but despite the blood smeared across his clothes, his lover was moving with ease while West and Ed were clearly hurt. They were his priority.

A cursory examination of West showed that he had a large gash across his thigh, thanks to getting strafed by a bullet. While messy and bloody, he needed little more than some stitches and painkillers.

He barked instructions to Charlie on how to bandage West up until they could get to a location where Will would be able to properly treat his wounds.

Ed, unfortunately, was another matter. The light inside the van was terrible, but it was enough to see that a bullet had torn through the meat of his shoulder and exited out the back without clipping bone.

"Give it to me straight, Doc Will," Ed said with a pained gasp as Will did what he could to clean the wound and staunch the bleeding. "Am I gonna lose my arm?"

"No, idiot, you're not gonna lose the arm," Will muttered under his breath as he dug through his bag for more padding. "But I can't properly stitch you or West up as long as we're moving. I'm just as likely to sew my fingers to you as I am to close the wound."

"Sorry, Doc!" Kairo called from the driver's seat with a frustrated growl.

"Ignore it! Keep going!" Charlie shouted.

"Are we being followed?" West demanded.

The van jerked wildly to the left, threatening to throw Will off balance, only to lurch to the right again, nearly tossing him into Ed. "Not that I can see. I think we're clear to go to the house." From Will's quick glance through the windshield, it looked as if they'd left the quiet neighborhood and were moving into a busier, more populous area. He didn't recognize it, but he didn't get out to see much of the city beyond the smaller neighborhoods where he saw his patients.

"That rental house?" Will's head popped up and his hands stilled on Ed's shoulder. "They have to know about it by now. They'll find us."

"Don't worry, Will." Ed grabbed Will's frozen wrist with his right hand and squeezed, drawing his gaze to the man in front of him. "We always have a fallback safe house before we launch a mission. Just in case things go to shit."

Like tonight.

"The only problem is that it's going to take at least an hour for us to get there," Kairo chimed in.

"Will? Are they safe waiting that long?" Charlie inquired, jerking his chin toward Ed.

"Yes. I've got the bleeding slowed enough and from what I

can see, no major arteries were hit. The sooner we get somewhere safe, the better, but I need time, light, and stability in which to work." Will dug into his bag again and found the bottle of morphine he was searching for. It wasn't his preference, but he didn't want Ed and West suffering through this bumpy ride. He quickly injected a dose into Ed, who released a relieved sigh. He then prepared a second syringe for West. The man didn't look happy about it, but at least he didn't fight.

Once that was taken care of, he ripped off the gloves he'd pulled on to treat his patients and tossed them to the floor of the van as he turned his attention to Charlie. He ran his hands over the man roughly and tugged at his clothes.

"Whoa! Whoa! I'm happy to see you, too," Charlie gasped, thrusting his hands into the air.

"I'm not groping you, asshole. I'm checking to make sure you're not hiding any injuries from me."

"I'm not!"

"Like I trust you to tell me the truth. I've seen those stupid war movies where the guy always says to take his buddy first, all while hiding his own worse injuries."

Both Ed and West broke into loud guffaws of laughter that helped to slow Will's questing hands enough so that Charlie could grab them.

"I'm not lying!" Charlie argued. "I'm seriously fine."

"Trust us, Charlie will be the first to tell you he's hurt," Ed chuckled.

"Loudly," West added.

"Biggest damn baby you've ever met," Ed continued. He slid a little lower in the seat that Kairo had used to work the equipment and braced his foot against the wall of the van. His eyes were partially closed and his mouth was in a lopsided grin. "Even if it's a splinter, he will bitch to anyone around to hear him."

"Thanks so much for your love and support," Charlie muttered.

"Baby," West snickered.

"Huge baby," Ed agreed, drawing the word out.

"Charlie?" Will braced his hand on the ceiling of the van to steady himself as Kairo deftly launched them onto a highway. He had no idea where they were going, and he truly didn't care just so long as it was somewhere safe.

Charlie placed his hand on the side of Will's neck and brushed a light kiss to his forehead. "I swear to you that I'm okay. At worst, I might have a little glass in my back because someone decided to take along C-4 to this stealth operation."

Ed giggled. "Danger Putty."

West even chortled. "That Danger Putty saved our asses."

Will sighed and squeezed his eyes shut against the swell of fear, panic, relief, anger, and exhaustion that rose in his chest. The scent of blood and sweat filled his nose, and he opened his eyes again to see that Charlie had taken a step closer, a strange look twisting up his features and digging lines around his eyes.

"Don't leave me yet. Just give me another chance," Charlie said in a choked voice.

"Leave you?" Will gasped and the entire van became oppressively quiet. Even the hum of the engine and the rush of the wind on the vehicle seemed to drop as if everyone was suddenly listening in on their conversation, but he didn't care. He needed to know what the fuck Charlie was even talking about.

"I know tonight was overwhelming and crazy, but I swear to you that this was a weird one. Nothing went right, and that almost never happens. Usually our missions are much smoother. We rarely get hurt," Charlie explained.

"It's true," Kairo called from the front of the van. "The last time any of us got hurt was when Ed fell down the stairs in Spain."

"It was three steps," Ed moaned.

"You still landed on your face," Kairo argued.

Charlie gave a growl at his companions and turned his attention to Will. His thumb rubbed along his jaw in the sweetest caress. "I'll never lie and say that what we do is safe, but we're very careful. We take a lot of precautions. We're good at what we do, I swear. Next time won't be like this."

Will barked out a harsh laugh. "We both know you can't possibly promise that the next time won't go batshit crazy like tonight." He stepped into Charlie, poking him in the center of the chest. "And I'm fucking insulted that you think I would run the first time things get crazy. I've *seen* some crazy shit in the past six years. You don't know what I've survived. I'm not gonna run because of bullet wounds and some little explosions. If anything, tonight proved to me that you *need* me. These two would probably bleed out before you got to your safe house, or you'd have to risk stopping at a hospital to get them help."

West giggled in the background. "He called your explosion 'little.' "

"Awww," Ed whined.

"You're not leaving?" Charlie asked, ignoring their banter.

"Because of this?" Will demanded, his voice jumping with his incredulity. "God! Sometimes you're a complete moron, Charlie. You need me to keep your head attached to your body. If I leave you, it'll be because of something you do like cheating on me or-or lying to me. I—"

Will didn't get any further. Charlie slammed his mouth over Will's, swallowing his words. This. He needed this to get balanced, to reassure himself that Charlie was safe. It didn't matter what his doctor brain told him. He needed to hold Charlie, to kiss him and feel that he was safe in his arms.

Unfortunately, the kiss broke off just as he started to fully lean into Charlie, deepening it so that he could get lost in the feel and taste of him. The van jerked and they pulled apart to keep their balance. Will flashed him an uneven smile, and Charlie stared at him with such warmth and open affection that Will's heart just sort of flopped over and sighed.

"Back to work," Charlie murmured as he made his way to the front of the van, where he dropped into the passenger seat. Will returned to Edison's side, checking the bandage on his shoulder. He needed to be sewn up, but the van was no place for such things.

"I'm okay," Ed reassured him with a crooked grin.

Will nodded, feeling the tension unwinding from his chest. "You will be. Though I'm thinking you might still need some physical therapy after you've healed to get full mobility in this shoulder."

"Wouldn't be the first time I needed a little PT. No big deal."

"What I want to know is, what the hell happened?" Charlie demanded gruffly.

Will checked on West before sitting on the floor with his shoulder braced against Charlie's seat.

"In short, they were expecting us," Kairo said with a heavy sigh.

"Definitely," Ed grumbled. "There's no way in hell he keeps that number of guards roaming around the compound on a daily basis. We moved too quickly."

"The other thing is that I underestimated the security system," Kairo continued. "He had a better IT team or maybe even another hacker on hand. Once I got inside, all my attention was on monitoring the cameras and giving you directions. I didn't notice that they were sending a virus back to disable my equipment and lock me out. It's my bad, guys. I'm sorry."

Charlie immediately reached over and placed his hand on Kairo's shoulder. "Don't. We got out safe."

"But—"

"Seriously, Kairo, don't," West snapped. "Shit happened.

That's the way it goes. We knew the risks were going to be higher because we were rushing this mission. Half of this shit wouldn't have happened if we'd taken more time to scope out the situation."

"Lesson learned," Ed chimed in.

"I'm sorry for asking that you try to do this so quickly," Will murmured.

"There's nothing you can do about this timetable, baby." Charlie gave Kairo's shoulder a final squeeze and dropped his hand to hold on to Will's arm. "Every job we take has its own unique complications. The fact is that we not only rushed it, but we also underestimated Perez. He's an arrogant, self-absorbed asshole, but we also took that to mean that he's an idiot. He's not, and we paid a price for that assumption."

They all fell silent for a long time. Will closed his eyes and rested his head against Charlie's chair, letting the feel of his fingers moving on his arm relax him. It was so freaking late. The sun was going to be rising in just a few hours and he still needed to finish patching up both West and Ed before he could actually get some sleep.

"I'm thinking that our crew isn't properly equipped for this mission," Charlie announced suddenly, shattering the quiet.

"What are you talking about?" Ed asked, sounding as if Charlie had woken him from a doze.

"I'm thinking we don't have enough stealth."

West snorted and even Kairo made a disgruntled noise. "Fuck you. I'm all stealth," the driver grumbled.

"Your best stealth comes from a distance. The same with West. You're both sneaky fucks, but you do some of your best work from a distance," Charlie argued.

A low, long chuckle rumbled up from Ed, causing Will to twist around to stare at him. "I see what you're getting at. You think he'll come?"

Will turned to look up at Charlie. "What? I don't understand."

Charlie shifted in his chair to smile at him. Exhaustion was digging lines in his face and making his eyelids droop. "There's no one sneakier in the world than a cat burglar."

Kairo cackled. "I dare you to repeat that where Alexei can hear you. I fucking dare you."

"No chance. That kid is psycho."

Kairo laughed. "I dare you to call him a kid to his face, too."

"I'm assuming you're talking about Soren," Will interjected since he was still feeling lost. "I thought you said he was vacationing with his boyfriend. Would he really leave that to come here?"

Kairo broke into another laugh, this one hard enough to make the van swerve slightly into the next lane. "Definitely. Soren might bitch and whine about it, but if he tells Alexei, they will be on the next flight." Kairo glanced over his shoulder at Will and flashed him a grin. "Ignore what Charlie is saying about Alexei. Yes, he's an assassin and scary dangerous, but he also loves Soren with every fiber of his being. He's really sweet, actually, and adventurous."

"Because he's twelve," Charlie spat out.

"He's twenty-three, which makes Charlie feel old and insecure," Kairo teased.

Twenty-three and an accomplished assassin? Who the fuck are his parents? Do they know what he's doing?

But Will got the feeling old and insecure part. Hearing about Alexei was starting to make him feel old and very insecure.

"Cat burglars are sneaky. Assassins are sneaky. Sounds like we'd be picking up a double threat if we can get them to come help," Ed said. "Make the call, Charlie. Ask Soren to bring his boyfriend to come play with us."

Charlie released Will and leaned over in his seat so he could pull his cell phone out of his back pocket. "I'll shoot him a text and see if he can stop screwing his boyfriend's brains out long enough to talk."

"Jealous," West muttered. His voice was low and husky like he was half-asleep.

"Fuck yes, I'm jealous," Charlie grumbled. "The second this nonsense is finished, I'm taking my boyfriend to some private beach and fucking his brains out. Somewhere none of you lunatics can find us."

Will cocked his head, looking up at Charlie with his eyebrows raised. "Boyfriend, huh?"

His lover's expression was completely unrepentant as he smirked at him. "Mine," he growled, and Will swore he could feel the vibrations of that single word across his soul.

19

CHARLIE SANDS

Charlie found Will sitting on the bench swing that hung in the small backyard. The doctor appeared to be staring off into space while the sun set just past the tall concrete walls that circled the property.

The place Kairo and Ed had lined up for them felt like it was in the middle of nowhere on a tree-lined street that the rest of the world forgot about. He'd learned long ago not to ask how they found these gems. During their time with the CIA, they'd all studied how to disappear and blend with the crowds. But Kairo and Ed always found a way to do it without sacrificing comfort, something he appreciated more with each passing year.

They'd been at the house for two days now, allowing Ed and Westin time to recuperate and Kairo to rebuild his stock-pile of technical equipment while they waited for Soren and Alexei. Everyone seemed to be relaxed, but Will appeared to be growing more anxious.

If he was being honest with himself, though, he was starting to wonder if reentering Will's life was the smartest thing. Assuming he kept running with Kairo, Ed, and West in their mercenary-for-hire enterprise. Wasn't he just dragging

196

Will into danger? It didn't matter if Will remained in the van or at the safe house, death, danger, and violence clung to them like a second skin. It would still find Will and threaten his life. That was the last thing he wanted.

Maybe it was time to leave this all behind.

What the fuck was he going to do with himself?

Will pushed the swing back and lifted his eyes to meet Charlie's, a slow smile forming on his lips.

He was going to do whatever Will needed him to do.

"I'm starting to learn that's your worried face," Will called with a tilt of his head to the side.

Charlie huffed a laugh and crossed the yard. Will slid to the far end of the swing, making room for Charlie to join him. The old wood creaked under Charlie's weight, and the metal chains clicked softly as he changed the rhythm of their movement, speeding it up a tiny bit.

"You know, I was just thinking that you seemed more worried," Charlie admitted. He stretched his right arm out, resting it on the back of the swing. To his extreme delight, Will leaned his body against Charlie's, cuddling closer and resting his head on Charlie's shoulder. Will chuckled, but he felt it in the shaking of his frame rather than actually hearing the sound.

"And that's the reason for your worried look?"

Charlie shrugged. "Among other things."

"What percentage of those other things are related to me?"

"Sixty percent?"

Will hummed softly as if that was what he'd expected to hear.

"How about you tell me what's got you worried, and then I'll tell you what I'm worried about?"

Will lifted his head and cocked it to the side, eyes narrowing on Charlie. "Seriously? You'll really tell me what's got you worried?"

197

"We promised we'd talk, right? Tell the truth so things don't go to hell all over again?"

"No, you're right. I'm just…surprised. I thought I'd have to fight you over it." He settled back against Charlie's shoulder and released a heavy sigh.

"I'm not claiming to be perfect at this. I'm going to forget or make the excuse that I'm hiding stuff to protect you. Then, you'll smack me and remind me that I'm being an idiot." Charlie leaned close, pressing his lips to Will's hair as he growled, "I'll get on my knees, beg you to forgive me, and show you exactly how sorry I am."

A shiver ran through Will from head to toe, and he burrowed closer into Charlie's larger frame. "Yeah, I bet you're going to be so good at begging."

"So, start talking. What's bothering you?"

"Carlos," Will immediately said.

"It's only been four days since you last saw him. How often did you visit him in the hospice?"

"Usually just once a week. He also has an oncologist who sees him regularly, and there's another doctor on staff at the hospice," Will explained. "The new doctor who's taking over the clinic is in town now, too. I've already talked to him on the phone, explaining that I'm having a family emergency myself and can't see any of my old patients. He was going to take them all over anyway. It's just happening sooner than anyone had planned."

"It sounds like everything is under control. What's the problem?"

Will shrugged his shoulders against Charlie. "I've done this dozens of times, but I've always been there to walk the new doctor through all my notes and share my insights. I could look them in the eye and answer their questions. This…it's all so fast and feels haphazard. People's lives are depending on me, and I feel like I'm shirking my responsibilities."

"No, you're staying alive." Charlie wrapped his arm

tighter around Will's shoulders, holding him even closer. "If you're spotted in Buenos Aires right now, you're going to get yourself killed. And probably one or more of us, because you know we wouldn't let you go alone right now."

"True." Will sighed.

"I'm sure this doctor is a professional. He's going to take good care of your patients. Everything is going to be fine."

"I know. I also talked to Carlos briefly. Told him that things didn't go well recently and that I had to leave town for a little while. He's been warned about the new doctor. I know he's worried about me, but he understands the situation."

Charlie grunted. "The man lived during the period of *Los Desaparecidos*. I'm sure he gets the need to lay low when things get too hot."

"Yeah, I just want to return to check on him as soon as possible." Will tipped his head up to look at Charlie. "I've been careful every time I made my weekly visit with him. No one has followed me or asked about my patients. I feel pretty confident that Perez doesn't know about Carlos."

The one thing Charlie didn't want to point out was that Will wasn't the only weak spot for Carlos. There was also Francisco. He could only hope that the man was truly out of town and avoiding all notice. They simply didn't have enough people on hand to protect Carlos right now. West and Ed were recovering but still needed more time. Kairo was busy rebuilding all his equipment for their next attack on Perez. And Charlie wasn't willing to leave his lover's side while he was still in danger.

"All right, that's what's eating at me." Will shoved into an upright sitting position and narrowed his eyes on Charlie. "What's bothering you?"

Charlie flinched. Five minutes ago, this had sounded like a brilliant idea. Now that he was sitting here, faced with actually putting into words the fact that he wanted to cover Will in bubble wrap and hide him away from the world, it seemed much harder.

"Say it out loud," Will pressed, clearly enunciating each word.

"I'm worried about your safety," Charlie spit out. "I'm worried about you getting shot. I'm worried there aren't enough of us to keep you safe. I'm worried that even after we're done in Argentina, all I'm going to do is bring danger and violence into your life. I'm worried that you're going to get tired of all the blood and bullets and danger. You'll get tired and leave—"

Will grabbed Charlie's face with both hands and pulled him into a long, deep kiss. Within seconds, the panic that had started to spiral out of control in his chest was dissolving and he was relaxing into his wonderful man.

After too little time, Will pulled back enough to lightly nibble on Charlie's lower lip. "Do you think I'm not worried about you getting shot or blown up?"

"I know, but I've been trained for this."

"Doesn't mean it can't happen. Look at Ed and West. They're professionals, and they still got hurt." Will's voice was surprisingly calm and sweet despite the topic. "I don't like the idea of you getting hurt, but I also know that you're doing an amazing thing for a dying man—something no one else can do. I also know that this kind of insane shit makes you happy. I want you happy, dearest."

That one endearment threatened to liquify Charlie's brain. It wasn't fair. He'd been called all manner of strange and clichéd endearments over the years by his other lovers, but Will was the only one to ever whisper that word to him. Those two syllables falling from those perfect lips made him stupid. He'd agree to anything Will said, and his lover knew it.

Charlie could feel his expression soften as he stared at Will. "It will be an adjustment. I just got you back. I'm not willing to do anything that would cause me to lose you again."

"We'll take things slow," Will reassured him.

"That reminds me. You were slated to finish up your time in Argentina about now anyway. What were you planning to do after this? Did you have another gig lined up?" He was only too happy to change the subject. He didn't want to think about losing Will to violence or his own stupidity. Let him just wallow in this happy moment a little while longer.

The laughter in Will's eyes showed that he knew exactly what Charlie was doing, but he let him. He settled his head on Charlie's shoulder and shrugged. "I didn't have anything lined up or specifically planned. I figured I would just head to the US and visit with my family for a bit while I looked for a new job. It's been almost a year since I was last there."

"You don't sound too excited about that idea."

Will made a noise that lacked all enthusiasm. "I'm not. Just tired of the guilt."

"So, if I were to kidnap you and take you off to some island where no one could find us, you wouldn't have a problem with it?"

Will chuckled and turned into Charlie, sliding his arms around his waist. "I would not have a problem with that at all. In fact, I—"

Charlie stiffened and held up one hand, halting Will's words at the sound of a car pulling into the driveway of the house. There should be only one person outside their immediate group who knew how to find them, but they couldn't be too careful.

"Go in the house," Charlie murmured. He pulled free of Will as he jumped to his feet. He grabbed the handgun resting in the holster snuggled against the small of his back. He automatically chambered a round and started toward the side of the house to check to see who had arrived.

Charlie was next to the building when he realized Will was following him instead of going inside as he'd instructed. He glared over his shoulder at the doctor, but Will returned the nearly snarling expression.

"It's just Soren, right?" Will countered.

"Possibly not," Charlie grumbled. He continued to the front, not wanting to argue about it now. At least the others were likely to have heard the car, and Kairo would be checking it out as well. No matter what, he and Will were going to have a very long discussion about following orders for his safety and the safety of the entire team.

As he reached the front of the house, he spotted a dark-navy sedan he didn't recognize. However, the man standing next to the open driver's side door with a killer tan was well-known to him.

"Sorry to disturb your vacation," Charlie called out as he lowered his gun to his side.

Soren's head whipped around, and a wide grin spread across his face, replacing the look of worry. "I'm hoping you'll make it worth our while." Soren then followed the direction of Charlie's narrowed gaze and sighed heavily. "Put the gun away, Angel."

"When he puts his up first," Alexei replied smoothly. The twink standing in the passenger-side door smirked at him. His pale-blond hair shone in the setting sun and his makeup was done in such a way to give him luxurious, smoky eyes, but when they turned to Charlie, they were cold and dead. The only time he'd seen the man's gaze warm was when his eyes were on Soren.

With an exasperated sigh, Charlie shoved his gun into his holster and lifted both of his hands to show that he was currently unarmed as he took a step away from the house toward the car.

"And what about your handsome friend?" Alexei pressed.

Will immediately stepped forward, his hands up and empty. "I'm completely unarmed, I promise."

"Holy shit! Will?" Soren gasped. "What the fuck are you

doing here? And with this idiot?"

Before Will could reply, Alexei stopped in the middle of tucking his own weapon away and squinted at the doctor. "That's the Will you told me about? Huh." The assassin then looked straight at Charlie and grinned wickedly. "He's a lot hotter than I thought you could snag. Not bad, old man."

Charlie sucked in a breath to shoot a snide remark back to the snot-nosed punk when Will's hand clapped over his mouth as he stepped in front of him.

"It's good to see you again, Soren," Will said loudly. "You're here because I find myself in a bit of a mess and Charlie volunteered to help along with Ed, Kairo, and West. Sorry to drag you in as well."

Soren stopped in his approach toward them, his eyes shooting a thousand questions past Will to Charlie.

Grabbing Will's hand, Charlie pressed a quick kiss to the palm and then pulled it down. "We told him everything."

"Oh, shit." Soren winced, his shoulders shrinking in a little as he lifted his eyes to Will. "I'm sorry…for any and all trouble that we caused you in Paris."

Will exhaled loudly, the sound rising from old wounds that were probably still healing on his soul. Charlie wrapped an arm around Will's waist and pulled him until his back collided with Charlie's chest. They were doing better, but it was going to be a long time before all the pain Charlie had caused him faded to a distant memory. That was fine. Charlie was going to be with him every step of the way.

"It's okay. Things happened. I'm just looking to move on from all of that," Will murmured.

"Alexei!" Kairo's voice rang out from the front porch.

Charlie chuckled as the young man's face transformed into an expression of pure delight as he slammed the door shut and raced up to greet the other man. While his and Kairo's time in Amsterdam hadn't been long, Kairo and the assassin had managed to bond over tech toys and guns.

Loosening his hold on Will, Charlie walked with his lover the last few feet to greet Soren. The cat burglar hugged them both prior to Soren formally introducing Alexei to Will. Something tightened around his heart to see Soren in Argentina with them. It was like getting the team back together. And while Alexei made him nervous, he couldn't deny that the assassin was a good asset to have on hand. He might be young, but he had a good head on his shoulders, even if he did fall for a reckless idiot like Soren.

After helping to grab their bags from the trunk, they all walked into the house, where Kairo was already introducing Alexei to West and Ed. Charlie swore Alexei and West exchanged a strange glance and a nod. It was as if some silent communication had passed between them and the two wolves had decided to be civil to each other. Completely different from the effusively warm greeting that passed between Alexei and Ed.

Of course, Ed had a way of being a ball of sunshine and liked everyone until you dared to hurt someone he cared about. Then you were just fucking toast.

"Okay, get me up to speed on this mess you've made," Soren demanded nearly three hours later. It had taken that long for them to catch up on stories from Amsterdam, Istanbul, and now Buenos Aires. Soren might have also taken some time to give Ed and West grief for getting hurt in the first place.

Charlie presented a concise recap of all the events that had occurred in Buenos Aires, the roadblocks they'd encountered, and the time crunch they happened to be facing. Soren nodded through it and glanced at his boyfriend when Charlie was done. Alexei was snuggled up against him, sipping some tea and looking very relaxed.

The assassin shrugged. "The mom."

"I agree. Benicio is the Picasso," Soren murmured.

"Totally," Alexei instantly agreed.

"I'm sorry," Will interjected. "I don't understand. What do you mean?" He shifted to the edge of the chair he was sitting on. Charlie moved a little where he was perched on the arm of the chair in case Will intended to get to his feet. A surge of joy rushed through his chest when Will placed his hand on Charlie's knee, keeping him right where he was.

"When you're hiding something really rare or valuable, you not only need a good security system, but it also helps to have a decoy or a distraction in place," Soren explained. "A Rembrandt or a Botticelli is a lot harder to get your hands on than, say, a Picasso. Something by Picasso is still worth a lot, but it's also easier to fake and not as big a loss as the Botticelli."

"You put the Picasso somewhere to draw a thief's eye while you hide the Botticelli. With any luck, he'll go after the easy target and tell himself that the other isn't worth his time," Alexei continued. "Benicio Perez is loud, flashy, and arrogant. It makes him the perfect target for anyone and everyone."

"But he's also younger with good health. It's easier to move him around and protect him," Charlie grumbled.

"Fucker is bait," West snarled. "And we went for it."

"He's done his job of being bait very well," Alexei said. He picked up one of Soren's hands and held it while setting his teacup on the table. "We can still go after him, but really, not killing him? That seems like a waste. It would just be easier if we kill him and then get the DNA sample you need."

Will's wide eyes snapped up to Charlie's face. His lover had been warm and welcoming from the moment Soren and Alexei appeared. He and the assassin had gotten along well. Now he'd gotten a real taste of Alexei's unique view of the world.

Before Charlie could speak, Soren was lifting both of Alexei's hands to his lips and brushing kisses across the knuckles. "Angel, it would be hard to go back to this Carlos and tell him that we've killed his nephew while confirming the dead man was, in fact, related to his beloved dead wife."

Alexei huffed an annoyed sigh and dropped his head against Soren's shoulder. "True," he agreed, his lips forming a pout. "He started with the lethal tactics first, though. He tried to kill Will. I say this is only fair."

And now Charlie was agreeing with the psychopath. Lovely.

It must have shown on his face, because Will squeezed his knee. "No, Charlie," he said in warning tones.

Fucker deserved to die for ever threatening Will.

"I've been trying to locate Catalina Perez, but I can't even confirm whether she's alive or dead," Kairo announced.

"In K's defense, he's also been stuck trying to hack Perez's defenses and support us for the compound infiltration," Ed argued. "It's not like he's been able to put all his resources behind the search."

Alexei bounced on the couch cushion as he turned to face Kairo next to him, his young face lighting up. "Let me help you. I've got a lot of experience finding people that don't want to be found. If we get really stuck, we could give my uncles a call."

"Oh yes, I'm sure they haven't gotten into any trouble in like…days," Soren teased.

"Your uncles are…?" Will's voice faded.

"Assassins," Alexei answered with a grin. "Mostly retired now, but they get bored and like to meddle in my life."

Will looked up at Charlie again. "This is your normal life?"

Charlie cupped the side of his face and ran his thumb across his cheekbone. "Sometimes. It doesn't have to be. After we finish in Argentina, you just say the word and we'll go to the States or Paris. You set up a practice, we buy a home, and have a Norman Rockwell life, if that's what you want."

The entire room became deathly silent. He could feel

every eye on them. No one moved. No one so much as breathed as they waited on Will's response. Charlie hadn't meant to drop this bomb on them—not like this—but they already knew Will was his world. He couldn't risk fucking this up a second time.

Luckily, Will didn't leave them hanging in suspense.

The doctor jerked his head back a little and wrinkled his nose as his upper lip curled. "Okay, we don't need to go quite that far into the realm of the mundane. I just need more time to adjust to the idea of people trying to kill me. And maybe, assassins." Will's head whipped around to Alexei. "No offense meant."

Alexei widely grinned and waved a hand at him. "None taken. My family and I take some adjustment."

Will returned his attention to Charlie. "I want to be with you on these crazy missions. I need to be there to watch out for you, Kairo, West, and Ed. Who else is going to patch you up?"

"Oh, thank God," Kairo groaned, sinking deeper into the couch.

"Seriously," Ed added. "Charlie is usually the one playing nursemaid, and his bedside manner leaves a lot to be desired."

"Fuck off," Charlie grumbled, but there was no heat in his voice. His eyes were still full of Will. Leaning down, he brushed a kiss to Will's lips. "We can talk about this more later." Preferably when Charlie was wrapped up in Will's relaxed, sweaty body in bed tonight.

He turned his attention to Kairo and Alexei. "Work your magic. Find Catalina Perez. If she's dead, we dig up her corpse. If she's alive, we hit wherever she's being hidden. We'll get the answer to this puzzle before Carlos passes."

"And if she is alive, we're not killing her," Will tossed out.

"Unless she deserves it," Alexei amended.

Charlie sighed and Soren cackled. This man was already proving to be a handful.

20

WILL MONROE

WILL SHUFFLED THROUGH THE INCREDIBLY QUIET HOUSE, following the scent of fresh coffee toward the kitchen. The sun was still inching above the distant horizon and as far as he could tell, West, Ed, and Kairo were asleep in bed. A glance out the front door showed Soren's rental car was missing—he and Alexei hadn't returned from Buenos Aires yet.

After two days of digging around to find any sign of Benicio Perez's mother, Alexei had stood up, announcing that he was restless and needed to move. So, he and Soren had gone to Buenos Aires for the night with the promise that they would behave and stay away from Perez. Will had known Alexei for less than three days, and even he was unwilling to believe that both of those things would happen.

But then, if Alexei was as good as Soren, Charlie, and Kairo claimed, he must know how to escape the notice of people. Maybe the sneaky man would be able to sidle right up to Benicio, get a DNA sample, and sashay back into the safe house like it was no big deal. That he didn't put past the man at all.

His bigger concern right now was Charlie—as in where the fuck was he?

Will had rolled over to find Charlie's side of the bed cold, and that was just wrong. Since they'd started sleeping together again, Will had woken up with Charlie stretched out alongside him, his arm wrapped around his waist. It didn't matter the time of day. Even if Charlie woke up well ahead of him, Charlie would remain in bed, holding him and watching him sleep as if he were afraid that Will would suddenly disappear from his life if he allowed Will out of his sight for a second.

Finding Charlie missing felt ominous. Uneasiness sat like a lead weight in the middle of his stomach, forcing Will out of bed and wandering through the house to find his lover. Both of the bathrooms were empty. A light touch to the carafe proved that the coffee was hot and fresh. He'd at least come this way. Charlie was as dependent on coffee as Will was. He glanced out the door of the kitchen to confirm that Charlie wasn't in the backyard.

Retracing his steps, he quietly opened the front door and immediately stopped when he heard the low rumble of Charlie's voice.

"I'm not sure what to do," Charlie admitted, which stopped Will cold. He couldn't remember the last time Charlie had stated out loud that he didn't know what to do. The man *always* had a plan.

"You tell him how you feel. This isn't rocket science, Charlie. This is Will we're talking about. You know him. Of anyone, you should know how he's going to react to something like that. Will is a sweet guy. Even if he's still pissed at you, he's not the type to just stomp on your heart for shits and giggles."

Will had started to close the door again to give Charlie privacy, but the new voice had him stopping. Well, the new voice and the mention of his name. But he knew this voice. He stood there, brow furrowed in concentration as he ransacked his memory for who the voice went with.

Stephen!

Charlie was talking to his younger brother, the psychiatrist. Will had spoken to him only a couple of times when he'd been dating Charlie the first time. He was an intelligent guy who happened to be a fantastic listener. He also had incredible patience if he was able to put up with Charlie's nonsense.

"That's not the problem. I told him how I feel. I think." Charlie paused and Will had to bite his bottom lip to keep from laughing. "Shit. Maybe I didn't say the words. I can't remember now. Everything has been insane. I think he knows."

Will was just barely holding in his chuckles. He knew. Charlie had said the words, but it was always more than the words for Will. Charlie showed it in dozens of tiny acts. He showed it in how he looked at Will, how he held him in his arms. Charlie threw all of himself into loving Will. He felt it now, and he'd felt it all those years ago in Paris. That was why their parting was so hard to swallow.

"Charlie—" Stephen said with a weary sigh. Will started to pull the door open, intending to reassure Charlie that he did know how he felt.

"No, my worry is that I've offered to give all this craziness up," Charlie interrupted before Stephen could say anything else. "To return to the States. He can set up a practice and we'll buy a house together. A normal life."

"Oh. That's…wow…that's not what I expected. Are you sure that's what you want?" Stephen replied, skepticism heavy in his voice.

"Of course. I want a life with Will. The longest period of time when I was happy was when we were together. This whole trip has been a nightmare, but I'm having the time of my life because I wake up every day to see Will. Even when he's pissed at me, I'm happy."

Will's heart did a happy somersault, but his joy wilted a little with Stephen's not-so-happy noise. "What did he say?"

"That he didn't want to give it up. That he wanted to travel with us and join me in this insane life I have."

Fuck. Now Will was confused. Why didn't Charlie sound happy about that? Shouldn't he be happy to continue the life he enjoyed with Will at his side? Did he not want to share this life with Will?

"Charlie, don't you see that you're making the same mistake all over again?" Stephen murmured.

"No, I'm not. In Paris, I lied about who I was and what I was doing. Since we've met in Argentina, I've told him all about my old job and told him what we're doing now. I'm not hiding anything from him," Charlie countered.

"Yes, the lying and secrets were a big problem, but that wasn't the only one. In Paris, you weren't willing or able to include him in your old life. You're doing that now. You're trying to change your current life to suit what you *think* he wants. But has he said that he wants to go to the States and settled down into this so-called normal life you've envisioned? No, he has told you that he wants to be included in your *current* life." Stephen sounded like he wanted to strangle his brother. Will wouldn't be surprised if Charlie had woken him up for this call.

"Stephen, this shit is dangerous. How could he want that?"

"I don't know. Why do you? From what you've told me, he's no stranger to a dangerous lifestyle. If it bothers you that much, you work with him so he's better protected from the dangers."

"What if he changes his mind? What if he decides this isn't the life that he wants?" Charlie asked, his voice so low that Will could barely hear.

"Then he changes his mind. People do that all the time," Stephen argued. "You've already said that you'd give it up with him. Does that offer have an expiration date? No. You try this for a while, and if it doesn't work, you try something else. That's what happens in a relationship."

"Yeah, yeah. It's not like I've had a lot of practice at these," Charlie grumbled.

Will finally pulled the door open and stepped onto the front porch. "That's why we talk about things. Like adults. No more hiding. No more lying. And no more secrets."

Charlie jumped up from where he was sitting on the concrete stairs and whipped around. "Shit. Will."

"Hey, Will," Stephen called out from where Charlie had him on speakerphone.

"Hey, Stephen. Good to hear your voice," Will replied, smirking at Charlie's shocked expression.

"You too. But it sounds like you've got a handle on this. I'll leave you to deal with Charlie. I'm going back to bed for a couple of hours."

"Thanks, Stephen. I'm sure we'll talk soon." Charlie's brother ended the call with a chuckle, leaving him alone with his wayward boyfriend.

Will closed the door quietly behind him and crossed the short wooden porch to place his arms on Charlie's shoulders. The man had been sitting outside in jeans and a hoodie, while Will had only pulled on a pair of pajama pants and a T-shirt. Cold air nipped at his bare toes, but it was already forgotten as he pressed his lips to Charlie's.

"What are you doing up?" Charlie asked as he moved his mouth to nibble at Will's jaw.

"I woke up alone and came to find you. Did you really call a shrink for relationship advice?" Will teased.

"I called my brother." Charlie's voice dipped into more of a pouting grumble. "But it's the truth. I don't know what I'm doing, Will. I'm terrified of fucking this up."

Will's heart whimpered and offered up a little sob. He knew the feeling, but they weren't going to make it if Charlie was walking on eggshells and Will was clinging to all the walls around his heart, just waiting for Charlie to hurt him again.

"Come here," Will murmured. He pulled out of Charlie's embrace and moved him so they could sit side by side on the stairs while the sun crept higher into the brightening sky. When Charlie was seated next to him, Will threaded their fingers together and rested his head on Charlie's shoulder. "You are going to fuck this up. It's as inevitable as the sun rising. I'm going to fuck this up. At some point, I'm going to make you so mad, you can't even look at me. But you're not going to leave me because of that. You love me too much."

"And you won't leave me because I'm an idiot over you?"

"No, dearest," Will whispered before taking his lips in a sweet kiss.

When it ended, he laid his head on Charlie's shoulder and squeezed his hand. His mind wandered for a moment until it finally settled on a thought. "You know, as much as it hurts to think about, I don't think we really stood a chance in Paris."

"Really?"

Will grunted. "We were in vastly different places in our lives. We wanted things that were driving us in opposite directions. No matter what, one of us would have likely had to sacrifice a dream for us to stay together."

"And one or both of us would have been resentful of that happening," Charlie agreed. "What about now?"

Will closed his eyes and rubbed his cheek against Charlie's shoulder. The familiar spicy scent of his body wash drifted past his nose, brushing away lingering tendrils of worry. "I think both of our dreams are more flexible than they used to be. We're more open to exploring and trying new things. If we had met now, instead of in Paris six years ago, we probably wouldn't have had half the problems we did."

"You think it would have been easier now?"

Will snorted and lifted his head to grin at Charlie. "No. But maybe you would have been more forthcoming about your life, and I wouldn't have been so scared to demand the truth from you."

Charlie's smile clung to his lips, but his eyes grew sadder. "I'm sorry you were scared to confront me. I know it was because you were sure I would walk out the door. I'm not leaving, ever. No matter how pissed or demanding you get."

"No more apologies. I don't want to live in the past anymore. Just tell me you love me."

"I love you. I love you completely. I love the amazing person that you were in Paris, and I love the idea of getting to know you all over again."

Will's throat tightened and his eyes burned with unshed tears. He'd truly never thought this would happen. It had taken him years to let go of all the hopes and dreams his heart had constructed around Charlie. It didn't want to accept that they didn't have a chance, that they couldn't make it work. He'd moved on, but he'd never been able to love another quite like he'd loved Charlie—with all of his soul.

He leaned in and kissed his lover because he couldn't get the words past the lump in his throat. Not yet, anyway. He let himself get lost in the feel and taste of Charlie. Strong arms wrapped around him, and he inched as close as he could.

"I love you," Will mumbled against his lips.

Charlie smiled, his beard scratching Will's cheek. "Let's go back to bed for a little while. It's still early."

Will didn't bother to reply. He just tightened his fingers around Charlie's and pulled the man to his feet as he rose. He led the way up the stairs with Charlie lightly chuckling behind him every freaking step, but he didn't care.

Unfortunately, they encountered a sleepy West in the hallway as they reached the top of the stairs. The man took one look at them and groaned.

"Fuck. Just try to keep the noise down. It's too early for this shit," West muttered.

"The coffee is fresh," Charlie said as if it were some small consolation prize for what West might have to endure.

Will knew he wasn't quiet. He couldn't be quiet when he was with Charlie. Everything his lover did turned him inside-out with pleasure—how could he possibly hold all of that in?

The second the door closed, they were on each other. A giggle tumbled from Will as Charlie tugged Will's T-shirt over his head and tossed it aside. It was as if they'd managed to slip back in time to recapture that frantic, crazed energy they'd had when they were younger and couldn't get enough of each other.

But each touch, each kiss was now deeper, tempered with the ghost of lost years and the ache of longing. There was no escaping the knowledge of how close they'd come to never having this again.

Their time was too precious to waste. No matter how much they drove each other crazy or how Charlie tried to protect him from danger, Will was never letting him go.

He shoved both hands under Charlie's hoodie, running his fingers through the thick hair covering him. Strong muscles jumped and flexed at his touch while nipples pebbled hard under his fingertips.

Their tongues tangled and retreated only to follow and fight again until Will finally submitted with a melting whimper. This was what he wanted, what he craved with every fiber of his being—to be possessed by Charlie, body and soul.

One hand slipped inside his loose pajama pants and wrapped around his cock, while the other squeezed a bare ass cheek, kneading tight muscles. Will moaned into Charlie's mouth, his mind liquifying at that touch. His body was trapped in an endless loop of pleasure that was winding him up closer to an explosion.

"Charlie!" he whined, thrusting his hips forward.

"What's wrong, baby? You need me to fuck that ass?"

"Yes! Now!" The bastard had reduced his brain to monosyllabic words. Pretty soon he was going to be nothing more than screams and nonsensical noises. He didn't care so long as Charlie was inside of him.

Charlie's warm chuckle wrapped him as they quickly shed the last of their clothes and Will was pushed onto the narrow full-sized bed. The thing would have been barely big enough for Charlie's broad shoulders, and it was definitely not big enough for the two of them. But they made it work each night as they tangled up in each other.

Will watched as Charlie snagged a condom and the bottle of lube from his bag that now lived beside the bed for the sole purpose of being close at hand when they needed it. Cold toes and morning chill were forgotten as Will took in the beauty of his lover. Sure, Charlie had fifteen years on him, but the man was built like a fucking gladiator, all hard muscle and golden skin.

His lover turned toward him and stopped, a slow smile spreading across his lips as his eyes moved down his body in an appraising caress that left behind tingles everywhere his gaze touched.

"What?" Will breathed. He shifted against the sheets, sliding his feet under the rumpled covers and parting his legs, giving Charlie a good view of everything. His entire body was restless and nerves on edge. He needed to be touched, licked, fucked until he didn't know his damn name any longer.

"You. So sexy." The low, rumbling voice was a drug, dragging Will into dark, sweet oblivion. His eyes began to shut but stopped when he saw Charlie's hand dip to his own cock and start to slowly stroke it while staring at Will. "I could come like this. Just watching you writhe on the bed, listening to you say my name over and over again."

Will grabbed his cock with his right hand while he slipped his left down to fondle his balls, giving his lover a good show. He grinned and licked his lips. "That might be fun, but don't you want to touch me? Don't you want inside of me? I'm so empty."

It was an old game they played, but the growl he got in answer to that question proved that it still worked.

Charlie immediately crawled between his legs and grabbed his wrists, pulling his hands away from his body to pin them to the mattress. At the same time, Charlie bent and sucked his cock down his throat. Will cried out and fought the urge to thrust deep. He shifted and moaned as pure bliss rippled through him. He tried to lift his hands to touch Charlie, but his lover only tightened his grip, keeping him trapped in the very best way. Brain cells were combusting while sweat slicked his skin.

"Fuck me, Charlie. God, fuck. Please fuck me now," Will begged, not caring if he was speaking complete gibberish at this point. His leg muscles trembled as he battled the need to move.

Slowly, Charlie lifted his head, letting Will's cock slide from his puffy lips while his beard tickled across his stomach. "So bossy. Don't you want to go slow?"

"No! God, no!"

Charlie released his hands but completely ignored his demands as he licked his way lower. He gripped the backs of Will's thighs and held him trapped as he sucked on his balls before moving down to use that too-talented tongue on his hole.

Will was utterly lost as Charlie placed Will's legs on his shoulders, so his hands were free to tease his ass and dick, keeping him constantly balanced on the edge of release, but never quite pushing him off. He thought he heard the condom wrapper and maybe even the snap of the lube cap, but he was delirious with pleasure. He couldn't be sure of anything anymore.

At last, Charlie shifted, kissing his way up Will's chest. As he moved, he pressed his thick cock inside of Will in one smooth, endless motion that squeezed all the air out of Will's lungs. Ecstasy and pain warred inside of him until he thought his heart was going to explode. Oh God, nothing had ever felt so good in all of his life.

Charlie kissed him with Will's legs still resting on his shoulders, his body nearly folded in half. Charlie was so fucking deep. There was no escaping him. This feeling of exquisite fullness had become his entire world.

And then he started to move.

Cries of pleading tripped from Will's parted lips. His cock was trapped between their bodies, rubbing against Charlie's chest. He gripped one of Charlie's biceps and grabbed the slats of the headboard with the other hand, trying to get just enough leverage to lift his hips to meet each of Charlie's thrusts. The man hit his prostate with every movement, shorting out Will's brain. No one knew him like Charlie. He could string him along until he was a taut rubber band on the verge of snapping and then bring him back.

He blinked open eyes to find Charlie's expression harsh, his features stark in his concentration even though pleasure and strain were vibrating through his frame. So beautiful. All his. Forever.

"I love you," Will whispered.

Charlie's eyes widened as if he'd not expected Will to say that. He grinned and thrust even harder, picking up the pace. "I love you too."

But Will barely heard it. There was only the racing of blood in his ears and the slap of their bodies. The orgasm crashed over him suddenly, muscles clamping on Charlie so that his lover cried out at the same time. The world whited out for a second and Will swore his heart jerked to a stop, but none of it mattered as everything spasmed in scorching pleasure.

Seconds later, Charlie lowered Will's legs to the mattress and collapsed on top of him, sweaty and panting. Some part of his brain warned him that everything was going to hurt later, but right now, he was floating on a warm river of rapturous delight. Nothing else mattered except for the man whose heart was thudding against his own.

"Baby," Charlie exhaled. "Sex with you is gonna kill me."

His smile felt crooked on his lips, but he was still trying to get his body to work again after that orgasm. Things definitely got fried in his brain with that one. "We…we could stop," he suggested.

Charlie snorted and turned his head to playfully bite on Will's collarbone. "Not a fucking chance."

"Thank God."

Several minutes ticked by as Charlie gathered enough energy to at least deal with the condom before it leaked everywhere. They wiped off with a T-shirt from the floor and then cuddled together in the bed, their hearts finally coming down from their impromptu marathon.

Will was just starting to doze with Charlie spooning him. One arm was under his head while the other was draped across his waist.

"So, you really want to join my team? Be our resident medic?" Charlie inquired. Will didn't miss the forced casual tone. The undercurrent of worry and tension was so easy to pick out. Or maybe he was getting better at reading this man, trusting his instincts when it came to Charlie as he let go of old fears and insecurities.

"You got an opening?" Will replied playfully, his mind instantly coming online.

"We do. We definitely need a doc who is good under pressure, has a cool head, and solid knowledge of weird injuries. Probably wouldn't hurt to have a good sense of humor and lots of patience."

Will turned in Charlie's arms to lie flat on his back while staring up at his lover. "Sounds like I'd be a damn good fit."

"I can guarantee the pay will be a hell of a lot better than what you're making now."

His eyebrows jumped toward his hairline. That was something he'd not even thought about, despite really needing to. His only concern was sticking close to Charlie and not letting him get away a second time.

Charlie threw his head back and laughed. "Did you seriously think you weren't getting paid for being our doctor?"

"Payment hadn't even crossed my mind."

Leaning forward, Charlie grabbed his lips in a quick, searing kiss. "Yes, you'll get paid, and what you deserve for your skills. Don't worry about that. We recently made a tidy sum on that job we helped Soren and Alexei with, so we all get paid a fair wage for our insanity. I'll take care of you, baby."

"I know you will. I never doubted that."

"We all vote on which jobs we take. Everyone gets an equal voice. If it's not unanimous, we don't do it. After that, I'm the lead and everyone listens to me. Follows my orders."

He liked that. He liked everything about that. An equal voice, but at the same time, Charlie was watching out to keep them all safe.

"Do the guys have to vote on whether to let me join the group?"

Charlie smirked and pressed a sweet kiss to the tip of Will's nose. "Baby, they voted days ago. They've been on my ass to get you locked down before someone else stole you away."

Will giggled and closed his eyes. "There is zero chance of that happening. You're stuck with me now."

"Not stuck," Charlie whispered as he cuddled him close. "Never stuck. You are my everything."

Will drifted off to sleep, a smile playing on his lips. He was home at last.

Now he just had to figure out how to deal with his one last secret.

21

CHARLIE SANDS

A WEEK LATER, CHARLIE FOUND HIMSELF CROUCHED BESIDE some bushes while staring at an enormous house more than six hours outside of Buenos Aires, with a sickening feeling of *déjà vu*. However, the big difference between infiltrating Benicio's house and this place was the fact that they'd spent nearly five days watching the secluded home. They felt confident that they knew the nightly routine of the occupants, the number of guards and their routes, and even had a strong handle on the security system.

At this point, he was sure Kairo was overthinking the job and being too cautious. Alexei and Soren had both started threatening to move without them if Charlie didn't pull the trigger soon. But after the disaster of the last attempt, Charlie couldn't help his hesitance. Kairo was of the same mind.

The night they chose was a bleak one with black clouds rolling across the midnight sky, blotting out stars and the sliver of moon. Cold wind swept across the flat grounds and angrily rattled bare tree branches.

Thanks to the somewhat frightening team of Alexei and Kairo, they discovered that Catalina Perez had been living in the middle of nowhere for nearly a decade. No one had seen a trace of her in Buenos Aires, and too many of her old acquaintances thought she was dead. The only thing that was unclear was whether her exile from the capital was voluntary.

"Are we a go?" Charlie whispered, his voice automatically picked up by the tiny mic pinned to his shirt.

"I'm in position. There's no movement at the front of the house," West immediately stated. The sniper's leg had healed enough that he could return to the field with only a minimal amount of fussing from the team doctor. West had already scaled one of the many trees on the property and was watching over the area through the scope on his rifle. He was providing the first line of backup if things went bad yet again and they needed to make a quick escape.

"Everything looks good on our end," Ed added, his voice coming in loud and clear in Charlie's ear from his position in the van. The demolitions expert did not get approved by Will, and he was just a touch salty about it, but at least he wasn't letting it bleed into his work now. "The interior of the house is quiet. Target hasn't stirred from the bedroom since she retired three hours ago. From our count, there are four guards inside the house, with two of them on rotation doing a patrol once per hour. One more is in the guard shack."

"I've got the guard shack in sight," Soren replied.

"I'm ready to take the security down." Kairo was hidden in another part of the large yard with his phone hacked into the house security system.

"Be careful, gang," Will murmured. His voice was strong and firm, but Charlie still felt as though there was a tremor of worry underlying it.

"We got this," Charlie stated. There was a chorus from the rest of the team mimicking the sentiment, and Charlie felt a swell of gratitude in his chest. He appreciated them watching out for the new guy. The inevitable hazing could wait until they were no longer worried about getting shot.

"Do it, K," Charlie ordered in a rough whisper.

The silence that followed for a few seconds left Charlie holding his breath. Kairo had claimed that the security system was far more simplistic than the one they'd encountered at Benicio's, and both Soren and Alexei had confirmed it.

Just as panic was sending a chill along his spine, Kairo spoke. "System is down. Everyone, move."

The four of them were approaching the house from different directions and would be entering from different spots. Kairo was at the back, while Alexei was bold enough to claim the front door. Charlie was moving toward a patio door that would let him into the kitchen. Assuming all went well with the guard shack, Soren was to follow Alexei through the front two minutes later.

The security system was attached to all the doors, and they would automatically unlock as Kairo crashed the system. Charlie ran in a partial crouch, muscles tensed against potential gunfire as he left the cover of bushes, trees, and thick shadows for the open ground.

Looming ahead of him was an enormous two-story house that looked as if it had been lifted straight out of Western Europe with its dark brick and black timber accents. As he got away from the line of trees surrounding the house, the main front lawn was decorated with perfectly sculpted hedges. Even a large fountain rose in the center of the driveway where it formed a circle before the curved staircase to the front door.

He thought he caught the tiniest glimpse of Alexei as he darted from one shadow to another, dodging the golden glow of the landscape lights. But then, it could have just been his eyes playing tricks on him.

The house was monstrously huge. How could this all be for one woman and her small security team? They'd tapped the interior cameras and had watched the house for days. No one came, and no one left. The count had to be accurate. Catalina Perez was living in the middle of nowhere in a giant house alone.

Shoving the thought aside, Charlie crouched down beside the patio door that was covered in windows and reached out for the handle. His breath became lodged in his throat as he tested it.

Unlocked.

He opened the door very slowly in case the damn thing whined or creaked on its hinges. It shouldn't, considering the wealth and extravagance of the house, but he was in no mood to discover the hard way that he'd used the one noisy door in the entire place.

Slipping inside, he closed the door again and swept his gaze over the enormous kitchen that was lit by only a small work light over the stove. He couldn't tell the color, but it looked pale in the dim light. An assortment of pots and pans hung from the ceiling over a center island covered in patterned tiles. There was a small table and two chairs in the kitchen that held salt, pepper, and sugar containers as well as a folded newspaper. Was that from the security team or from *Señora* Perez?

"Security guard headed your direction, Charlie," Ed stated in a low, calm voice.

Charlie nodded, assuming the man likely had him visible on one of the house cameras. Each step was quick and silent as he darted over to the center island, staying out of sight of the two main entrances to the kitchen.

A couple of seconds later, a man in a dark suit strolled into the room, his attention locked on his phone, not even aware of his surroundings. Charlie barely kept from rolling his eyes as he lifted his gun and placed two slugs neatly in the man's chest. The suppressor screwed on the front of the weapon kept the noise to a minimum, but the guy wasn't small. It was as if half the house shook when he slammed into the counter and fell to the floor.

"One down," Charlie murmured.

"One in the hall. Sneaking up the stairs," Alexei immediately replied, sounding far too giddy about the entire thing. That time, Charlie did roll his eyes.

"I think they heard something. We've got one of the guards on the move from the guard station, headed to the kitchen," Ed warned him.

"The other one?" Charlie eased around the island and carefully stepped over the sprawled legs of the dead man.

"Still in the guard office, but I think he might have noticed that there's something wrong with the cameras. He's popped his head out twice to look at the camera just outside the office."

"I'll be in the front door in less than thirty seconds," Soren chimed in. "I'll swing by the office on the way to the second floor."

"East wing of the house is clear. Moving into the foyer," Kairo chimed in.

Charlie grunted, his attention turning to the guard who was headed in his direction. He moved quickly, hoping to take the guy by surprise. His heart thudded heavily and adrenaline coursed through his system. This was the kind of thing that he lived for. Yes, he'd give up the excitement and danger for Will, but it was even better that he could have both in his life. At least for a little while longer.

As he reached a corner, the sound of footsteps grew louder as the guard approached. Charlie popped out just before the man reached him. The guard halted in shock. He'd been lifting his phone to his ear but stopped halfway up. Charlie adjusted his aim and put a bullet through the phone in case the man had been calling in some kind of trouble and then put one into his forehead.

"Problem eliminated," Charlie growled.

"Soren just entered the house. Hold position."

Charlie dropped into a shadowy niche within the hallway so that he wasn't directly in the line of sight if someone else were to come through the hall. He glanced at the shiny wood floor and the ever-expanding pool of blood. He probably should have felt some kind of remorse for ending the lives of the two security agents who worked for Perez, but he couldn't summon any up. His mind just kept replaying the image of Will running down the block as gunshots were fired at his back.

If one of those men had been a better marksman, if he had gotten there just seconds later, Will would be dead right now. That idea silenced any feelings of doubt or regret he might have suffered. No, Benicio Perez took this to deadly levels first. Charlie wasn't going to feel any regret because he was better at playing this game.

Barely a minute later, a soft pop echoed through the hall.

"Security is down," Soren murmured.

"Good. We——" Charlie's words were cut off by a loud gunshot from the second floor. The only ones who were supposed to be up there were Alexei and Catalina Perez, and Alexei's gun was equipped with a suppressor just like the rest of them.

"Alexei!" Soren screamed. Charlie flinched as his voice filled his ear and echoed through the house.

"I'm fine!" Alexei called, speaking in a normal voice. "I'm fine!"

Charlie raced down the hall, following Soren's pounding footsteps to the main foyer. There was a dead body at the bottom of the stairs, left there by the assassin. Soren was just ahead of him on the stairs, gun drawn, moving cautiously as they searched for the person with the weapon they hadn't accounted for. Kairo waited for Charlie at the bottom of the stairs for directions.

"West? Front still clear?" Charlie demanded, pausing with his free hand on the ornate wood banister.

"Clear."

Charlie turned his attention to Kairo. "Return to the rear

of the house. Keep an eye out for anyone approaching the house from that angle."

Kairo nodded and bit out a quick, "Got it," before running down the hall again on nearly silent footfalls.

"Um…we need Will in here," Alexei stated a few seconds later.

"You're hurt? You told me you were fine!" Soren snapped.

Alexei sighed so heavily Charlie could feel his eyes roll. "I'm fine. I'm not hit. It's Grandma here. She's demanding to talk to the one who has been troubling her son. She says she'll keep firing until the police get here if we don't let her talk to him."

Charlie halted midstride, his head cocking slightly to the side as he tried to process what Alexei had said.

"What? Catalina Perez is the one who fired the gun?" Kairo demanded across the comm system.

"I'm coming in," Will announced.

"Wait! No!" Charlie barked.

"She's demanding to see me. I'm sure we have mere minutes until the cops are here. It's only fair," Will argued. In the background, Charlie could clearly hear the sound of the van side door rolling open. "I'm the one who started this. I want to talk to her."

"Shit," Charlie swore under his breath. He didn't like this. He didn't want Will anywhere near Catalina Perez on the off chance that she turned out to be just like her son.

"Don't worry, Charlie." West's low voice came across smooth and confident. "I've got your boy in sight. He's jogging up the drive now. No one will have a chance at him. We're currently alone out here."

That was a small comfort at least.

"Tell Perez he's coming," Charlie ordered as he turned on the stairs and descended to the first floor again. He waited by the front door and stared out the sidelight window, watching for his appearance. A couple of minutes ticked by until Will appeared at the top of the curved stairs. He jerked open the door as Will gave him a crooked grin.

"This is an unexpected development," Will said.

"I don't like it," Charlie complained. Before he could say more, Will tilted his head up and brushed a kiss to the corner of his mouth, instantly erasing his frown.

"It'll be fine. If she knows someone has been troubling her son, I'd be interested to hear what else she's been told." Will slipped by Charlie only to have his steps stumble slightly as his eyes fell on the dead man.

"Will—" Charlie started, placing a gentle hand at the base of his spine while trying to position himself so that Will's view was blocked.

Will smirked at him, his eyes still sad. "It's okay. Doctor, remember? I've seen plenty of dead bodies."

That didn't mean Charlie wasn't going to attempt to protect him as much as he possibly could.

They climbed the stairs together, Charlie sticking as close to the doctor as he could. The house might seem empty, but he wasn't taking any more risks than necessary with Will's life. It was bad enough that he was in the house.

When they reached the second floor, they turned left and headed down the long hall where Alexei and Soren were stationed on either side of a pair of double doors leading into the master bedroom. One of the doors was open, and only thin light was leaking out from the interior. The hallway itself glowed with just a night-light near the baseboard in the middle of the corridor.

"*Señora* Perez?" Will called out as he reached the doors. "I'm sorry to trouble you this late in the evening. My name is Dr. William Monroe."

An older woman's voice rang out strong and firm from the interior of the room. "You're the one who broke into my son's house and set it on fire?"

Will winced and glared over his shoulder at Charlie. At

least Charlie managed to look a little remorseful about that. The situation had completely gotten out of hand, but he was happy to blame at least some of that on Benicio.

"That would be my fault, *Señora* Perez," Charlie answered before Will could.

"And who are you?"

Will threw a repressive glare at Charlie. "That would be my overprotective boyfriend, *Señora* Perez."

Charlie thought he heard a soft chuckle from the older woman, but he couldn't be sure. There were several seconds of silence and then she continued, "Is this about who my parents are?"

"It is. May I come in and explain the situation to you? I truly don't mean you any harm. I swear, no one will harm you," Will promised.

This time Charlie definitely heard the laugh. "I'm supposed to believe this when I'm pretty confident that you killed all the bodyguards in the house."

Will winced and glanced over at Charlie, his eyes full of questions. How the fuck was he supposed to respond to that? She had no reason to believe his reassurances.

"No matter. They were my husband's men. No great loss. They were more jailors than bodyguards. You can come in."

Will moved to the door and Charlie instantly followed. There was no way in hell he was allowing Will into the room without him. Will shoved at him and harshly whispered that he needed to back off. He ignored him as he shoved his gun into the holster on his hip and lifted his hands into the air to show that he was unarmed.

The bedroom was elegantly decorated in shades of pale, soft pinks as if they'd stepped inside a flower while the floor was covered in thick white carpet. Immediately in front of them was a massive king-sized bed with a hand-carved head-board and a mountain of pillows resting against it. The size of it made the slender woman sitting on the edge look all the more tiny.

She was wrapped in a pale-blue dressing gown, and her dark hair was slightly mussed from sleep as it hung down to her waist. They might have woken her, but her gaze was piercingly sharp, and her hand was steady as she held the gun on them. This was definitely Benicio's mother. There was no missing their similar brows and eyes. Charlie was even sure they had the same cheekbones. However, her son's mouth was a cruel slash and his nose was larger—probably traits he'd gotten from his father.

"Which of you is the doctor?" Catalina inquired.

"I am," Will replied and Charlie immediately stepped in front of his lover, putting his body in the path of the bullet if she decided to shoot.

Catalina's gaze slowly traveled up the entire length of Charlie's body. Her pale lips tilted into a smirk. "I guess that makes you the overprotective boyfriend."

"I am," Charlie said firmly as if daring her to shoot. There was no fucking way he was letting this woman harm Will.

"Not bad, young man. Not bad at all."

To his utter shock, Catalina heaved a deep sigh and tossed her gun onto the mattress, beside her. She slid to her feet and crossed the room, moving away from the bed to a small sitting area with a sofa and a pair of chairs. She paused to turn on a floor lamp, adding more golden light to the room, then turned to look at them as they continued to hover near the open doorway.

"Come along. Let's get this done. I'm sure I'll still need to deal with the police tonight, and I would like to get some sleep before sunrise."

Charlie could only blink at her as she settled on the sofa and tugged at her robe so that it better covered her legs. As he was trying to wrap his mind around the strange development,

Will darted past him and claimed one of the chairs, while Charlie settled in the other one.

"Because it is so late, I will try to be brief." Will leaned forward, bracing his forearms on his knees with his hands folded together. He stared straight into Catalina's eyes as he spoke in a calm, measured tone. "The wife of a dear friend of mine was searching for her niece, who happened to be one of the children of *Los Desaparecidos*. The wife's name was Emilia Lopez. Her sister, Martina Ruiz, and brother-in-law, Valentino Ruiz were taken in 1977, while she was six months pregnant. Martina and Valentino were discovered dead, but the baby was born. Emilia, unfortunately, died ten years ago without ever discovering what happened to her dear sister's child. Her husband is now on his deathbed, and he is desperately trying to fulfill his wife's final wish before he, too, passes."

Charlie watched as the older woman's eyes turned glassy and she lowered her gaze to the floor. She swallowed hard once and nodded. "You think I'm the daughter of Martina and Valentino Ruiz." There was no question in her voice, as if she'd expected this.

"I do," Will stated without an ounce of doubt in his voice. "The research was done long before my arrival in Buenos Aires, but I've checked it over carefully. You are the correct age. I've also seen pictures of both Emilia and Martina. You have similar features to those women."

A strange expression crossed her face and she made a sound like a choked laugh. "This is that Carlos Lopez's doing, isn't it?"

"You know him?" Charlie asked.

Catalina finally lifted her eyes to look at them and shook her head. "No. He contacted me once about ten years ago in an email, asking questions about my parents. I was debating whether to answer him when my husband suddenly decided that it wasn't good for my health to remain in Buenos Aires. A couple of days later, I was packed off to this gilded prison cell." She waved to the room they were in, her thin lips twisting into a bitter smile. "Since that day, all my emails and phone calls have been closely monitored by his people. I'm not permitted in Buenos Aires or to leave the country."

"He knows," Will snarled. "He knows you're one of the *Los Desaparecidos*, and he's kept you a prisoner here."

Catalina's thin shoulders lifted in a lackadaisical shrug. "He's always known that I was adopted, but my parents have very official-looking papers, claiming they went through proper channels." She snorted inelegantly. "Everyone knows how easy it is to get official documents that say any number of lies. I wondered when I was growing up, but I never gave it much thought until Lopez contacted me."

Charlie sighed and sank back in his chair. "Your son and husband have made it look like you've completely disappeared. Most people think you're dead."

"It's why I tried approaching your son in the first place," Will admitted. "If I couldn't have access to your DNA, his was the next best thing."

"Little monster," Catalina grumbled. "Takes after that bastard of a father." She narrowed her gaze on Will, who straightened under those dark eyes. "Okay. What do you need? Some blood?"

Charlie laughed, confident that he couldn't be more impressed with the older woman. She looked like she was ready to open a vein right then and there for him.

Will jumped to his feet, his body practically vibrating with his excitement. He pulled a small plastic test tube out of his jacket pocket and held it up so she could see that there was a cotton swab sealed inside of it. "Actually, all I need to do is swab the inside of your cheek. Just a bit of saliva is plenty."

Shock had the older woman blinking at him for a second. "Your friends weren't planning to kill me?"

"Oh God, no!" Will gasped.

"We figured you'd be asleep, so we were going to send

someone in to steal your hairbrush and toothbrush," Charlie explained.

Catalina sniffed at him. "That would work, I guess, but this has been more interesting."

That was an understatement.

At Will's direction, she opened her mouth and the doctor very carefully swabbed the inside of her cheek, treating her with incredible care. When he got what he needed, he carefully returned the swab to the test tube and screwed it shut.

"How long will it take for you to run your test?" Catalina inquired.

"If I can pull some strings, we should get the answer inside of a week." Will paused and cocked his head to the side. "Would…would you like to know the results?"

The older woman stared off into space, a frown starting to tug down the corners of her mouth. "You said that Lopez is on his deathbed?"

"He is. Terminal cancer. He doesn't have long. Maybe days. Maybe weeks," Will replied, his words barely more than a whisper.

"And his wife, the woman who might be my aunt…she's already dead?"

"Yes. I'm sorry."

The silence stretched for several seconds, and she finally gave a small nod. "I still want to know." She stood and walked across the room to a small writing desk positioned in front of a wall of windows looking out on the lawn. She pulled over a small notepad and scribbled something down before tearing the sheet of paper off. Returning to the sitting area, she handed the paper over to Will. "This is an email address my husband doesn't know about. Your message can be a simple yes or no. I'll understand what it means."

Will accepted it and held one of her hands in both of his. "Thank you, *Señora* Perez. You don't understand what your help means to me and Carlos. Even if this isn't a positive match, it is enough to lift the weight from his shoulders. He'll know that he did everything he could to find the truth for his wife."

"Thank you for fighting so hard for your friend. I'll be anxiously awaiting news."

Will tucked the paper away and crossed the bedroom toward the doors to leave. Charlie started to follow right on his heels, but Catalina grabbed his elbow, stopping him. Charlie stared at the diminutive woman who'd narrowed her eyes on him in warning.

"You keep a close watch on him. Take good care of him. Be worthy of that kind of love and devotion," she advised him.

Charlie grinned. "That's not going to be a problem at all."

With a nod, she released his elbow so he could leave.

However, he didn't get more than a few steps before she called out in laughing tones. "If the test does come back positive, it would be just a horrible shame if that information was released to the media."

Will stopped at the doors and whipped around on a gasp. "Are you sure?"

Charlie chuckled as he also stared at the older woman. "It could be fun. But are you sure you want to stay here for something like that? Considering the steps your son took to stop us, it could be dangerous for you."

Catalina returned to her seat on the sofa, her chin held high and proud. "After being trapped as a prisoner for ten years? I wouldn't miss it for the world. I want a front-row seat."

He couldn't blame her one tiny bit, but he couldn't shake the worry that gnawed at his stomach. She'd helped Will. He could extend her the same courtesy.

His mind made up, Charlie crossed to the same writing desk and quickly scratched out a secret email address they kept for jobs on the same pad of paper she used. He ripped off the sheet and took her the paper.

"What's this?" she inquired.

"In case you change your mind and need help leaving the country. My team and I are good at arranging things like that."

"Thank you. I'll consider it. Now get out of here. I need to call the police about a robbery. Do me a favor. On your way out, can you grab some of the Chinese antiques from the front parlor? At least make this appear to be a robbery."

"On it!" Soren shouted from the hallway before two sets of footsteps whispered down the hall toward the stairs.

Charlie sighed but kept his comments to himself. Looks like they were getting paid for this job.

Will was giggling as they hurried out of the house, the test tube clutched tightly in his fist and a bright light shining in his blue eyes. As they ran across the yard together, he held up his hand in front of Charlie's face. "Are you ready to discover the truth?"

"Yes, I am." He was ready for anything so long as Will never stopped smiling at him.

22

WILL MONROE

WILL BIT DOWN ON HIS BOTTOM LIP TO KEEP FROM SMILING AS
he glanced over at Charlie. His lover drove with both hands
tightly clenching the wheel, his brows gathered over his nose
in a scowl. Charlie was *not* happy about Will demanding to see
Carlos in person in Buenos Aires.

It had been a week since they spoke with Catalina Perez
and got the DNA sample. Will made endless phone calls and
pulled every string he could to get the material in for analysis,
which had required him to go to a lab in Buenos Aires. The
entire team had accompanied him on the brief trip before
they retreated again to their backup safe house.

Now they had the results at last.

Will was determined to deliver the news to Carlos in
person. It was just because they'd gone through so much
together, but Will also knew this was going to be his last
chance to see the old man.

"I get why you need to do this in person rather than over
the phone," Charlie grumbled. His shoulders slumped a little
and he finally looked over when they stopped at a red light. "I
don't want you to think I'm this overprotective monster who
doesn't believe in you or that I want to control your life."

Will slumped in his seat and laughed. "I don't think that at all, dearest." Just tacking on that endearment to his statement had some of the lines disappearing from Charlie's face and the worry clearing from his dark eyes. "I know I'm still in danger from Benicio Perez. Probably his father too. I need to tell Carlos in person. I need to say good-bye."

Charlie released the wheel with his right hand and reached over to place it on Will's thigh. "I know. I'm sorry."

"It's okay. You're just protecting your client," Will added with a smirk. "Why else would you bother wearing an earwig today?" Will tilted his head toward the right, his eyes sliding over to the mirror on the door. "And I'm pretty sure I spotted Soren and Alexei in their sedan about three cars back."

When he glanced over, it was to find Charlie's lips twisted into something that was like half a smile and half a disgusted frown. "I thought you two knew how to be sneaky," Charlie stated, clearly talking to whoever was listening on the earwigs.

There was a short pause followed by Charlie's chuckle. "Alexei says it's not his fault. He never should have let Soren drive." Charlie rolled his eyes and sighed. "They're all arguing now. You should be grateful you can't hear it."

Charlie relaxed a little more on the rest of the drive through the city to the hospice, while Will's mind turned to Carlos. He'd spoken to the man almost every day since they left Buenos Aires, and he'd chatted with the doctor who'd replaced him, getting regular updates on Carlos's condition. His health had deteriorated again, but it appeared they'd managed to stabilize him for now. Time was running out.

As they pulled up to the hospice, the quiet building was bathed in warm sunlight against a crystal blue sky, almost making it seem like summer, if it weren't for the somewhat chilly temperatures. The second they parked, Charlie hurried to Will's side of the car and wrapped an arm around his shoulders, pulling him tight into his larger frame as they walked up to the front doors.

237

Olivia greeted them warmly as usual, even if she was a little surprised to see them both again. Will explained that he'd come back for a final visit before he left town. She wished them well and even came out from behind the front desk to give him a hug.

Walking down the hall, Charlie threaded his fingers through Will's and squeezed, offering up a compassionate smile. He was glad Charlie was there. Will had seen death plenty in his life. It was part of his job, but it didn't mean that he'd ever grow entirely numb to it. Carlos was still too full of life and passion to go now, but he knew the man had made peace with his death. He was eager to see his wife. And just maybe, close out a lost chapter of his long existence.

The door to Carlos's room was open and his TV was on. Some insane game show was filling the screen in a riot of colors and activity. Will needed only to glance at Carlos to see that he wasn't doing well. What color he'd had in his face had left entirely while his eyes and cheeks appeared even more sunken. A tube for oxygen was directly under his nose. It was good that it wasn't a full mask, but there was no doubt in his mind that it was coming very soon.

Forcing a grin on his lips, he knocked on the doorframe. The noise jerked the old man's eyes to him and his expression morphed into one full of delight. He laughed and waved a withered hand at him, beckoning him inside.

"Dr. Monroe! Come in, come in!" he rasped.

"I hope you don't mind that I brought Charlie with me," Will said, grasping the man's hand in greeting.

"I was expecting him." Carlos winked up at Charlie, his grin growing a little devilish. "It's easy to see he knows a good thing when he sees it."

Charlie placed a hand on Will's shoulder and squeezed. "Never letting this man out of my sight again."

"We won't take up much of your time. I just wanted to talk to you about the DNA results," Will informed him as he settled in the chair by the bed. Charlie continued to stand just behind his shoulder, a silent wall of support that Will appreciated more than he could explain.

Carlos settled on his pillows and drew in a few shaky breaths before he finally nodded. "Give it to me straight, doc. It's okay if it came up negative for a match."

"The test results are positive. Catalina Perez is, in fact, the daughter of Martina and the niece of your wife, Emilia," Will answered quickly, forcing the words past the sudden tightness in his throat. "You found her. You found your wife's niece."

Tears immediately glistened in Carlos's eyes, and he struggled to draw in air. Will jumped to his feet and grabbed a couple of tissues from the little pastel box on the nightstand. He handed them over to Carlos while he pulled over the full oxygen mask. With Carlos choked up, the man wasn't going to get enough oxygen, but before he could get anything settled, Carlos was waving him off.

"Sit down. Sit down. I'm fine. I swear. I'm fine." His words were breathless and halting, but still strong.

Will hesitated for a second before returning the mask to a hook and sitting in his chair again. They sat in silence as Carlos wiped at his eyes and nose, the smile never leaving his thin lips.

"You said on one of our calls that you saw her? You talked to her?" Carlos pressed when he could.

"I did. She looked to be in good health. She was a very strong, confident, intelligent woman. I was very impressed with her," Will happily described.

"Very no-nonsense with a good sense of humor," Charlie added.

Carlos closed his eyes and sighed. "Sounds just like her aunt. Wonderful."

"I sent her an email, giving her the results of the test as well. I don't know if she'll come visit you. With her husband and son being the way they are…" Will's words drifted off. He didn't know how much Carlos might have hoped to meet Catalina before he died, but he wanted to set some realistic expectations. It simply might not be safe for either of them.

Carlos opened his eyes and started to lift his hand as if to wave Will off. "I understand. It would be nice, but it's enough that I can tell Emilia that I found out the truth for her."

"It's not all good news, you know," Charlie interjected. Carlos lifted a questioning gaze to him, and Charlie smirked. "It does mean that Little Shit, Benicio, is your great-nephew."

A loud cackle erupted from Carlos and he slapped the bed several times. Will tried to give his lover a repressive glare, but Charlie just smiled at him, trying to counter his troublemaking with cuteness. Sadly, it was working, and Will couldn't be mad if his silliness was making Carlos happy.

"Yeah, well, we can't pick our relatives, unfortunately," Carlos said when he stopped laughing and could catch his breath. "At least Catalina turned out all right."

Their conversation died off and they fell into a comfortable silence for a couple of minutes. Will was happy to let Carlos digest the new information and regain his strength. They needed to leave soon. The man had to be exhausted.

But Carlos had one more surprise up his sleeve.

With a twist of his lips, Carlos turned his attention to Charlie and announced, "Dr. Monroe tells me that you've been searching for me."

Will dropped his face into his hand and groaned. After everything he'd done for Carlos, the old bastard just chucked him under the bus for laughs. He so easily could have rephrased that so it had nothing to do with Will, but no, of course not.

"I'm sorry. What?" Charlie demanded. Will looked up to see confusion digging lines across Charlie's forehead as his eyes bounced from Will to Carlos.

"You can be a real asshole, you know that?" Will muttered, earning a new cackle from his former patient.

"I like to stir the pot. Gets the blood pumping and keeps life interesting," Carlos countered.

"My life is plenty interesting, thank you very much. I don't need the help."

"Will? What's he talking about?" Charlie interrupted, trying to get them back on track.

Will sat up straight and directed his most pleading gaze at his lover, inwardly praying he was understanding. "Charlie Sands, I would like to formally introduce you to Thiago Vergara."

Charlie's eyes went impossibly wide, and his mouth fell open as he looked at Carlos again. The smug prick just grinned broadly at Charlie and gave a little wave of his hand.

"Are you shitting me?" Charlie growled.

Will grabbed Charlie's hand in both of his and squeezed, the words tumbling from his lips in a wild torrent. "No, I'm not. I'm sorry I didn't tell you sooner, but I swore to Carlos that I wouldn't tell a soul. I was trying to protect his life. Besides, it wasn't my secret to tell."

"Yeah, you can't get pissed at him. He was keeping his promise to me," Carlos said sharply.

"What? No, I'm not angry. Surprised. Shocked. Confused. Not angry." Charlie stared down at Will. "You knew when I told you I was hunting for Vergara?"

"I did. I'm sorry. I needed to get Carlos's permission before I said anything to you."

Charlie managed a small smile and squeezed Will's hands. He turned his gaze to Carlos. "I'm just confused. What happened to you? How did Yusuf Badem end up with your paintings in his private collection?"

A wistful grin spread on Carlos's lips and he motioned for Charlie to sit. Will started to get up to give his chair to Charlie, but his lover just settled on the arm of the chair, wrapping one arm around Will's shoulders, holding him blissfully close.

"Lord, it had to be in '77 or '78. Fuck, I'm old." Carlos

paused and shook his head. "Anyway, my work was just taking off. I was making more money than I had sense and mouthing off to the wrong people." He snorted and grinned. "Sleeping with all the wrong people, too. But it worked out. The night I was supposed to be taken, this general's wife got wind of it and got me out of town before they arrived. We bounced our way through Argentina and into Chile a little, having fun and ignoring what was happening in the rest of the world. After about three years, she heard her husband was dead and decided to return to Buenos Aires."

"You didn't return with her?" Will inquired.

Carlos shook his head. "Nah. It wasn't love. Just a fling. Plus, it wasn't safe for me yet. I waited another three years. After the military dictatorship fell, I decided to return to Buenos Aires under a new name. The world had largely forgotten about Thiago Vergara anyway. When I got to town, there was a new air of hope in the city. I decided to start painting with this crazy idea of remaking myself and framing my work with this new hope. I figured that if I could make it big once, it couldn't be hard to do it all over again." He paused and his gaze grew distant.

"What happened?" Charlie prodded.

Carlos's smile spread and softened. "I fell in love. I'd never met anyone like Emilia. She was all fire, passion, and drive. No one could stand in this woman's way. She'd lost her sister and brother-in-law to the dictatorship and was determined to find out what happened to them as well as her unborn niece. After meeting Emilia, nothing else mattered. Her cause became my cause. I put all my energy behind the groups determined to find all the missing people and children."

Charlie shifted on his perch, leaning forward a bit. "That makes sense, but where does Yusuf Badem come into the picture?"

Carlos chuckled softly, but it fell into a cough. Will slipped out of Charlie's grasp and picked up a glass of water. He helped Carlos get a drink and resettled him against his pillows. He didn't want to keep pulling information out of him, but he had a feeling Carlos wanted to tell his story as much as Charlie was dying to hear it.

"Yusuf was a devilishly smart man. Will told me he passed away recently. Damn shame. We got to meet only a couple of times, but we corresponded for years," Carlos murmured, seeming to talk mostly to himself before finally lifting his eyes to Charlie. "I started painting again, but under my new name. They were selling, but nothing like what I saw as Thiago. That was fine. It was enough that I could give any profits over to the organizations that Emilia supported. But somewhere along the way, Yusuf Badem saw my work and he was convinced that it was the same style as Thiago Vergara. He sent me letters, but I ignored him. Next thing I know, the sneaky bastard is standing on my doorstep, demanding to talk to Thiago Vergara."

"No shit!" Charlie exhaled.

Carlos laughed, but it was light and breathless. "He knew from just the brushstrokes who I was. Only one ever to put it together. He stayed in Buenos Aires for two weeks. We talked art constantly. We also talked about *Los Desaparecidos*. He got it. His home country had seen more than its share of turmoil over the years. He worked out a plan to help get my Carlos work in front of more people. The price of my work went up, and I could pour more money into the cause. Yusuf and I got to be good friends over the years."

Will picked up the glass and offered Carlos another sip of water. "And the paintings in his collection?"

"A gift," he said between sips. When he was done, he motioned for Will to put the glass on the table. "The ones I made for him were in my old Thiago Vergara style. I knew if he ever needed money, he'd be able to sell them for a fortune. But he was also a big fan of my old work. I knew he'd appreciate them."

"I think he did. He had six pieces of your work and he never showed them to anyone. His nephew said that he thinks they were precious to him." Charlie paused and winced. "We had them authenticated. I'm sure it's only a matter of time before it circulates around the art world that lost Thiago Vergara paintings were found."

Carlos closed his eyes and smiled. "I'm glad. I'm glad he had a chance to enjoy them. His nephew can do whatever he likes with them. As long as they gave Yusuf joy, that's all that matters to me."

"I believe he's planning to loan them to a museum so the world can enjoy them now."

"Good...good..."

They didn't stay much longer after Carlos told his story. A nurse came in to check on him and they left. Will swallowed hard, knowing he would never see Carlos again, but there was also a sense of joy in his heart. He'd managed to give Carlos the answers he'd been seeking as well as allow him a final chance to share his story. Carlos knew that his work was going to continue to give the world happiness. That was a good life.

As they stepped outside the hospice, Charlie wrapped an around Will's shoulders, pulling him in close. "You knew. You knew Carlos was Thiago."

Will leaned his head on Charlie, cringing just a little. "Sorry. I couldn't—"

"I know. I'm just teasing. I'm not angry." Will looked up at him, his skepticism clear on his face. "I'm serious! I'm not angry. You protected his secret and his life. I respect that."

"The rest of the guys know?"

Charlie smirked and nodded. "They overheard enough. I'll fill in the rest of the details when I get back. We've got to finish packing and find out what flights Kairo has booked for us."

Will moved ahead of Charlie and leaned against the driver's side door. He tilted his head up and grinned like the utter fool that he was. Unexpected joy was bubbling up inside of his chest like fizz from a shaken soda can. He grabbed both sides of Charlie's jacket and pulled him in between his legs.

"Speaking of flights and such, what is the plan? I haven't heard any talk about next jobs or where we are supposed to go. Didn't you say that we vote on everything? Do you see me as a junior member? Am I not allowed to vote yet?"

"No, baby, nothing junior about you," Charlie purred. He started to lean in but stopped suddenly. He made a disgruntled noise as he dug the little plastic device out of his ear. After shoving it into his pocket, he turned his attention to Will. "They don't need to listen in to this part, and I don't need feedback from the peanut gallery."

Will tipped his head up to rest on the roof of the car and laughed. He could only imagine what the others were saying. As it was, Soren and Alexei were somewhere close by getting a show already.

"No job is currently lined up. Ed is planning to go to the States for a little bit, visit family and go through some PT for his shoulder. Kairo mentioned seeing family too. West said something about getting into trouble with Soren and Alexei," Charlie listed.

"Wow. That leaves you with no one to babysit," Will teased.

"No, that leaves me with a very sassy doctor I want to spend some time getting to know all over again," Charlie corrected.

Why is this man so endlessly smooth?

He was melting. Will didn't want to melt. He wanted to be just as cool and smooth when it came to Charlie, but even though they'd been apart for six years, Charlie still knew him. He knew what buttons to push. He understood what was important to him.

"I was thinking I'd take a page out of Soren's book. Let's go to an island for a week or two. No guns. No explosions. No insanity. Just us being together." With his hands planted on either side of Will on the roof, Charlie leaned his head down and brushed the sweetest kiss to the center of his forehead. "I think I need to spend the next thirty to forty years holding you, Will. Do you think we could do that? Just let me hold you."

Will wrapped his arms around Charlie's waist and pulled his lover in tight. "I want that, too."

"You know once I start, I'm never letting you go. No matter what," Charlie warned.

"Please, don't. I love you, Charlie. Don't ever let me go again."

Charlie placed his hand under Will's chin, tipping his head up. "I love you, Will Monroe. You will always be mine." He captured Will's lips in a deep, searing kiss. He felt it all the way down to his soul—the promise of forever. Charlie Sands was truly his, heart and soul. No matter where they went, what insanity they faced, they would finally do it together.

And Will couldn't wait.

EPILOGUE
KAIRO JONES

Kairo lurched forward, coughing and choking on his beer, as Soren delivered the punchline to his story about sneaking into the bedroom of a known arms dealer and being harassed by his four cats. Ed slapped him hard on the back, possibly knocking Kairo's lungs up into his throat.

"You okay?" Edison asked, tears of laughter still gathered in the corners of his eyes.

"Yeah, fine," Kairo rasped. He took a delicate sip of his beer to clear his throat. This was what he got for attempting to drink while Soren was in the mood to tell stories.

Alexei was proving to be just as creative, though, as he told of his own insane adventures. Someone so young should not have experienced the things he had.

When he caught his breath, Kairo sank into his chair and stared down the long table they'd claimed in the restaurant. Shortly after Charlie and Will returned from meeting with Carlos—aka Thiago *fucking* Vergara—Kairo informed them that he'd acquired tickets for a ferry headed a short hop, skip, and a jump across the Atlantic to Uruguay. Specifically, the small, historic town of Colonia. They'd grabbed hotel rooms and were now settled in a restaurant serving delicious drinks and lots of meat, which allowed them to watch the fireworks in Buenos Aires from a safe distance.

As they boarded the ferry, Kairo just might have sent off countless packets of information revealing the fact that Lorenzo Perez was married to a child who had been stolen from a couple who had been kidnapped during the era of the military dictatorship. His wife was one of the very people whose existence he was trying to deny in the first place. The Argentine media was exploding with this news, and it even seemed to be getting picked up across different news agencies across South America.

Oh, yes. This was looking very bad for Lorenzo Perez and his asshole son. His chances at the Argentine presidency were dwindling by the second.

Kairo took one last glance at the news headlines on his phone and then tucked it away with a soft cackle.

Lorenzo Perez was a small fish in terms of the people they'd taken down in the past, but that didn't mean it didn't feel good to see him stopped. The people of Argentina suffered under the military dictatorship, and while everyone wanted to move on and be happy, it was important to never forget what had happened. That was just a direct route to it happening all over again.

"Everything good?" Charlie asked from his seat directly across from him.

Kairo lifted his beer and smiled. "We're all good. Appears the Perez boys have got their hands full managing the mess we created. I don't expect them to come searching for us. It's way too late for that now."

Will paused, a forkful of steak halfway to his mouth, when he glanced over at Kairo. "What about Catalina Perez? Has she emailed Charlie?"

Kairo's heart ached a little as he shook his head. "Nothing yet."

Charlie reached over and placed a hand on Will's slumped shoulder. "Honestly, I'm not expecting her to. She's pissed at her husband and son for what they've done to Argentina and to her. She wants to stand and watch them burn."

"Besides, if she suddenly disappears from the country, they could use it to shove all this back under the rug," Kairo pointed out.

"But if she does happen to reach out and need help escaping, we'll be right there for her," Ed interjected. "She helped us. We're not gonna leave her stranded."

Will nodded, looking a little more settled, even if some of the sadness and worry lingered in his eyes. Was there a chance that Lorenzo would have his wife killed over this? Yeah, a pretty good chance. But if Catalina wanted to face her husband head on, who were they to get in the way of what she wanted?

Kairo swallowed the rest of his beer and placed an order for another when the server returned to check on them. He usually wasn't a big drinker, but they were celebrating closing two mysteries and reuniting Will with Charlie. If that wasn't a reason to get completely shit-faced, he didn't know what would be.

Relaxing in his chair, he just smiled at the man who had been his boss for more than a decade now. Sure, since parting ways with the Company, they'd agreed they were equal members of the team, but deep down, they all still knew that Charlie was their fearless leader. He was the one they all turned to for answers when a plan went to hell or they were low on ideas of what to do next. Charlie Sands just had that confident leader aura around him. People *wanted* to follow him. And it didn't hurt that he usually had damn good ideas.

But since Charlie had been forced to walk away from Will, it was as though a large chunk of the man's soul had been missing. He'd gone through the motions for years—partied, drank, and slept with plenty of willing people—but it wasn't until Kairo spotted Charlie looking at Will that he noticed the light was back in his eyes. He was lit inside by pure love for this man, and maybe Kairo was just a tiny bit envious.

Who didn't want to find love like that?

It was why none of them had felt any anger when Charlie stated that he was willing to leave the team for Will. The doc made Charlie happier than any of them ever could. There was no way in hell any of them would stand in the way of his happiness.

But Kairo wasn't going to deny that he was happy that Will was joining them. Not only would the man make their oldest friend happy, but he'd probably help to temper some of Charlie's crazier impulses. There was no sense in being utterly reckless when you had a hot doctor waiting for you to come home.

"What's next for everyone?" Will inquired when the conversation had fallen quiet. He leaned over into Charlie, his head partially resting on his lover's shoulder. "Charlie says we're escaping to an island, but he won't tell me which one."

"Knowing Charlie, it's probably Alcatraz," West called out with a smirk.

"Hey!" Charlie snapped, pointing a finger at the sniper. "Don't ruin the surprise."

Will snorted and elbowed Charlie. "Idiot. As long as it has a beach, I don't care."

"Home to North Carolina for me," Edison announced. "Thought I'd get a little of my sister's home cooking and a couple of weeks of PT. I've got a friend who's a licensed therapist who can help get this shoulder back in shape." He lightly lifted his left arm, which was still in a sling.

Will sat up, his expression turning serious. "Definitely get an MRI while you're in town. Get an orthopedic surgeon to look you over to make sure I didn't miss anything."

Ed winked at him. "No worries, Doc Will. I'll be good.

You just keep an eye on that one." He finished with a jerk of his chin to Charlie.

"We've got a line on a possible job in Geneva," Soren broke in. He motioned with his thumb toward West. "We thought we'd drag this one along for the fun of it. We're worried Charlie isn't exercising him enough."

"Asshole," West muttered, glaring at Soren from across the table.

Alexei leaned forward, a wide grin on his beautiful face. "Come on. It'll be fun. We promise to find lots of interesting things for you to shoot. We might even invite my uncles. Gabriel gets cranky if he's not shooting or stabbing enough bad people. He starts using my other uncle as target practice."

To Kairo's surprise, West's scowl softened a little and a hint of a smile started to perk up one corner of his mouth. It wasn't hard now to warm to Alexei. The young man was full of boundless energy and mischief. Of course, he was also deadly, ruthless, and scary when he wanted to be, but there was zero doubt in his mind that Alexei would keep Soren and West safe.

"What about you, K? Any plans yet?" Will inquired and Kairo inwardly flinched, wishing the sweet man had forgotten about him completely.

"Back to see my mom, actually," he admitted with a sigh.

"Where's that?"

"She's still in Boston, right?" Ed supplied.

Kairo shook his head. "She's teaching at the University of Cambridge right now. They've got her on loan or something for the next few years."

"You don't sound excited…" the doctor hedged cautiously.

Kairo shrugged and forced a grin he didn't feel. "My last memories of the UK aren't the best, so I can't say that I'm all that eager to return. And my mom wishes I'd devoted my life to academia rather than what I'm doing now."

That was a fucking understatement. Dr. Elaina Jones was the foremost expert on Egyptology and no matter how many years passed, she still went out of her way to express her disappointment that her only son failed to follow in her footsteps. Her favorite argument was that it was part of his heritage, but she didn't care to recall that he was more than a bunch of people who had been dead for millennia.

"Should I ask what she thinks you do now?"

Okay, so that brought about a much bigger grin. "IT specialist."

Will tipped his head into Charlie's shoulder and groaned loudly while several people around the table laughed.

The trip to see his mom wouldn't be so bad once she got her needling and harping out of the way. It would be nice to just kick back and relax for a little while. And if he got bored, it wouldn't be hard to just jump onto a plane and head off to somewhere more interesting.

After a few more rounds and way too much meat, Kairo stumbled toward the bathroom. The alcohol was definitely starting to make his brain fuzzy, while the most delightful sense of well-being was coursing through his veins. Everything was right in the world at last. Charlie was happy and in love. The team was together. It even sounded like Soren and Alexei were planning to hang out with them for a while.

Kairo finished his business and shuffled out of the bathroom again. It was time to head to the hotel and sleep some of this off. They were driving to Montevideo early in the morning to catch flights to various parts of the world.

As he turned to walk down the narrow hallway to the main seating area of the restaurant, he found his path blocked by a man as big as a mountain. He would have towered over Ed by at least six inches, and his shoulders were wide enough that they nearly brushed both of the walls on either side of him. The man's head was shiny and bald, but there were tufts of black hair sticking out from just above the top button of his shirt.

Kairo paused and blinked at the large beast a couple of times, his sluggish brain trying to figure out how he was going to get past this mountain. Did he back up? Did the other guy? Should he try to climb over him? No. Climbing would be bad. He might fall.

"Are you Kairo Jones?" the stranger inquired in a low, rough voice.

Kairo's thoughts scattered and he stared up at the stranger. His first reaction was surprise that the man knew his name. His second was even more surprise that he had spoken in English rather than Spanish. And his English was heavily accented…like Greek. That was weird.

"Yeah. Who are you?" Kairo asked, trying very hard not to slur his words.

The guy grunted with a little nod. "Sorry about this."

Kairo's brow furrowed as he frowned at the stranger. He was about to ask what he was apologizing for when something incredibly sharp stuck him in the side of the neck. He hissed and tried to jerk around while slapping his hand to the spot that stung. Was that a damn bee? How did a bee get in the restaurant?

As he twisted, he saw only a glimpse of another person behind him before his knees turned to water. He was falling and darkness was swallowing him whole.

Fuck. Someone drugged him.

He sucked in a breath to shout for Charlie. Ed. Someone. Panic flared in his chest, sending a surge of adrenaline through his body.

But it was too late.

The darkness enveloped his mind. They had him.

BE SURE TO CATCH *KAIRO'S BILLIONAIRE*, BOOK 2 OF SHADOW Elite!

Discover who has kidnapped our sweet Kairo and what their wicked plans are.

Grab your copy now!

ABOUT THE AUTHOR

My book-loving friends,

Your ratings and reviews are more important than I can ever express to you. Those little stars and thoughtfully written words not only help other readers discover my books, but they directly impact my sales numbers. The more book sales I get, the more books I can write. It's a great arrangement that benefits us both!

The best possible support you can give is to post an honest review, even if it's just clicking those stars to rate a book!

Thank you so much for all your support over the years. I can't wait to share the next adventure with you.

New York Times Bestselling author Jocelynn Drake loves a good story, whether she is reading it or writing one of her own.

Over the years, her stories have allowed her to explore space, talk to dragons, dodge bullets with assassins, hang with vampires, and fall in love again and again.

This former Kentucky girl has moved up, down, and across the U.S. with her husband. Recently, they've settled near the Rockies.

When she is not hammering away at her keyboard or curled up with a book, she can be found walking her dog Ace or playing video games. She loves Bruce Wayne, Ezio Auditore, Zhou Zishu, travel, tattoos, explosions, and fast cars.

Check out all her books at JocelynnDrake.com or join her newsletter and get regular updates on all upcoming books.

Join the fun in her Facebook Group, Jocelynn Drake's Darlings. Exclusive giveaways, cover reveals, and sneak peeks!

ALSO BY JOCELYNN DRAKE

Shadow Elite

Stephen's Translator (novella)

Charlie's Doctor

Kairo's Billionaire

Edison's Professor

Westin's Prince

Exit Strategy

Deadly Lover: Special Edition

Vengeful Lover

Final Lover

Forbidden Lover

Accidental Lover

The Godstone Saga

Steal the Wind

Breath of Life

Wake the Dead

Wings of Fire

Embrace the Light

City of Blood

Lords of Discord

Claiming Marcus

Saving Rafe

Waking Bel

Embracing Winter

Healing Aiden

Visiting the Variks

Ice and Snow Christmas Series

Walking on Thin Ice

Ice, Snow, & Mistletoe

Snowball's Chance

Defrosting Jack

By AJ Sherwood and Jocelynn Drake

Scales 'N' Spells Series

Origin

Breath

Wish: A Novella

Blood

Embers

Wings 'N' Wands Series

Dawn (free novella)

Ruins

By Jocelynn Drake and Rinda Elliott

The Unbreakable Bonds Series

Shiver

Shatter

Torch

Devour

Blaze

Fracture

Ignite

Rialto

Unbreakable Bonds Short Story Collections

Unbreakable Stories: Lucas

Unbreakable Stories: Snow

Unbreakable Stories: Rowe

Unbreakable Stories: Ian

Ward Security

Psycho Romeo

Dantes Unglued

Deadly Dorian

Jackson

Sadistic Sherlock

King of Romance

Killer Bond

Seth

Wicked Outlaw

Pineapple Grove

Something About Jace

Drew & Mr. Grumpy

All for Wesley

Weavers Circle

Broken Warrior